"Gotcha..."

Ivy Rutherford's gaze snapped up to the cowboy's. Her throat was dry. Her palms damp.

She could still feel the warmth of his breath against her skin; the single word was triumphant. A challenge.

Oh, she was in so much trouble here.

Something passed between them. Something heated and tangible and, on her part, wholly unwanted. Damn it. Damn it! She wanted him to touch her again. Wanted to do some touching of her own.

"It's cute that you think so," she murmured, keeping her tone even. Her eyes steady on his. "But don't be getting delusions of grandeur."

If possible, his grin amped up a few degrees, all cocky and pleased with her response. She shouldn't have found it so attractive. "Aw, darlin', you wound me."

"You don't seem like the kind of man who cares much for being subtle."

"You're right. I prefer the direct approach." He scanned her face, taking his time before meeting her eyes again. "Makes it that much easier to get what I want."

There was a strange fluttering in her chest, just under her heart. It was clear enough what he wanted...

Dear Reader,

I'm thrilled you picked up a copy of *About That Night*. When I first started writing the In Shady Grove series, I had planned to focus solely on the four Montesano siblings—a close-knit Italian-American family with strong ties to their beloved hometown. But something happened during *What Happens Between Friends*, the second book in the series, that changed everything.

Kane Bartasavich arrived.

As soon as he appeared on the page, I knew he was perfect for Charlotte Ellison. What I didn't know was that during the writing of their story (*Small-Town Redemption*) I'd fall head-over-heels for Kane's three brothers. I love family dynamics, and writing their stories gives me a chance to explore the relationships between the brothers. As with most families there are frustrations and irritations, sibling rivalry, shared memories and genuine— though at times, grudging—affection.

C. J. Bartasavich, the eldest brother, is a man in control of his life. Until he gives in to desire and spends a passionate night with sexy, cynical waitress Ivy Rutherford. When he learns Ivy is pregnant, he returns to Shady Grove. But he has his work cut out for him trying to convince Ivy they should build a life together and be a family. Luckily for him, he's a man used to getting what he wants!

I had such fun writing C.J. and Ivy's story. The sparks flew between them from the moment I put them on the page together. I hope you'll look for the next In Shady Grove book later this year featuring handsome attorney Oakes Bartasavich.

Please visit my website, bethandrews.net, or drop me a line at beth@bethandrews.net. I'd love to hear from you.

Happy reading!

Beth

BETH
ANDREWS

—

About That Night

HARLEQUIN® SUPERROMANCE®

ISBN-13: 978-0-373-60912-3

About That Night

Copyright © 2015 by Beth Burgoon

Printed in U.S.A.

www.Harlequin.com

Romance Writers of America RITA® Award-winner **Beth Andrews** writes edgy, emotional contemporary romance for Harlequin Superromance. She loves coffee, hockey and happy endings. Learn more about Beth and her books by visiting her website, bethandrews.net.

Books by Beth Andrews

HARLEQUIN SUPERROMANCE

In Shady Grove

Talk of the Town
What Happens Between Friends
Caught Up in You
Small-Town Redemption
Charming the Firefighter

The Truth about the Sullivans

Unraveling the Past
On Her Side
In This Town

His Secret Agenda
Do You Take This Cop?
A Marine for Christmas
The Prodigal Son
Feel Like Home

Other titles by this author available in ebook format.

For Andy

CHAPTER ONE

CLINTON BARTASAVICH JR. tipped his Stetson in thanks to the toothy brunette who'd escorted him from the front desk of King's Crossing Resort—Shady Grove, Pennsylvania's equivalent of a four-star hotel. They stopped outside closed wooden double doors, the placard to the right stating Bartasavich/Ellison Party. "I appreciate the help…" He glanced at the small name-tag on her chest. "Allison."

He probably could have figured out how to get to this room—a distance of about a hundred feet straight down the main hallway—on his own. But when a pretty woman offered to lead the way, he didn't argue.

Allison let out a high-pitched giggle that was grating enough to make a man's ears bleed. "Oh, you're very welcome, Mr. Bartasavich."

He bit back a grimace. He hated having his name butchered. "Actually, it's Bart-uh-sav-itch."

Not Bart-as-a-vitch.

With a soft gasp, complete with a hand to her heart, she blinked at him so rapidly, he half expected her to start hovering above the ground.

"How silly of me." Sending him a look from under her eyelashes, she edged closer, her voice turning husky. "Maybe there's…some way I could make it up to you?"

He'd eat his hat if she meant extra mints on his pillow.

"No harm done. It's an honest mistake."

One not made in Houston where the Bartasavich name was well-known. Even revered in certain circles.

Her lower lip jutted out in a pout no one over the age of six should attempt. "Well, if there's anything else I can do for you," she said in a whispery tone, "—and I do mean an…ee…thing—you just let me know."

He cocked an eyebrow. Seemed Houston wasn't the only place where his family's name, power and wealth were known.

While he didn't have any objections to casual sex—the more casual the better—he didn't play games. No subtle hints about what either of them wanted. No coy looks or innuendos trying to convey what could be easily said with a few simple words.

And definitely no simpering.

But even if she'd held his gaze and told him in no uncertain terms that she was interested in him, attracted to him and ready, willing and eager to prove how much, he'd decline.

Having women throw themselves at him because of his name had long ago lost its thrill. He was his father's son. Not his clone. And while Senior had always been more than happy to take whatever was offered to him, C.J. preferred knowing, for certain, that a woman was in his bed because of him.

Not his money.

"I'll keep your offer in mind," he said. Then he pulled off his hat and used his free hand to open the door.

And stepped into his own private version of hell. A very crowded, very loud, very *pink* hell.

It was as if Valentine's Day had exploded, leaving hearts everywhere. On the walls. Dangling from the ceiling. Scattered on the tabletops. There were big ones, small ones. Flat ones, poufy ones. Some with scalloped edges, some with straight. But all were shiny or sparkly and in shades ranging from the palest pink to the brightest fuchsia.

A long banner draped across the doorway wished the happy couple Heartfelt Congratulations on their engagement. Long streams of twisted pink, red and white crepe paper hung from the rafters.

Any hope he'd held on to of missing the entire party died a cruel and violent death. Because the ballroom wasn't just filled with hearts. It was also filled with people.

Damn. He should have gotten a later flight.

He turned to his right, scanned the bar where

several men and women gathered, talking and laughing, ignoring the hockey game that was being shown on the large TV on the far wall.

No hearts there. Not one flash of pink. He could set his ass on that empty stool in the corner, have a drink or two and pretend he wasn't here. That most of his crazy family wasn't in the next room creating only God knew what sort of havoc.

But pretending had never been his style. And he didn't ignore his problems. He faced them head-on.

Anytime the Bartasavich family was together, there were problems. The only questions were how many—and what did C.J. have to do to fix them.

"You," a familiar female voice said, the tone dripping with scorn, "are, like, in so much trouble."

C.J. turned to find his seventeen-year-old niece glaring at him. Always happy to see her—even when she was giving him the stink eye—he grinned. "Now, darlin', everyone knows getting into trouble is your daddy's job. Not mine."

From the time Kane had been born, it'd been C.J.'s job to watch over him. To keep his younger brother out of the trouble he attracted like a freaking magnet.

He'd failed.

"You're three hours late," Estelle Monroe said, the very picture of an affronted, pissed-off female who knew she was right—a man's worst nightmare. "Three. Hours. That is, like, so rude."

"Some of us have to work. Keep the family living in the style to which you all have become accustomed." Ever since his father's stroke ten months ago, it'd been up to C.J. to make sure Bartasavich Industries continued to run smoothly.

Estelle rolled her eyes. She was a beauty like her mother. Long, blond hair, big blue eyes and the face of an angel. Her scowl, on the other hand, was all her father. "It's Saturday."

"A Bartasavich's work is never done." There were no weekends off. Running a multimillion-dollar company took commitment, dedication and full-time focus. Every goddamn day.

At least for him. His eyes narrowed as he took in her dress. "Does your father know you're wearing that?"

She tossed her hair back. Smoothed a hand down her hip. "Of course. *He* isn't the one who's three hours late. Why?" she asked, her tone daring him to actually answer.

"It's too…" *Short. Tight. Revealing. Adult.* "…red."

"How can something be too red?"

He wasn't sure, but hers qualified. Did she have to wear such high heels? And so much makeup? "I'll give you a thousand dollars to change," he told her, only half kidding. Hell, he'd offer her two grand if he thought it would work. "Preferably into something with a high neckline, a boxy shape and a floor-length hem."

"I'll have you know I've had, like, a hundred compliments on this dress tonight. Evan even thought I was twenty-two."

"Who is Evan?"

She nodded toward the five-piece band rocking a cover version of Bon Jovi's "Living on a Prayer." "Chimps on Parade's drummer."

"No drummers," C.J. growled. "Ever."

"Evan says age is just a number and that I have an old soul. Besides, nine years really isn't all that big of a difference."

C.J.'s hands closed into tight fists. "Excuse me," he ground out from between his teeth. "I'm just going to go and have a little chat with Evan."

She gave a life-is-so-hard-and-unfair-for-a-pretty-pretty-princess-such-as-myself sigh. "Don't bother. Daddy already said something to him, and now Evan won't even look at me."

"Good to know your father can be counted on for something." They must have taught him how to act big and tough in the army. Christ knew he hadn't learned it growing up.

"Come on," Estelle said, slipping her arm through C.J.'s. "Grandma Gwen's been asking about you."

She tried to tug him along but he planted his feet. "I think I'll grab a drink first. Get ready to face all that pink."

Though he'd been joking—a little—her lower lip jutted out. Trembled. She could give Allison lessons on the proper way to make a man feel like shit. "You don't like the decorations."

"Of course I do," he said, remembering too late that Estelle was, officially, the hostess of this little shindig for her father and his fiancée. "They're very…festive."

"They're supposed to be romantic!" she wailed loudly enough to make several of the bar patrons glance their way.

He put his arm around her shoulders. Squeezed. "Hey now, you know I'm clueless about decorating."

She sniffed and shrugged him off. "It's not just that."

He glanced around, but no one was there to explain what the hell he'd said wrong. "Then what is it?" he asked, not sure he really wanted to know.

"You don't even want to be here."

He'd flown halfway across the country, left the civilized world of Houston—where he had work, work and more work—to be in this small town thirty miles south of Pittsburgh to celebrate his brother's engagement. A brother he'd barely spoken to in the past fifteen years. An engagement C.J. highly doubted would make it to the altar.

Hell no, he didn't want to be here. But he was. He always put his family first. Didn't that count for anything?

"What I want doesn't matter," he told her.

"It's just—" she threw her hands into the air, beseeching the heavens to help her cope with the disappointment "—I tried so hard to make this party special for Daddy and Charlotte, but it's a disaster. First Uncle Zach texted me that he wasn't coming and then you were late. Granddad's been an absolute grump all night, making angry noises and thumping his good hand. I'm not sure if it's because he doesn't want to be here or because Carrie's drunk and been hanging on Uncle Oakes. Then there's Grandma..." Estelle shivered dramatically. "Well, you're going to have to see *that* for yourself." Her eyes welled. "I just wanted everything to be perfect, and instead, it's ruined."

He sighed. Hung his head. Women. Care about one of them too much and they'd get their hooks into you—either by the balls or by the gut. Either way, once they had you, you were never free.

He hoped like hell that, if he ever had children, he followed in his father's footsteps and had all boys.

He held out his arms, but Estelle lifted her chin.

Stubborn as her father.

C.J. amped up his grin by a few degrees. "Come on, darlin'. Don't tell me you're going to stay mad at your favorite uncle."

"At the moment, Uncle Oakes is my favorite," she said, prissy as a princess to a peasant. But then she relented enough to step into his embrace. Wrap her arms around him for a hug.

He squeezed her hard. Kissed the top of her head. Damn, but he was crazy about her.

"Oakes is everyone's favorite," he said, not offended in the least to be usurped by his brother. If she'd wanted to go for the jugular, she would have picked Zach.

There wasn't anything he could do about his youngest brother not showing up, but he could take care of the rest for her. He looked over her head and scanned the room. People laughed and conversed around the round tables or stood in small groups, eating hors d'oeuvres and sipping tall flutes of champagne brought around by the waitstaff. Others had paired off, swaying to the band's acoustic rendition of Guns N' Roses' "November Rain," the lead singer's smoky voice giving the song a slow, seductive quality.

Among the dancers, it was easy enough to find his brother Kane and his new fiancée, Charlotte Ellison. Hard to miss Charlotte, with that bright beacon of short red hair. Usually more cute than beautiful, she was a knockout tonight in an emerald-green dress that showed off her long legs and gave her thin figure the illusion of curves. For his part, Kane still looked every inch the badass he pretended to be. One of only a few men without a suit, he'd tied back his too-long hair into a stupid, stubby ponytail and wore dark jeans and a white button-down shirt that covered his tattoos.

"For a disaster, everyone seems to be having a good time," C.J. said.

Estelle stepped back and nodded toward the room. "Look again."

He followed her gaze to the far window where Carrie was pressed like a second skin against a pale, grim-mouthed Oakes. Though Carrie was doing her best to get a reaction, Oakes stood still as a statue, his eyes straight ahead and not on her impressive breasts, which were spilling out of her pale yellow dress.

Poor bastard looked as though he'd been cornered by a pissed-off bobcat and not a perky blonde.

C.J. would have laughed if that perky blonde hadn't also happened to be married to their father.

Problem number one.

"You say Carrie's drunk?" C.J. asked Estelle.

"The way she's been groping Uncle Oakes all night, she'd better be drunk. God. It's, like, completely disgusting. And with Granddad right there, too."

It was then that C.J. spotted his father, his once robust form slumped to the side of his wheelchair. The stroke Senior had suffered almost a year ago had stolen his ability to speak and paralyzed the right side of his body. But judging from the glare he was shooting at his wife and third son, his mind was still in working order. Behind him, Mark, his large bald nurse, took a hold of Senior under the arms and lifted him straight.

Senior slid down again. His mouth moved, his body jerked, and C.J. knew he was trying to say something, more than likely giving Mark, Oakes and Carrie hell.

Problem number two.

"But that's not the worst of it," Estelle said.

C.J. sent his niece a sidelong glance. "It gets worse?"

"Much." She looked so solemn. So serious. Not expressions she wore often. C.J. bit back a groan. What sort of fresh hell had he walked into? "Like, catastrophically worse."

She pointed to the dance floor. The band had started another song, this one an upbeat pop song. People bounced and danced along.

And there, surrounded by a circle of dancers, his mother did a slow bump and grind against a tall, dark-haired man.

C.J. grabbed the back of his neck. Squeezed hard. Worse, indeed.

Estelle nodded. "I know. It's gross." She made the mistake of looking at the dance floor again only to whirl back, horrified. "Ugh. Grandma Gwen just totally, like, groped him. In front of God and everybody." Estelle leaned forward, her voice a harsh whisper. "Like, her hand was on his butt squeezing and—and stroking. I'm going to have to have my brain sprayed with bleach in the hopes of taking the memory out of my head. You have to do something, Uncle C.J. You're so good at fixing things."

He snorted. Right. He should be good at it. He'd had enough practice. He wouldn't mind a night off every now and then, but he couldn't refuse his niece. Couldn't refuse to do what had been his responsibility since birth.

Take care of his family.

"What would you suggest?" he asked.

"Make her stop."

If only it was that easy. But then, for Estelle, life was simple. She asked for something and got it. She was indulged at every turn, her every wish granted.

Tonight was no different.

He patted her hand. "I'll handle it."

She smiled and threw her arms around him for another hug, this one more enthusiastic and warmer than before. "Thank you, thank you, thank you! I know Daddy and Char will appreciate your help, too."

C.J. doubted that, but it wouldn't stop him from doing what was right.

His mother took that moment to rub her ass against her date's pelvis.

C.J. winced. He'd have to tag along when Estelle had her brain scrubbed.

"Excuse me, darlin'," he drawled to a teenage

waitress as she passed. "You wouldn't happen to have any forks on you, would you?"

"They're just mini quiches…" Frowning, she tipped her head to the side, her ponytail of light brown corkscrew curls bouncing with the movement. "Is that the proper plural form of *quiche*? Or is it one of those words like *deer* or *fish*?"

It took him a moment to realize she was talking about the food on her tray. And that her question hadn't been rhetorical.

"I think either form is correct," he said.

"But you don't know for sure. What if it's one of the questions on the SATs? I mean, I doubt it, but you never know. Leighann—my best friend—took them last fall, even though you really don't need to take them until the spring of your junior year, but she's always trying to be The First, you know? Which is why I think she finally gave in and slept with her boyfriend, so she'd be the first of our group to lose her virginity."

C.J. blinked. Blinked again. "Uh…"

"My stepmom says it's because deep down, Leighann's insecure, and she overcompensates by acting overly confident. Like men with little—"

"I hope like hell you're about to say wallets," C.J. said quickly. "Or brains."

"No," she said slowly. "But if it'll make you feel better, I can just say men who aren't quite as endowed—"

"No. That doesn't make me feel better at all. How about we skip that part in its entirety?"

She lifted a shoulder, then switched the tray to her other hand. "Anyway, Leighann said there were a ton of arbitrary questions on the SATs, most of them not having to do with real life at all. What if the plural form of weird words is one of them?"

"Sorry, darlin'. *Quiche* isn't exactly a word I use very often. In any form."

She nodded sagely. "That's good. They're pies of death, if you think about it. All those eggs. And cream. And cheese. Really, it's a heart attack waiting to happen. Or at least, high-cholesterol levels. Plus, it's not natural—humans eating products made from cow's milk. Except I'm not allowed to—" she made air quotes with one hand "—preach about my personal views to guests." Another set of air quotes as if closing what must have been a direct order from her supervisor. "So I'll just say I'm sure these appetizers are extremely delicious. At least, I'm guessing they are. I wouldn't know personally, as I don't eat any animal products." She frowned. "Usually. And, best of all, you don't need a fork to eat them. They're small enough to just pop into your mouth."

She lifted the tray higher, obviously expecting him to do just that.

How she managed to get so many words out with

so little breath was beyond C.J. But get them out she did, all the while holding his gaze innocently.

Amazing.

Back in Houston, people treated him with a certain...reverence. Because of his father's last name, his father's money. The old man had always eaten it up. Had loved having servants fawn all over him, unable to make eye contact, bowing and scraping as if it was all nothing less than expected. Deserved.

But Clint's ego was just fine. It didn't need to be stroked.

No matter what Kane said.

"I don't need the fork to eat. I wanted to use it to stab my eyes out." He nodded toward the dance floor where his mother gave a loud whoop and threw her arms in the air, lifting the hem of her short dress so high C.J. quickly averted his gaze lest he see parts no one but Gwen's gynecologist should see. "Anything sharp and pointy will do."

The waitress followed his gaze. "Yes. That is disturbing." She shifted the tray to her hip. Studied him closely. "Is she your date?"

He flinched, but he couldn't blame the kid for thinking Gwen was younger than her actual age. She saw her plastic surgeon more often than her own sons. "My mother."

"Oh." Then she shocked the hell out of C.J. by giving his forearm a quick squeeze. "I'm sorry."

He raised an eyebrow as amusement flowed

through him. Not many felt sorry for him. He was a Bartasavich, after all. People usually envied him—his looks, his money, his business acumen.

He nodded his thanks. "Wish I could say you get used to it, but that'd be a lie."

His mother caused drama wherever she went. If C.J. had to guess, he'd say tonight's show was all for his father's benefit. But Senior was still staring at Carrie. C.J. doubted Senior even knew what Gwen, the first in a long line of Mrs. Bartasaviches, was doing. How hard she was trying to prove she was over him.

How hard she was trying to make the old man jealous.

The waitress watched his mother do a pelvic thrust that should have been illegal, then bend at the waist, stick her ass in the air and shake it.

The waitress scrunched up her face. "Eww. Mothers should never twerk. Something like that could scar a person for life. Have you tried therapy? It might help."

He chuckled, surprised he could laugh at this. "After tonight, I just might need it."

He helped himself to a couple of the quiches. Pie of death or not, he was hungry. He'd worked through lunch and hadn't bothered with dinner before catching his flight to Pittsburgh.

He was still chewing the first one when Kane approached him. As they had so many times throughout their lives, they sized each other up.

There'd been a time when C.J. could read every thought in Kane's head. When he'd known his little brother's strengths and weaknesses as well as his own.

Those days were long gone, killed by Kane's drug addiction and subsequent stint in the army. Kane was now clean and sober—had been for years—and even owned a local bar called O'Riley's. But there was too much hostility, too much anger to ever mend the bond that had been broken between them. There were days C.J. could admit he regretted that. That he missed his brother.

But he'd be damned before he'd ever say it out loud.

"Estelle said you were here," Kane said, his expression closed, his eyes hooded. "I'm surprised you could tear yourself away from your desk."

Not as surprised as C.J. had been to hear about his brother's engagement. He hadn't known Kane and the redheaded ER nurse he'd gotten involved with last year were that serious, until Estelle had told him they were engaged as she'd hand delivered his invitation to this little soiree.

Kane had spent the past twelve years doing his best to avoid any ties whatsoever to anyone—except Estelle. What the hell made him think he was ready to commit to one woman?

"I wouldn't have disappointed Estelle," C.J. said, eating the second quiche. "Or miss the chance to get to know your fiancée better." He wiped his hands on a paper napkin and crumpled it in his hand as he scanned the ballroom. Spotting his future sister-in-law across the room, laughing at something a pretty, very pregnant blonde said, he sent Kane a grin. "Charlotte seems like a nice woman. A smart woman. Too good for the likes of you. I'll have to do my best to make sure she realizes that before she makes the biggest mistake of her life and goes through with this marriage."

"I think you're safe," the waitress told Kane. "I mean, look at you." She swept her hand up and down in front of him. "You're gorgeous. And you have that whole bad-boy vibe going on, which most women find irresistible but, personally, I don't get. No offense or anything."

"None taken," Kane said, looking torn between amusement and horror at the girl's assessment of him.

"Yes, my brother sure is a fine catch." As long as a woman didn't mind being tied to an ex-addict with a bad attitude and a ton of emotional baggage. "He's a real prince among men. All the women fall for that pretty face. Want to smooth out those rough edges."

Kane's mouth thinned. He made a show of looking around. "Couldn't find a date, Junior? All the big-haired, big-breasted debutantes in Texas busy this weekend?"

"Between Mom and Carrie, I'd say there are

two too many here now. I'm not sure this party could handle another one." He nodded toward Oakes, who was valiantly trying to hold a conversation with an older man while Carrie clung to his arm, her hand caressing his bicep. "You try to put a stop to that?"

Kane followed C.J.'s gaze and shrugged. "Oakes is a big boy. He can handle himself. He'll give Carrie a gentle brush-off, something that will save her from being embarrassed."

Kane's way of dealing with problems was to avoid them until they went away on their own. Or someone else took care of them. Oakes's was to be patient, to pick and choose his words and actions carefully and hope for the best.

"She's humiliating Dad," C.J. said. "And getting more than her fair share of attention for it. You need to go over there and tell her to back off."

"Not my job. Being in charge of everyone and everything, being a huge pain in the ass, is your thing."

C.J.'s fingers tightened on his hat. Kane could give lessons in being a pain in the ass. "I take charge," he said, "because no one else ever steps up."

"Why don't you just beat the crap out of each other and get it over with?" the waitress asked. Why was she still there? "That's what my brothers do when they're mad at each other. Then, while the blood is drying, they're suddenly best friends again."

"We're not friends," C.J. assured her, not taking his eyes off Kane.

But at one point they had been. Less than two years apart in age, they'd spent every moment together. Had been playmates. Confidantes. And as close as two brothers could be.

Those days were long gone. No sense wishing them back.

Or regretting the distance between them now.

"Guys are so weird," the waitress murmured while C.J. and Kane continued to glare at each other. "This is what's wrong with the world, by the way. Too much testosterone. Especially in leadership positions. I'm seriously considering forming a society consisting solely of women. Sort of like the Amazons but not as bloodthirsty. I wonder how much my own island would cost?" she asked in a thoughtful tone as she walked away.

"I'd buy her an island," C.J. muttered, "if we could convince Estelle to live there with her."

"A society with no hormonal teenage boys?" Kane asked. "Or horny adult drummers? I'd pitch in for that."

They shared a grin. Too bad their moment of brotherly bonding was interrupted by another of their mother's enthusiastic "whoop-whoops," this one accompanied by a fist pump.

"That's your cue, Junior," Kane said, his grin turning into a knowing smirk. "Go save the day."

C.J. wished the waitress hadn't taken off. He could use more food. And a drink. A strong one.

He'd need one to deal with his mother.

With nowhere to leave his hat, he stuck it back on his head, then crossed the dance floor, weaving his way through the jostling bodies. "Excuse me," he said, tapping Gwen's date on the shoulder. "Mind if I cut in?"

"C.J.!" Gwen trilled, her voice somehow carrying over the blaring guitar riff, the pounding bass. Tottering on her four-inch heels, she flung herself into his arms. "You're late."

C.J. wrapped an arm around his mother's waist so she didn't do a face-plant on the floor. Looked like someone had had a few too many dirty martinis. "So I've been told."

Linking her hands behind his neck, she leaned back, studying him with none-too-clear eyes. "Darling, you look absolutely horrid."

C.J.'s left eye twitched. He'd come to save her from herself and all he got was grief. No good deed went unpunished. Not in his life anyway.

He took in her black leather minidress and matching thigh-high boots. "You look…" *Like you're trying way too hard. Desperate. Needy.* "…beautiful as ever."

She smiled and patted his cheek. "Such a charmer. Just like your father."

"Not quite the same."

His father had spent his entire life making promises to women. Vows of love and fidelity that he'd broken, over and over again, without a second thought.

C.J. didn't make promises he couldn't—or in his father's case, wouldn't—keep.

"Oh, you have to meet Javier," Gwen said, craning her head to seek out her date with such determination, C.J. was surprised she didn't twist it clean off. "Javier." She held out her hand. "Darling, come here. C.J.," she continued when her date joined them, "this is my dear, dear friend Javier Ramirez. Javier, my eldest son, Clinton Jr."

Tucking Gwen to his side, Javier flipped his hair from his eyes. "Dude," he said, offering C.J. a fist bump.

C.J. stared at Javier's hand until he slowly lowered it. "My mother needs some coffee," he told the younger man. His mother was dating a man younger than her own sons. Then again, his father's last two wives had also been younger than him. Maybe he could fix Javier up with Carrie. Get them both of out his hair. "Black. And plenty of it."

Before Javier could respond, C.J. gently tugged his mother away from him and escorted her to a table in the corner. Helped her into a chair.

She frowned at him the best she could with a forehead full of Botox. "Are we done dancing?"

"We're taking a break," he told his mother, sitting next to her. "Your *dear, dear friend* is going to get us some coffee."

She patted his knee. "Javier is such a sweetheart. He's an aspiring model, you know. Though his true love is the theater."

A model. That explained the thick neck, gelled hair and blindingly white teeth. "I hadn't realized you were seeing anyone," C.J. said casually. "Or that you'd be bringing a date."

"Javier and I met weeks ago at a yoga class," she said with a wave of her hand, her red, talon-like nails almost taking out C.J.'s eye. "I enjoy spending time with him. He's attractive and attentive. I hadn't realized how advantageous it was for a man to be so limber until we made love in the backseat of the Bentley. Of course I'm referring to his limbs being flexible," she said, leaning forward and patting C.J.'s hand reassuringly, "not his penis, which is quite straight, thank goodness." She wrinkled her nose. "Though, just between us, it could use another inch or two."

C.J. sat frozen, his mouth hanging open, a strange buzzing in his head. Forget the forks in his eyes. He'd much rather use them to dig his mother's words from his ears.

She was often thoughtless with her words, careless with her deeds, but the alcohol had obviously washed away any and all filters between her brain and her mouth.

No doubt about it. He really was in hell.

"Please," he managed to choke out, holding up his hand as if that would stop her from talking, "I'd like to keep up the illusion that you don't have a sex life, and that would be easier to do if you didn't share details."

He made a mental note never to ride in her car again.

She laughed and slapped his arm. "Don't be silly. Just because you're my son doesn't mean you and I can't be friends, as well. And friends tell each other such things."

"I will never tell you such things," he promised solemnly. "Ever."

"Well, just know that you can. But I do hope you won't divulge anything I've said to your father."

Her voice had been casual, her expression clear. If C.J. hadn't looked carefully, he would have missed the calculation in her eyes, the small, satisfied smile turning up the corners of her mouth. As if all she needed for her evil plans to come to fruition was for C.J. to regale his disabled father with stories of her sexual escapades, causing Senior to become insanely jealous, toss aside his latest bimbo and finally come crawling back to Gwen.

C.J. had an entire lifetime of experience when it came to Gwen and her manipulations. As a kid, he'd fallen for her act too many times to count.

Had run to his father every time Gwen had a date, had told Senior about the days she'd spent locked in her room, crying over him. But no matter how hard C.J. had tried, no matter how much he'd begged, his father had never come back.

Damn it, Kane should be the one handling this. The one hearing all about their mother's love life with her white-toothed, greasy-haired, flexible, less-than-well-endowed boy toy.

C.J. jerked to his feet, intending to find his brother and force him to take responsibility for what happened at his engagement party. He turned blindly, took a step and slammed into a waitress.

He grabbed hold of her upper arms to keep her from falling. Opened his mouth to apologize, only to have the words catch in his throat when he raised his head.

Trouble.

That was his first coherent thought. The kind of trouble that had a man forgetting all about his goals, self-preservation and his pride. The kind that brought a man to his knees and made him beg for more.

Her hair was long and tumbled past her shoulders in soft, flaxen waves. Her mouth was lush and red. Her eyes the color of smoke. As he stared at her like some moron who'd never seen a woman before, those lips curved. Her gaze sharpened. Stayed direct and knowing.

His gaze skimmed down the long line of her

throat, lingered briefly at the V of pale skin and hint of cleavage visible above the button of her white shirt. While the other waitresses wore pants, she'd chosen a black skirt that hugged her hips, showcased the indentation of her waist and ended midthigh.

Definitely trouble.

The very best kind.

"Sorry, cowboy," she said, her husky, seductive voice matching her looks. "Not going to happen."

The humor in her tone, the glint in her eyes snapped him out of his reverie. "Excuse me?" he asked, sounding as formal and disapproving as the old biddies who congregated at the country club. Next thing he knew, he'd be adding a *bless your heart* at the end of his sentences.

She smiled, all feminine power and confidence. "You looked like you were ready to take a big old bite out of me. But I'm not on the menu."

He wanted to snatch his hands away, stick them in his pockets like a schoolboy who'd been admonished to look but not touch. She couldn't be serious. He couldn't be the only one feeling the slow burn of desire, the heat of pure, unadulterated lust.

The instant connection.

He frowned. No. Not *connection*. Connections weren't instantaneous. They were made over time, through common ground, parallel goals. Love at first sight was a myth, one invented by starry-eyed romantics who couldn't admit what they were really feeling was human nature at its most basic. Sexual hunger. Need.

He wanted her.

And she stood there, seemingly unaffected.

Testing her, needing to know for sure, he loosened his grip. Slowly drew his hands down the silky material of her sleeves, let his fingertips trail over the soft skin on the back of her hands before dropping away.

Her expression remained cool and amused. But he heard her small, quick intake of breath. Saw the awareness in the depths of her eyes. The answering desire.

He grinned and ducked his head, catching a tantalizing whiff of her spicy perfume as he whispered in her ear.

"Gotcha."

CHAPTER TWO

GOTCHA.

Ivy Rutherford's gaze snapped up to the cowboy's. Her throat was dry, her palms damp.

She could still feel the warmth of his breath against her skin, the single word triumphant. A challenge.

Oh, she was in so much trouble here.

Something passed between them. Something heated and tangible and, on her part, wholly unwanted. The music and sound of background conversation faded until it was nothing but a low hum. He edged closer and she breathed in his scent, something crisp and musky and undoubtedly expensive. Damn it. Damn it! She wanted him to touch her again. Wanted to do some touching of her own.

Gotcha, indeed.

Crap.

He needed to back up. He was close. Too close. Closer than was appropriate, especially for a waitress and a customer.

Way too close for her comfort.

Pride held her immobile. Forced her to stand

her ground instead of stepping back the way she wanted and putting some much-needed distance between them.

"It's cute that you think so," she murmured, keeping her tone even. Her eyes steady on his. "But don't be getting delusions of grandeur."

If possible, his grin amped up another few degrees, all cocky and pleased with her response. She shouldn't have found it so attractive.

"Aw, darlin', you wound me."

"I doubt that."

He nodded, rubbed his chin, his eyes narrowing as if he was in deep thought. "How about, you can't blame a man for having such delusions when faced with you?"

She had to fight to hide a smile. "Better."

"I was going to say when faced with one of God's greatest works, but that seemed like overkill."

She pointedly eyed his hat. "You don't seem like the kind of man who cares much for being subtle."

A middle-aged man brushed past them, and the cowboy stepped aside to give him more room, a handy excuse in Ivy's mind to shift closer to her. "You're right. I prefer the direct approach." He scanned her face, taking his time before meeting her eyes again. "Makes it that much easier to get what I want."

There was a strange fluttering in her chest. It was clear enough what he wanted.

Her.

He wasn't the first. Wouldn't be the last. Men were simple creatures, after all. They saw a pretty face, a curvy body and wanted them. If a woman coddled them a bit, stroked their…ego…and gave their friends something to envy, even better. For that, they'd put in the time, the effort to chase a woman, to make her his.

Until the thrill of that chase waned and the next woman came along.

"Didn't your mother ever tell you you don't always get what you want?" Ivy asked.

He laughed, low and long, as if that had been the most ridiculous question anyone had ever asked him.

Glad to know she could amuse him so.

"No," he finally said when he'd contained his mirth. "My mother never told me that. No one has."

"It's like a dream come true," she said drily. "Finally meeting a man brought up to believe that ordinary, mundane things such as failure and rejection are below him. Your mother didn't do you any favors, did she? And since she didn't, let me be the one to pass on this extremely valuable lesson. There comes a time in everyone's life when there's something they want, but it's just out of their reach. That time has come for you."

His grin sharpened. The gleam in his eyes turned downright predatory. "That sounds like a challenge."

Dear Lord, he was right. She had been challenging him. Baiting him.

Flirting with him.

Okay, yes, she was attracted to him. She wasn't dead, was she? And he was gorgeous—even with the cowboy hat. But she didn't lose her head over things like a sharply planed face, wavy golden hair and a pair of broad shoulders all wrapped up in a perfectly tailored dark suit.

Men lost their heads over her.

She'd been twisting males around her little finger from the time she could talk, had learned at her mother's knee how powerful a smile or glance could be. Yet, with this man, she felt unsure. Nervous that if she continued to play this dangerous game, she'd lose.

It was the way he watched her, she decided. As if he sensed the truth beneath her words. Could see what she so desperately needed to hide—her interest in him, how much she was enjoying him, his smile and humor, his confidence and looks.

You don't always get what you want.

No, she certainly didn't. That was life. One long journey of trying and trying and trying. Of mediocre triumphs and spectacular failures. She had no qualms about going after her goals, wasn't afraid to fall on her face during a long, hard climb. But just because you wanted something, just because you busted your ass, kept your focus and worked hard every day didn't mean you'd succeed.

Just because you wanted something didn't mean it was good for you.

"Let me get you a drink," the cowboy said, glancing around as if searching for a waitress—when one was right in front of him. "We can talk. Get to know each other better."

"Yes, that sounds like a great idea. And I'm sure none of my coworkers, or my supervisor, will care if I sit down in the middle of my shift and toss back a few with a customer."

He frowned. Scanned her from head to toe, as if suddenly remembering she should be getting him a drink. Not the other way around. "What time do you get done?"

"You're persistent. I'll give you that." It was flattering. Knowing he was willing to work a bit to get her time and attention.

That she was seriously considering telling him she'd be done by midnight annoyed her to no end. She didn't date customers, never hooked up with men she waited on. It set a bad precedence. Gave them the crazy idea that she'd serve them in bed, too.

An unsteady blonde in leather tottered over to them. Pressed against his side. "Darling," she said, tugging at his elbow, "don't flirt with the help. It's unseemly."

Ivy bit back a wince. Damned her cheeks for heating.

The help.

Well, if that didn't put things into perspective, nothing would.

"Yes, *darling*," Ivy said, mimicking the older woman's slightly slurred, superior tone, "listen to your date. One must always remember one's station in life."

Ivy never forgot hers.

The blonde's smile was none-too-sober and as fake as her boobs. "Aren't you sweet?"

Ivy matched her toothy grin with one of her own. "Not particularly."

"She's not my date," the cowboy said, keeping a hand on the woman's upper arm. "She's my mother."

His tone was pure resignation with a bit of embarrassment thrown in for good measure. Ivy could relate. Her mother had never been able to grasp the concept of acting—or dressing—her age, either.

"I'll have a dirty martini," his mother told Ivy as she clung to her son's arm—though Ivy guessed that had less to do with maternal love and more to do with her being three sheets to the wind. If she let go, she'd probably fall on her surgically modified, freakishly smooth face. Though that huge helmet of teased and sprayed hair might protect her from brain damage. "Three olives."

"And damn the calories," Ivy said under her breath, taking in the woman's ultrathin frame. Looked as if those olives were tonight's dinner.

She turned to the cowboy, was taken aback by his easy grin. Guess he'd heard her. She wanted to return his smile, but *the help* were to be seen, not heard. Ordered about, not engaged in small talk or flirtations. At least, not publicly.

She shook her head. She really needed to cut back on those reruns of *Downton Abbey*.

"And you, sir?"

His eyes narrowed on the *sir*, which, admittedly, she'd emphasized. No harm reminding them both why they were there. Who they were.

But she hated seeing that smile fade.

"Bourbon," he said. "Neat."

She inclined her head. "Right away."

Ivy brushed past him. Could feel him watching her as she crossed the room toward the bar, but she refused to look back. Though she possibly added a bit more sway to her hips.

"Table 15 needs drinks," she told her coworker Vanessa. "Could you handle that for me? Dirty martini for the Dancing Queen. Three olives." They'd all seen the blonde shaking her ass in that leather dress. "Bourbon, neat, for the cowboy."

Setting cocktail napkins on her tray while Kent,

the bartender, filled her order, Vanessa shook her head, her short, artificially red hair swinging. "Don't try to pawn your butt-grabber off on me. I've gone the entire evening without any pats, rubs or pinches. I'd like to keep it that way. Preserve the record."

Ah, the life of a cocktail waitress. People thought the goods being displayed were theirs to touch. Even a subdued, family-type gathering such as an engagement party could get out of hand once the alcohol started flowing.

"He's not a butt-grabber," Ivy said. A man who looked like that, with that deep, subtle twang, didn't have to resort to creepy tactics to get a woman's attention.

"I was talking about the woman," Vanessa said. "She looks capable and more than ready to eat anyone alive. And there must be a reason you don't want to deliver them yourself."

Many, many reasons. The number one being self-preservation.

"Trust me," Ivy said. "Your butt is safe. And the reason I don't want to deliver them myself is because it's my break time."

"Fine. I'll switch you table 15 for table 8."

"Done." Ivy skirted the bar and snagged a flute of champagne from a tray before pushing through the door to a small hallway. She walked past the kitchen on her right, then, farther down, a small break room on the left and kept going until she reached the metal exterior door.

She pushed it open and stepped out into the night. The cold stung her cheeks, stole her breath. Still, she kept going, her high heels echoing on the pavement as she crossed the dimly lit parking lot to her ancient car. She climbed behind the wheel, shut the door and stared blindly through the windshield.

What was that? What the hell was that?

The cowboy had flustered her. Unnerved her. Worse than that, he'd known it.

She'd given him power. Control. Had pretty much handed them over to him on a platter along with her good sense and a portion of her pride.

She took a gulp of champagne. Bubbles exploded inside her mouth, the taste light and expensive, but it did nothing to wash away the bitterness rising in her throat.

Men never flustered her. Why should they? They were simple souls with simple needs. Basic needs. When they saw her, they saw opportunity. What she could do for them. What she had to give them. How she could make them feel.

Why shouldn't she turn that around—twist their desire for her, their attraction to her—to her advantage? A warm smile, a light, friendly touch to an arm, some harmless flirting could all increase her night's tips.

And she was always—*always*—the one ruling the game.

Until one tall, green-eyed cowboy had to come along and mess things up.

She finished the champagne. Wished she'd helped herself to two glasses.

Or at least had had the foresight to grab her coat.

The cowboy's fault, as well. He'd scrambled her thoughts. Her attraction to him had thrown her for a loop, but that was over now. No man got the better of Ivy Rutherford.

The passenger door was yanked opened and she squeaked in surprise, her breath hanging in the air a few inches before her face like a tiny cloud.

"What are you doing out here?" Ivy asked seventeen-year-old Gracie Weaver as the teenager flopped onto the seat and shut the door. "And where's your coat?"

Ivy shook her head. Great. She sounded like a mom. Not Ivy's mother, of course. One of those sitcom moms who always had time for their kids, cared about whether they were warm enough.

One of those moms who loved their daughters instead of blaming them for ruining their lives.

"Brian said he saw you leave," Gracie said, her teeth already chattering. "I figured you'd be here."

"That still doesn't explain why *you're* here."

"One of the guests wants to speak with you. Said it was important."

Ivy's fingers tightened on the glass so hard, she was afraid it'd shatter into a million pieces. Slowly, carefully she set it on the console next to her sunglasses and an empty to-go coffee cup.

"Oh?" Her voice sounded strangled, so she cleared her throat. "Which guest?" she asked, though she already knew.

Oh, yeah, she knew.

"The guy in the cowboy hat."

"Tall? With blond hair and green eyes?"

"Yes and yes. Plus, he's the only guy in the building—probably in the whole town—wearing a cowboy hat. Not sure how else to narrow it down for you." Gracie frowned and rubbed her hands together, then blew on them. "Do you think it's acceptable to wear a cowboy hat indoors? Because my grandma would have a fit if Dad wore his baseball cap inside the house."

"Let's focus on the topic at hand, shall we?" If Ivy didn't keep Gracie on track, the kid could veer so far off topic, they'd never find their way back. "I'm sure whatever the cowboy wishes to discuss, he can do so with Wendy." It would serve the cowboy right if Ivy sent her uptight supervisor over to see what he wanted. "Besides, I already switched tables with Vanessa. She's more than capable of getting his drinks."

"But he wants to talk to you," Gracie said.

"He seems like a guy well used to getting his way." She remembered the confidence in his eyes, bordering on arrogance. The way he held himself, as if he owned the room and everything—and everyone—in it. "This will be a great life lesson for him."

"What if he gets upset?"

"He'll get over it. A little disappointment never killed anyone."

"I wouldn't disappoint him." The teen was all innocent earnestness and dreamy sighs. "He's completely hot. And nice. We had a very interesting conversation earlier, and he didn't come across as creepy at all."

Ivy smiled. Leave it to Gracie to put her in a better mood, no matter what the situation. "Well, noncreep or not, I have no intention of doing his bidding."

"I'm just saying he seems decent. And," Gracie continued, pulling something from her pocket, "he gave me this for finding you."

Ivy raised her eyebrows at the one hundred dollar bill currently being waved in her face. "Really? He bribed a minor to do his dirty work?"

Gracie wrinkled her nose. "I think it was more of a tip. Which means he's generous."

"What it means is that he's willing to pay any price to get his way. That he doesn't mind throwing his money around."

"You could give him a chance. Maybe he just wants to get to know you."

"Yes, I'm sure that's it," Ivy said blandly. "After

speaking with me for less than five minutes, he's intrigued by my mind. Attracted to my sparkling personality."

Oh, to be so young and innocent in the ways of the world.

Ivy almost envied the teen.

"It's possible," Gracie insisted. "Who knows? Maybe he's your soul mate. And if you don't go back there, you could miss your chance with him."

"Honey, I believe in soul mates as much as I do Santa Claus and the Easter Bunny." She softened her tone, squeezed Gracie's arm. "But, to go along with your soul-mates-and-fate theory, we'll just say if it's meant to be, then it'll be. I could ignore him for the rest of the night, and it wouldn't change anything. We'd still end up together."

As long as they ended up together on her terms. Not his.

"I just find it sad," Gracie said with all the melodrama of a soap star, "incredibly, momentously sad, that you're so…so…"

"So…pragmatic?" Ivy asked when the teenager struggled to find the right adjective. Which was unusual as Gracie typically had no trouble with words and loved using as many as possible. "Practical? Reasonable? Realistic?"

Gracie's sigh was a work of art. Long-suffering and heartfelt. Ah, to be seventeen and a master of sarcasm. And a slave to emotions. "Cynical."

"Well, that cuts deep, doesn't it?" Giving her

coworker a thoughtful frown, Ivy kept her tone somber. "But I've now seen the error of my sensible ways, thanks to your amazing grasp of syntax and the perfect amount of pathos in your tone." She lifted the champagne flute in a mock toast. "Pink lacy hearts, huge diamonds and chocolates for everyone."

Tucking one leg under the other, Gracie turned and studied Ivy with her too-intense gaze. "Molly says sarcasm is a defense mechanism used when someone hits too close to the truth."

"Molly has six sons under the age of eight, one of them a newborn. It's obvious your stepmother is a few kale leaves short of a pound, so we're not going to take anything she says to heart."

Another sigh from Gracie, this one just a few notches below resignation. At least all those heavy exhalations were warming up the car a bit. "Don't worry. Someday, you'll get over it."

"If the *it* you're referring to is my common sense, then sorry, but you're going to be majorly disappointed. If a woman doesn't have her wits about her, she has nothing." Ivy dug out a pen and crumpled napkin from the console. Handed them to Gracie. "Write that bit of wisdom down so you remember it."

Gracie didn't even glance at the offerings in Ivy's hands. "*It* being your broken heart. Someday, when you're ready, it will mend, and you will be able to live your life free of all that anger and pain you carry around." She tipped her head, her ponytail bouncing, and studied Ivy some more. "I'm surprised you don't know this. You should have better self-awareness."

Ivy laughed. She got such a kick out of this kid. "Honey, there's not a woman alive who is more self-aware than I am."

Gracie meant well, but she was way off base. Ivy had gone twenty-six years without suffering from a broken heart, and she planned on keeping that streak alive for…oh…forever sounded good.

She already knew the damage heartbreak could cause. It wore you down and stripped you of your pride, leaving you angry, resentful and so hurt, you never got over it.

She may not have experienced it firsthand, but she'd heard about it plenty, had witnessed its effects up close, thank you very much. Her mother had spent her entire life jumping from relationship to relationship, happily swallowing the lies men fed her, believing their promises only to be let down again and again.

So, yeah, Ivy knew all about the frailty of emotions. How they tricked you into believing foolish myths about happy endings and forever after. No other person could complete you or make you happy.

Give away your truth and you gave away the upper hand. Share your secrets, your hopes and dreams and desires, and you lost all power. The idea of true love looked good on paper, but in reality, it was complicated, often messy and, in many cases, downright ugly.

Loving someone made you vulnerable. Weak.

And any weakness led to pain.

GRACIE WATCHED IVY pick up the empty champagne glass, lift it to her mouth and tip it back. When nothing came out, Ivy held the glass out and glared at it, as if she'd expected bubbly wine to magically appear.

"Are you okay?" Gracie asked. She tucked her hands under her legs to warm them. Her nose was starting to run. She sniffed. "You're acting…" *Weird. Flustered.* "…not like yourself."

Ivy was not only possibly the most beautiful woman Gracie had ever seen in real life, she was also the coolest. Always in complete control of her emotions. Her actions.

Gracie knew her well enough to know it was a defense mechanism of some sort, a facade she kept up in order to keep people at bay. Still, she couldn't help but admire Ivy for it.

"I'm fine. Come on. Let's get back inside before we freeze to death."

"Thank goodness." They climbed out and crossed the parking lot, their steps quick, the click-click of Ivy's heels ringing. Pressing her hands to her aching ears, Gracie hurried to keep up, though how Ivy could move so fast in those high heels—

let alone how she wore them during her entire shift—was beyond Gracie. "Do you think there's a correlation between low temperatures and hearing loss? I mean, the cold can affect blood circulation. Extreme heat can affect brain function."

"I have no idea. I'm sure you could find out, though."

That was the thing about Ivy. She never got frustrated with Gracie's questions, was never short with her when she started talking, never interrupted her and told her to condense what she had to say and wrap it up already.

She listened. Really listened. And she believed in Gracie, in her ability to seek out her own answers. To find her own way.

Ivy opened the door, and they stepped into the blessedly warm hallway.

"I have a few more minutes left on my break," Ivy said. "I'm going to grab a bite to eat."

"Okay." Gracie took the one-hundred-dollar bill from her pocket. "I suppose I should give this back to the hot cowboy."

"Why would you do that?"

"He asked me to get you. I didn't."

"He asked you to deliver his message to me. Which you did."

Gracie bit her lower lip. She could use the money, no lie. At the rate her parents kept having kids, they wouldn't be able to afford to pay for her college tuition until she was sixty. "It doesn't seem right."

Ivy looked as if she was about to argue, but then she smiled. "It's up to you. Follow your heart." She picked a tiny silver piece of heart confetti from Gracie's sleeve and handed it to her. "No pun intended."

They parted ways at the end of the hall, Ivy heading into the kitchen, Gracie going back to the main room. The band was playing a slow country song long on melody and short on substance, repeating how love had saved some poor guy.

Gracie wanted to kick the lead singer in the shin. Get him to just stop already.

She was sick of love songs. Yes, it was an engagement party, so she supposed they were fitting, but add the songs to the fact that it was Valentine's Day, and it was all just too much.

V-day. It was so dumb. All that pink. All those hearts and the sappy commercials telling you the only way you were worth anything was if you had a significant other.

It was ridiculous. Being single wasn't a bad thing. You had to be comfortable being alone before you could fully be with someone else anyway.

And she'd keep telling herself that until she finally believed it.

The cowboy was still where she'd last seen him, but now he was talking to a beautiful blonde in a clingy red dress. The woman turned, gestured wildly with her hands, and Gracie realized she wasn't a woman, but a girl around her own age.

A girl with the body of a twenty-five-year-old swimsuit model and the face of a beauty queen. The dress showed ample amounts of toned, tanned thighs and above-average boobs. Her hair fell, thick and straight, to her shoulders, the strands glossy and smooth.

Gracie touched a coarse, loose curl at her temple, tucked it behind her ear.

Nothing like seeing perfection standing effortlessly in a pair of four-inch heels to make a girl feel inadequate.

Gracie frowned. That was just silly. A person's worth should never be based on their looks. So what if the blonde was one of "those girls," the kind who probably never went anywhere— including gym class or a quick trip to the grocery store—without full makeup and high heels. Who rolled out of bed with nary a snarl in their hair or a pimple on their chin.

It took all kinds.

A dark-haired guy tapped the blonde on the shoulder. Something about the color of his hair, the shape of his head seemed familiar. Before Gracie could figure out if she knew him or not, the blonde turned and squealed as if he'd spent the past ten years on a deserted island with only a volleyball for company, then threw her arms around him. Hugging her back, he turned, giving Gracie a clear view of the huge smile on his face.

His handsome, lying face.

Gracie stumbled and rammed her hip into a chair, bumping it so hard against the table, the glasses on it wobbled. Her face flamed. "Sorry," she mumbled to the cowboy, but from the corner of her eye, she saw Andrew Freeman's head jerk up, felt his gaze on her.

The cowboy motioned for her to join him by the large window overlooking the front lawn. She went gratefully. It was better to have that bit of distance between her and where Andrew embraced the beautiful girl.

Better, but not enough. Not nearly enough.

"Couldn't you find her?" the cowboy asked.

Gracie pursed her lips. He didn't seem angry. More like he couldn't understand why she hadn't done what he'd wanted her to do. Ivy's words about him being willing to pay to get his way floated through Gracie's head. Yes, he was nice. And no, he wasn't yelling at her—like some other guests might have done. But he was obviously used to getting his way.

Maybe Ivy had been right to keep her distance.

"I found her," Gracie admitted. "I told her you wanted to speak with her, but she declined."

He raised his eyebrows as if that was a turn of events he'd never expected. "Excuse me?"

"She declined. It means to politely refuse an

invitation. But that's just in this case. Decline could also mean to become smaller or a gradual loss of strength, numbers, qual—"

"I know what *decline* means," he said, exasperation edging his tone.

She got that a lot.

"You looked totally confused, so I wasn't sure."

He rubbed his forehead, bumping the edge of his hat. "Did you tell her I wanted to see her?"

Hadn't she just said that? "Yes. I was very specific. She said you weren't used to being turned down. That this would be a good life lesson for you. So here—" Gracie held out the money. "You can have this back."

He flicked his gaze from her hand to her face. "That's yours."

"But I didn't earn it. And it doesn't feel right, keeping it. Plus, now that I've had time to think about it—" and time to let the excitement of that much money fade "—I realize it's sort of icky, a middle-aged man—"

"Middle-aged?" He looked pained. "I need another drink."

"Giving a teenage girl that much cash. I mean, you don't look like the kind of guy who'd try to bribe young girls to do, well, *things*—if you know what I mean…"

He shut his eyes. "I wish like hell I didn't."

"But then, everyone said Ted Bundy didn't look like a psycho serial killer, either, so I think it's best if I just give it back. Trust me," she continued when he just stood there. "It's better this way. For both of us."

He finally took the cash, and she hurriedly turned away before he decided he was willing to double or triple his offer. She loved Ivy, but Gracie was only human. And if the price were right, she just might be tempted to drag Ivy over here by her hair.

"Hey, Gracie," Andrew said, having disentangled himself from the blonde. "How's it going?"

Gracie pulled up short. Darn it. Why had Andrew approached her? Why was he talking to her?

She wanted to hate him for giving her that lopsided grin of his, especially after bestowing the same smile on another girl not two minutes ago. Wanted to hit him for looking nervous, as if he was scared she was going to start ragging on him. Or worse, ignore him.

She wished she could. But that would make him think he still had the power to hurt her. That she still cared about him.

"I'm fine, thank you," she said, shooting for cool and polite but coming across as uptight and possibly deranged. She tried to work up a smile but figured it would only make things worse. "How are you?"

"Uh, fine. Good. Really good." Andrew cleared his throat, flipped his head to get his stupid floppy dark hair out of his eyes. "I, uh, didn't know you worked here."

Why would he? It wasn't as if they'd had long, involved chats about their lives. Or anything at all. They were neighbors. Not friends.

Even if she had naively believed otherwise not so very long ago.

"I started here a few months ago," she told him.

"Cool. That's...cool."

Thick, uncomfortable silence surrounded them. Which was weird, since the party was still going on, the band still playing, people still talking and laughing.

He shoved his hands into the pockets of his khakis. He was wearing a dress shirt, too, a light blue one that brought out the color of his eyes. She tried to ignore how cute he looked, but she'd pretty much have to take after the cowboy and stick a couple of forks in her eyes for that.

"So, uh, are you doing anything for Spring Break?" he asked.

"No."

"Oh. Me and my mom and Leo—uh, Coach Montesano. You know him, right?"

"Only by sight." Which wasn't a bad way to know the firefighter-slash-high-school-football-coach. He was one beautiful man. And Andrew's mom, Penelope Denning, was dating him.

Lucky woman.

"Right. So, anyway, we're going skiing in Colorado," Andrew said. "Have you ever been?"

"The only places I've been are Pittsburgh and Erie."

He shook his head. "I meant have you ever been skiing?"

"No."

"It's fun." He took his hands out of his pockets. Put them back in again. "Maybe we could go together sometime. I could teach you."

"Why would you want to do that? And why on earth would you think I'd ever agree to it?"

Color swept up his neck and into his cheeks. She refused to feel bad about it.

Not after what he'd done.

He shrugged. Dropped his gaze. "I thought maybe we could, you know...start hanging out again. Like before."

She went cold all over, a deep freeze that chilled her to the bone. She couldn't breathe through it, couldn't move for fear that she'd shatter into a million pieces.

"You want to hang out?" she managed to say through stiff lips. "Like before? God, you must think I'm an idiot."

She turned, but he caught her arm. "No! No," he repeated, more softly this time as he glanced around. "Not like that. I just meant...you know. As friends."

"I don't want to be your friend." Her voice was

even. Dismissive. A miracle as there was a scream building inside her, one she was terrified would escape if she didn't get away from him. "I thought I made that clear the last time we spoke."

He flinched and dropped her arm. "Sorry. I thought..." He sighed. Ran his hand through his hair, leaving it all messy and, yes, sexy. "I thought maybe you'd have forgiven me by now."

She clamped her teeth together to hold back the ugly words in her throat. She didn't owe him anything. Refused to justify her feelings or explain her thoughts.

"Andrew," the blonde girl called. "Come here. I want you to meet my uncle."

He gestured he'd be a minute, then turned back to Gracie. "I, uh, guess I'll see you in school."

She didn't respond. Just walked away.

Of course they'd see each other. She could hardly avoid it in a school the size of Shady Grove High, especially as they shared a few classes.

But she wouldn't acknowledge him. Wouldn't make eye contact or speak to him.

I thought maybe you'd have forgiven me by now.

Her fingers curled, her nails digging into her palms. She'd already forgiven him for pretending to like her, sleeping with her and then treating her like dirt. She'd had to. Hating him hadn't made her feel better. Hadn't stopped the pain or the tears that had come when she'd thought about how stupid she'd been. How gullible.

In the weeks after his betrayal, she'd spent countless hours imagining ways she could exact her revenge. Things she could do or say to humiliate him. To hurt him.

The way he'd hurt her.

But being angry at him had only given him even more power over her—over her thoughts and feelings. So she'd forgiven him and moved on. But she hadn't forgotten.

And she never would.

CHAPTER THREE

IVY HAD THOUGHT about the cowboy all night, like some hormonal teenager in the throes of her first crush. Or a stalker with a new obsession.

She jabbed the elevator's button with her knuckle, tapped her foot impatiently as she waited for it to arrive. Worse than thinking about him? She'd sought him out. Had caught herself scanning the ballroom, the bar—even the hallway for God's sake—more than a few times, hoping to catch a glimpse of him.

There had been plenty of good-looking men there tonight, an abundance of pretty faces for a woman to ogle, but had she stared at any of the Montesano brothers—a trifecta of dark-haired, dark-eyed, handsome men? Or taken a few minutes to appreciate the beauty that was Kane Bartasavich, with his long hair and that hint of danger in his sexy grin?

No and no. She'd skimmed her gaze right over all of them in search of one green-eyed cowboy.

Yeehaw.

The elevator doors opened and she stepped inside. Chose the top floor. Mooning over him was complete idiocy of course. And a total waste of time. She'd given him the brush-off, and he'd respected that. Despite his initial persistence, he hadn't pushed. Hadn't attempted to talk to her again.

She'd figured that would be the end of it. That one of those too many times she'd glanced his way, he'd be pulling out the charm for some other woman. Men. Such fickle, sensitive creatures. She was sure that, after her rejection, he'd move on. Forget all about her.

He hadn't. He'd watched her, just as much as she'd watched him. Throughout the night, she'd felt his gaze on her, warm as a flame, insistent as a touch. And when she'd made the mistake of meeting his eyes, even from across the room, those damn sparks she'd felt when he'd grasped her shoulders were still there.

The elevator dinged as it opened on her floor, and she walked down the empty hallway, her footsteps muffled by the thick carpet. She stopped at room 801, stared at the door. Biting her lower lip, she realized she'd forgotten to reapply her lipstick. Hadn't even taken the time to check her hair. Crap. If those weren't signs that she should turn her little self around and get back in the elevator, she didn't know what was.

Except her body didn't seem to be getting the message. Instead of turning, she raised her hand, curled her fingers into a fist. Instead of walking away, she knocked softly on that door.

He'd sent her running. And that would not do. It was demoralizing to realize she'd been such a coward. He was just a man. A gorgeous, confident, sexy man who was obviously interested in her. The day she couldn't handle a man was the day they needed to take away her high heels and shove her into a pair of mom jeans.

She knocked again, louder this time. Shifted her weight from her right side to her left. The attraction between them was undeniable and mutual. There was nothing to be afraid of.

As long as she was the one in control.

The door opened and there he stood, in all his six-feet-plus glory. And my, my, my, what glory it was. Heaven had blessed the man, that was for sure. His shoes, coat, tie and hat were gone, the sleeves of his shirt rolled up, the top three buttons undone. His hair was shorter than she'd realized, the conservative cut highlighting the strong line of his jaw.

She missed the hat. Wondered if she could talk him into putting it back on.

He skimmed his cool, green gaze over her, his lips curving into a cocky smirk. It took all her willpower not to bolt down the hall as if the hounds of hell were chasing her.

But then his lips flattened, his gaze lingered—

not on her boobs or her hips, but on her mouth—
before he raised his eyes to hers.

Not so cool, not so disinterested, after all.

Silly man. Did he really think he could one-
up her?

She smiled. Oh, she was going to enjoy this.

"I didn't order room service," he said, nodding
toward the champagne in her hand.

"On the house. Looks like it's your lucky day,
cowboy."

"That so?" he murmured, the huskiness in his
voice causing her scalp to prickle. "Funny, but it
doesn't feel that way."

Ivy waved her free hand in the air. "All of that
is changing. You, my friend, are about to have a
reversal of fortune and in the very best way possible."

"Because I get free champagne?"

"Even better." She tipped her head to the side,
her lips curving in an unspoken invitation. "You
get to have a drink with me, after all."

"Just you?" he asked drily. "Or you and that
healthy ego you're carrying around?"

Her smile was quick and appreciative and completely unembarrassed. "We're a package deal."

But when she stepped forward, he leaned against
the door frame, all casual grace and stubbornness,
blocking her. "To what do I owe this reversal of
fortune?"

"Good karma?" She shrugged, didn't miss the

way he glanced at her breasts before yanking his focus back to her face. "Clean living, perhaps?"

He studied her. Looking for whatever answer he needed to hear to let himself get over her earlier rejection. Let him look. She kept her thoughts and her secrets well hidden.

"If you're waiting for me to beg," she said, her tone threaded with humor and a hint of nerves she prayed he couldn't detect, "you're going to be very disappointed."

"I've never been into making people beg," he told her. "For any reason. I'm waiting for you to tell me why you changed your mind."

"Does it matter?"

"Yeah," he said slowly. "I'm afraid it does."

"Most men wouldn't question their good fortune. They'd either accept it as their due or run with it before that luck turned again."

"Well, now, darlin', here's the thing." Leaning toward her, he spoke directly into her ear, his words quiet, his breath warm against her skin. "I'm not most men."

"I guess you're not. But since it's not enough for you that I'm here, that I've changed my mind, which is a woman's prerogative as I'm sure you know, maybe I should just…change it again."

A dare. A challenge. One meant to inspire him to let her off the hook. To accept what she was willing to give, no matter what her reasons.

Or watch her walk away again.

He shifted, bringing their bodies close but not touching. The urge to move back was as strong as the one to step forward. Doing neither, she tipped her head to maintain eye contact.

"I'm not asking for a lot," he said. "Just the truth."

Her laugh was part snort of disbelief, part oh-you-simple-man-you. "Ah, but the truth is the most powerful thing out there."

Their gazes locked. She didn't know whether to laugh or shout in frustration. They were at an obvious impasse. And how had that happened? Men didn't argue with her, for God's sake. They didn't question her motives. Didn't care about those motives, as long as they got what they wanted in the end.

I'm not most men.

That was why she was here, she reminded herself. What attracted her to him.

And wasn't *that* coming back to bite her in the ass?

It didn't matter what he decided, she told herself. Didn't matter that she was holding her breath waiting, that her palms were growing damp. If she walked away, he'd be the one kicking himself for letting her go.

Her pride nudged her to get moving already. Reminded her that she wasn't some pathetic woman in need of a man's approval or his attention. She was strong. Independent. Brave enough to go after what she wanted.

Of course, her pride was also what had pushed her to come to his room in the first place.

Stupid pride.

"Your loss, cowboy," she said, though she wondered if she wasn't losing, as well. She turned, but before she could take a step, he snatched her wrist, held it loosely.

"Don't."

It wasn't an entreaty, more like a command.

Looked as if she wasn't the only one who refused to beg.

Ducking her head, she indulged in a small, triumphant grin before facing him. She flicked a glance to his hand on her, then back up to his eyes. "You have a choice here, cowboy. A very simple one. You can spend the night alone, holding on to your grudge. Or," she continued, sliding closer until her knee bumped his leg, her breasts inches from his chest, "you could spend the night holding on to me." She lowered her voice to a soft, seductive whisper. "What's it going to be?"

Her breath was caught in her chest. Anticipation and nerves warred inside her. His mouth was a grim line, his chest rising and falling steadily as if he were completely unaffected by her nearness. Her words. The image she'd invoked of them together.

As if he really was going to send her on her way.

She needed to leave. To make her exit with as much dignity as possible.

To make it before he took the choice away from her.

But when she tried to tug her wrist free, his grip tightened. She swallowed. Her hand trembled.

He stepped aside and pulled her into his room.

THE WAITRESS SMILED, a small, self-satisfied grin that was incredibly sexy, as she brushed past him. "I guess your mama didn't raise any fools, after all."

C.J. forced himself to let go of her. Shut the door.

He didn't compromise. Didn't negotiate. And he sure as hell didn't give in.

And yet, the fact that she was standing here said otherwise.

"My mother would punch me in the throat if I dared call her mama," he said. "Plus, she helped raise my brother, and he's an idiot."

The waitress tipped her head to the side, making all that abundant hair slide over her shoulder. "Ah, yes, the groom-to-be."

"You know Kane?" He wasn't sure if that was a point in her favor. Or against it.

"We're not acquainted, if that's what you're asking. Although I did go to school with Charlotte."

"Then how did you know he's my brother?" Another thought occurred to him, one he would have considered much earlier had she not scrambled his thoughts so easily. Too easily. "How did you know which room is mine?"

"Oh, I have my ways," she said with a wink. Then she turned and walked farther into the suite, as if expecting him to trail after her like some sort of puppy, eager for her time. A pat on the head.

His eyes dropped to the sway of her hips, the way her skirt hugged her ass.

And he followed.

Not his fault. He was, underneath the wealth, a simple man.

"When I stay at a hotel," he said as she set the champagne on the wooden bar next to the window, "I expect my privacy to be respected."

"Not much privacy in Shady Grove, I'm afraid. Or, I'd guess, in small towns in general. Pretty much everyone knows everyone else. If you don't, you can still get the information want. You just need to pay attention." She bent, searched under the bar for a moment, then straightened with a cloth napkin in her hand. Unwrapped the foil from around the bottle and loosened the wire cage. "People say all sorts of things in front of— as your mother so charmingly described me— *the help.* When a guest needs something or has a complaint, we get all the attention. But most of the time, we're invisible, just ghosts delivering drinks and cleaning up messes."

She didn't sound bothered by it, more as though she was stating a fact.

He skimmed his gaze over her face. No hardship there. He'd spent the greater part of his evening wanting to get another close-up look at her. He wasn't going to waste one moment of it. Not when he'd given up hope of seeing her again.

"You could never be invisible," he told her, his voice gruff. "And you know it."

A small smile playing on her lips, she inclined her head as if in thanks. Or agreement. "Either way, I hear plenty. Probably more than people realize. And you, Clinton Bartasavich Jr., were a hot topic of conversation."

"Is that so?"

He got enough gossip in Houston. He sure as hell didn't need it following him to this Podunk town.

"Now, don't be getting all sensitive," she said, obviously detecting the irritation in his tone. She covered the cork with the napkin, pressed the bottom of the bottle against her hip and neatly twisted until there was a soft *pop*. "If you hadn't wanted people to talk about you, you probably shouldn't have worn that hat."

"I like my Stetson," he said easily.

She made a humming sound. Pulled out two wineglasses from the shelf. "Yes. So did plenty of the women at the party. Trista Macken's grandmother wondered what you would look like in it… and nothing else."

The back of his neck warmed with embarrassment. He glanced at his hat, sitting on the desk next to his open laptop. "Someone's grandmother imagined me naked? I might never wear the damned thing again."

"If it helps, I think the only reason she said it was because all the chardonnay she was guzzling loosened her tongue and her inhibitions."

Frowning, he considered it. Shook his head. "Nope. Doesn't help."

"Don't be too hard on Mrs. Macken. She was actually the one I overheard say you were Kane's brother." The waitress poured champagne into the glasses. Picked them up and sashayed toward him, a siren in high heels and tiny skirt, certain of her appeal, confident of the effect she had on a man. "Though I'd already guessed you two were related, given the resemblance between you."

"That still doesn't explain how you knew which room was mine."

"Now, that's where my amazing deductive skills come into play." Stopping in front of him, she offered him a glass. After he took it, she sat on the sofa and crossed those long legs, her foot swinging idly. "It's obvious no regular room would do for someone like you—"

"Someone like me?" he asked, eyes narrowed. She vaguely waved a hand at him. "The designer suit, diamond cuff links and that air of privilege and entitlement surrounding you make it clear you only accept the best. The best suites at King's Crossing are all on this floor, the top floor. The best rooms, the best views of the river... It was all pretty simple, really."

"And you knocked on every door on this floor until you found me?"

"Not quite. Come," she said, patting the spot next to her. "Have a seat and I'll tell you a secret. You can keep a secret, can't you?"

He sat, his thigh pressed against hers. Let his gaze drop to her mouth for one long minute before meeting her gaze again. "If the price is right, I can."

"I asked a coworker who works the front desk to find your room number."

"Which coworker?" It had to have been a man. What warm-blooded, heterosexual male could refuse her anything?

"So you can get him fired?" She shook her head. "I don't think so."

He set aside his untouched champagne. "Maybe I want to thank him."

She laughed, a slow, sexy sound, which did nothing to help his already screwed-up equilibrium. "You don't. You want to march down there and hand him his ass."

"More of your deductive skills at work?"

"More like good, old-fashioned common sense.

It's clear you're a man used to getting what you want. You don't ask for anything. You demand it. And when you don't get it, there's hell to pay."

"These theories you have about me are fascinating."

"You don't really think so, but there's more. For instance, when I asked if you could keep a secret, you said *if the price is right*, which tells me you don't do anything free. No favors from you."

"Favors come with strings attached."

"I won't argue. People are inherently users. They'll take and take and take until a person has nothing left to give. Then they'll move on to the next poor soul they can suck dry."

"A cynic."

She lifted her glass in a mock toast. "A realist. Something we have in common. You're also neat—no clothes lying around, cluttering up your space, no shoes to trip over. A place for everything and everything in its place, if I had to guess. You have a hard time separating yourself from your work," she continued, gesturing to his laptop and the contract he'd been reading when she'd knocked on his door. "How am I doing?"

His shoulders went rigid. He didn't like her reading him so clearly when he couldn't get a handle on her. Hell, he didn't even know her name.

"You have me at a disadvantage," he said tightly.

"Only one?" she murmured before sipping her champagne. "I must be losing my touch."

He had to bite back a sudden grin. Damn it, but he appreciated her quick mind. Her self-assurance and intelligence.

Shit. He was in so much trouble.

"You seem to know quite a bit about me," he said. "But I don't even know your name."

"That's easy enough to fix." Shifting forward in a movement that did some really interesting things to her breasts in the tight, white shirt she wore, she held out her free hand. "I'm Ivy."

It didn't suit her. It was too innocent, too sweet, when she was all female power.

He held her hand, liked the feel of her palm against his. "Ivy," he repeated softly, and her eyes darkened. He rubbed his thumb against the back of her hand, wanting to see if he could fluster her the way she'd flustered him. "Just Ivy?"

"Is that a problem?" Her gaze was steady, her expression amused. Not flustered in the least.

But when he let go, he noticed the unsteadiness of her hand, how she curled her fingers into her palm.

"I like to know who I'm talking to." Wanted to know more about her.

"You're talking to me."

"I could find out easily enough," he pointed out. All he had to do was make a call to the front desk or ask to speak to the restaurant's supervisor.

"You could, but there's no reason to. You and me? We aren't going to be friends."

"We're not?"

"Hardly. Look, we both know there's a...pull between us. A strong one. I didn't come up here so we could get to know each other better, just as you didn't ask me to have a drink with you within five minutes of meeting me so we could swap life stories. We want to explore this attraction between us. Why pretend it's something other than what it is? I don't need it prettied up. I don't need small talk, persuasion or seduction, and I sure as hell don't need promises." She laid her hand on his arm, scooted closer, her fingers warm, her scent surrounding him. "I want you, Clinton," she said, drawing his name out as if tasting it on her tongue. "Tonight, all I want is you."

Desire slammed into him like a wildfire, threatened to burn away his willpower and common sense. Her agile mind and sharp sense of humor intrigued him. Her face and body attracted him. But it was the combination of everything—her looks and personality, her intelligence and wit— that left him speechless. Breathless.

Made him want her with a hunger that bordered on desperation.

She was dangerous to his self-control. His pride.

He had to figure her out. Had to do whatever was needed to gain the upper hand.

Even if part of him was screaming at him to take what she was offering and leave it at that.

"You declined to have a drink with me," he reminded her. "Refused to even speak to me."

"Still stuck on that, huh?" She patted his knee. "How about you build a bridge and get over it?"

"You changed your mind when you found out my last name."

Letting her hand rest on his leg, she raised her eyebrows. "Wow. I'm not sure if you're giving yourself too much credit. Or not enough."

He grinned. "Believe me, darlin', I give myself plenty of credit."

"Just not everyone else. Or maybe," she continued softly, "it's just me you don't think too highly of."

What he thought was that she was just like everyone else. No matter how much he wished she wasn't. He had to question everything. Everyone. He was a Bartasavich.

And he had to know that wasn't why she was here.

"Weren't you the one who said people were users?" he asked. "I need to know who you are. Why you changed your mind."

IVY WASN'T SURE whether to smack the man upside his too-handsome head or laugh outright. She was practically in his lap, her hand on his thigh, and he wanted to talk about why she was there?

There was obviously something wrong with him. And, possibly, something amiss with her, as well, since she was enjoying their verbal battle so much. When they finally came together, it was going to be explosive.

A thrill shot through her, anticipation climbing. She could hardly wait.

She smoothed her hand up his leg an inch. His muscles tensed, and he grabbed her hand to stop her from exploring any farther.

Too bad. She liked the feel of him. Solid and warm. She sensed there was an edge to him underneath the expensive clothes, a power he kept carefully contained.

She couldn't wait to be the one to make him lose that control. "The beauty of a situation like this is that I can be whoever you want me to be."

"I want you to be honest."

She almost scoffed, but then she looked at him, really looked, and saw that he meant it. He was attracted to her, yes, that much was clear, but he wasn't going to give in to his desire. Not until he got what he wanted.

Silly, stubborn man.

But he wouldn't be the only one who was going to lose if he sent her on her way. And really, telling him what he wanted to hear wasn't a big deal. She was still in charge. Still the one deciding how much to share. And how much to keep hidden.

It didn't have to change anything, didn't mean there was anything between them other than sex. Uncomplicated, no-strings-attached, possibly mind-blowing sex. A one-night stand between two virtual strangers who would go their separate ways in the morning.

That last realization cinched it. She didn't have to worry about opening up, just the tiniest bit, to a man she'd never see again. Nothing she told him would matter after tonight.

"There's more to you than you let on," she said.

He frowned. "Excuse me?"

"You wanted to know why I changed my mind. You think it's a game, and it's not. Well, maybe not completely." Her throat was parched, so she took a long drink then set her glass down. Tugged her hand from under his. "I had every intention of keeping my distance from you. I thought you were exactly as you seemed. Arrogant. Bossy." She pursed her lips as she considered him. "Entitled. Uptight—"

"I get it," he said, his tone all sorts of dry.

But he didn't correct her or try to claim he wasn't those things. She could appreciate a man who knew his strengths as well as his weaknesses.

"As the night went on you surprised me. You didn't flirt with other women after I turned you down, which makes me believe you weren't out to get laid."

His laugh was a quick burst of sound that scraped pleasantly against her skin. "Let's not get carried away."

She returned his grin. "You weren't *only* out

to get laid. If you were, plenty of women at the party would have been willing to give you anything you wanted. So I knew you weren't just out to scratch an itch. Plus, you did your best to keep your mother sober—and off the dance floor—and you tolerated her thick-necked date, which means you feel responsible for her well-being or, at least, her reputation, and care about her feelings. You sat with your father for almost an hour, which means you're patient."

And she didn't even want to think about what it said about her that she'd noticed how long he'd sat by the wheelchair, talking to the uncommunicative man. How upset he'd seemed.

"You came to my room because I'm a good son?" he asked, clearly not buying it.

Except it was the truth. Just not all of it.

She edged closer, her knee pressing against his. "I realized it was unfair of me to make assumptions about you based on how you looked."

People did that to her all the time. They saw her face, her body, her clothes and thought they knew her.

She'd long ago stopped trying to get them to see her as something more than her looks. Why bother? It wouldn't change anything. It was easier to play along.

"And in doing so," she continued, "in walking away from you, I'd miss out on seeing where this attraction between us led."

One corner of his mouth turned up, making him look younger. More approachable. But the heat in his eyes, the way he watched her reminded her that he was still a dangerous man. A potent one. "So you're admitting the attraction was mutual from the start."

"I don't deny the obvious. But now it's your turn."

"My turn to admit the obvious?"

Keeping her eyes on his, she shook her head slowly. "Your turn to make the next move."

CHAPTER FOUR

CLINTON STUDIED HER, as if he was trying to get inside her head, see into her soul. As if he wanted to know her thoughts, feelings and secrets.

She'd chosen to share a few of those with him, but the rest were hers to keep.

Such as how hard it had been for her to come here, to knock on his door. How she wasn't sure which had been a bigger mistake—refusing him earlier or changing her mind. How scared she was that he was going to send her on her way.

How she didn't want to be alone tonight.

But he couldn't know any of that. She kept her expression clear. Waited while he looked his fill, while he made up his mind.

"You're trouble," he finally said.

Tension burst out of her in a short laugh. That was his big revelation? "So I've been told. What's wrong with a little trouble?"

He looked at her as though she'd asked what was wrong with a little nuclear war. "I don't do trouble."

But he was getting closer to it. Literally. Leaning forward, he wrapped his big hands around her upper arms. Pulled her gently toward him.

"No?" she asked softly, her heart racing.

He shook his head, his eyes dark with want. "I fix things. Make the trouble disappear."

She'd noticed. Had watched him put out one small fire after another at the party, taking care of his parents, getting the busty blonde who'd been hitting on his brother to back off. Dancing with his niece when she pulled him onto the dance floor.

Ivy let her gaze drop to his mouth, linger there as she ran her tongue across her bottom lip. "Do you really want me to disappear?"

His fingers tightened, his nails digging into her skin. Though it killed her not to touch him, not to close the distance between them and press her mouth against his, she kept her hands in her lap. Stayed perfectly still. She'd meant it when she'd said the next move was his. He may not like playing games but he was participating willingly in this one. And far be it from her to take away the man's belief that he had the upper hand.

As long as she was the one holding the best cards.

His hands slid up her arms slowly, across her shoulders. He stabbed his fingers into the hair at the nape of her neck, his thumbs nudging her chin up. Her mouth parted. Her breathing quickened.

He tugged her forward. Later, much later, she would worry about that. About how he'd turned the tables. How, instead of coming to her, he was bringing her to him. But for now, with his palms warm against her cheeks, all she could think about was his touch. His kiss.

His head came closer, his features blurring. She wanted to shut her eyes, to lose herself in sensations, but she couldn't look away. He paused when their mouths were inches apart. The air surrounding them stilled. Thickened. All she could see was his face, all she could hear was the blood rushing in her ears.

All she wanted was him.

His breath washed over her, and she made a sound in the back of her throat that could only be described as needy. Dear Lord, he hadn't even kissed her yet, and she was already acting like a fool, her brain fogged with desire. It was humiliating, needing him this much. It was dangerous, being this weak for a man. If Ivy wasn't careful, she'd lose her good sense and her pride.

She couldn't make herself care.

She lifted her hands to his chest, curled her fingers into his shirt and yanked him to her.

Yes, she thought as their mouths met. This was what she wanted. The flash of heat. The heady desire. His kiss was hard and hungry, his lips firm. Beneath her hands, he was solid. Warm. She'd expected finesse. Control. After all, he had both in spades. But what she got was an answer to her own desire, one that matched it. A heat that threatened to consume her.

His fingers tightened on her hair, the bite and tug ramping up her excitement as he tipped her head to the side to deepen the kiss. She slid her hands over the hard planes of his chest, up to his shoulders. Down his arms. He tasted of whiskey and smelled like heaven. She wanted to rub against him, imprint the feel of him on her skin, absorb his scent into her pores.

She pushed him back, trapping him between her and the back of the couch. His hands raced down her back, then smoothed up her torso, his thumbs brushing the sides of her breasts. She shifted, lifting her leg only to give a grunt of frustration when her skirt trapped her. Not breaking the kiss, she rose onto her knees and pulled the material up her thighs, then straddled him so they were connected, chest, belly and pelvis. He lifted his hips, had the hard ridge of his erection pressing against her.

She playfully bit his lower lip, then ran her tongue over it before fusing her mouth to his again. He felt wonderful. Even better than she'd imagined. All lithe muscles and carefully contained strength and power.

She couldn't wait to make him lose that control. To be the one to unleash that power.

He pulled her shirt out of her waistband, slid

his hands under the fabric, his nails lightly scraping her spine. She tore at his buttons, her fingers clumsy. Frantic. One button snagged, and she jerked it clear, leaving it to dangle by a string. She worked the rest free, shoved the shirt down his arms, where the sleeves bunched at his wrists.

Breaking the kiss, he sat up and yanked the shirt off, tossing it aside. He leaned back, the ridges of his abs bunching, his pecs well-defined. She smoothed her hands over his shoulders. Combed her fingers through the springy golden hair covering his broad chest.

She kissed him. His lips. His cheeks and chin, then along the sharp line of his jaw. His cologne was intoxicating, the taste of his skin enticing. She nipped at the pulse that was beating rapidly at the side of his neck, then slid lower, her belly brushing his hard length as she worked her way down his chest. She flicked her tongue over one nipple, and he groaned, so she repeated the action on the other side. Opened her mouth over it and rubbed it with the flat of her tongue. His breathing quickened. His hand shot to her head, his fingers digging into her scalp.

With a satisfied smile, she trailed her mouth lower. She swirled her tongue, tasting his skin, then leaned back so she could watch her forefinger follow the light trail of hair disappearing into his pants. She dragged her finger up to his belly button then added a second for the return trip. Up and down again, two fingers became three. This time when she went up, she laid her hand flat on him, felt his muscles jump under her touch.

She lifted her gaze to his. He watched her through hooded eyes, his chest rising and falling rapidly. She drew her hand down, down, down. When she reached his pants, she raised the heel of her hand, her fingers skimming over his belt buckle before she settled her palm on him.

He inhaled with a sharp hiss, pushing himself harder into her hand.

Indulging herself for a moment, she cupped his impressive length, reveling in his groan. She slid down to kneel between his legs, her fingers at his belt, loosening the buckle, eager to feel the heat of his skin, the weight of him.

He stood suddenly, in one smooth move, and she squeaked and grabbed hold of his shoulders as he lifted her. His hands went under the backs of her thighs, urging her to wrap her legs around his waist as he strode toward the bedroom.

She complied, looping her arms around him and threading her hands in his hair as she pressed her face against the crook of his neck. "I was just getting to the good stuff."

"Bed." The word was more of a growl than actual speech. She lifted her head. Grinned. She'd reduced the man to barely decipherable, monosyllabic grunts.

She shouldn't be so pleased, but damn it, she was.

He stepped into the room, shifted her weight to one arm and flipped the switch on the wall, turning on the lamp next to the king-size bed.

"For what I want to do to you, cowboy," she murmured, flicking his earlobe with her tongue, "we don't need a bed."

His step faltered—not a lot but enough for her to notice. His fingers tightened on her legs. "We do," he insisted as he carried her across the room and followed her down to the mattress, "for all the things I'm going to do to you."

Her stomach churned. From excitement, she told herself. Okay, and maybe just the tiniest bit of fear, but not because she was afraid he'd hurt her. Because she was afraid of not being able to keep control.

He kissed her again, his mouth voracious, his hands seeking. She tried to get her control back, to keep the power firmly on her side, but his mouth was hot and hungry. He made it hard to resist responding with no care to the little sounds she was making, to how her hands were clutching him, how her head was spinning.

He tore his mouth from hers, and she almost cried out. Tried to pull him to her again, but he resisted, began working the buttons of her shirt, sliding them through the holes one at a time, his moves slow and controlled. His eyes followed each new inch of exposed skin.

She reached to help him, to hurry him—and he lightly slapped her hands away. Gave his head a quick shake. "Mine."

The one word, grumbled and insistent and possessive, went through her, making the hairs on the back of her neck rise.

Mine.

Her arms fell to the bed, as if boneless. Panic suffused her. She couldn't breathe, couldn't think, not with his hands on her, his palms skimming her rib cage as he opened her shirt. Not with that word echoing in her mind.

Mine.

He slipped a finger under the front clasp of her bra, tugging it away from her skin, stroking his knuckle between her breasts.

"I'm not yours." She winced. Her words had come out in a croak and not the flirtatious, aren't-you-cute-to-think-so tone she'd wanted. She swallowed. Tried again. "No delusions of grandeur, remember? I don't belong to any man."

He kept up with the stroking, his other hand lightly holding her waist. "No, you don't belong to me. But right here, right now, you're mine." He flicked open her bra and she wasn't sure whether to be amused, impressed or irritated he did so with one hand. "You're mine," he repeated gruffly. "Just for tonight."

She wanted to argue, she really did, but he slid one hand up, taking his sweet time, until he reached the edge of her bra. He separated the cups, pushing them aside, exposing her breasts to his hungry gaze. Then his hands were on her, and all ability to speak disappeared. He held her, his palms large and warm against her breasts, and she prayed he couldn't feel the hammering of her heart. That he didn't suspect what he did to her, how weak he made her.

With a moan of appreciation, he lowered his head and licked one nipple before taking it in his mouth and sucking hard. He worked her other breast, his clever fingers pinching and tugging until she was gasping for breath. Until she was squirming beneath him.

She touched his head, loving the feel of his hair, like cool silk, as the strands slid between her fingers. He kissed his way down her abdomen, held her hips as he dipped his tongue into her belly button. Her heart raced, her skin heated and became overly sensitive to his touch, to the light abrasion of his whiskers, the feel of his lips, the rough pads of his fingers.

He pushed her skirt up in that same slow way— as if savoring every moment with her, every touch of her skin, every sound she made—bunching the material at her waist. His eyes narrowed as he reached out and lightly traced the edge of her black lace panties.

"Pretty." His voice was a low hum that seemed to reverberate inside her.

Hooking his fingers in the sides of her panties, he pulled them down. When he reached her feet, he lifted her right ankle, took her shoe and the panties off then repeated the action on the left. She wanted him to hurry, needed them to get back to where they'd been in the living room, was desperate for that flash of heat, the bite of hunger.

She started to sit up, only to have him settle his hand between her breasts and gently push her back.

"I want to look at you."

She opened her mouth to remind him of the lesson she'd given earlier, about not always getting what he wanted, but then she noticed that while he kept one hand on her ankle, as if he couldn't bear to break contact, the other was fisted. A muscle jumped in his jaw, and she knew he was as affected as she was.

Smiling to hide her nerves, she eased back. But it was torture, lying there while his gaze raked over her. She'd never felt so exposed. So vulnerable.

"You are so beautiful," he said, his voice low and rough.

Her throat clogged. Her chest ached. She'd been called beautiful before, too many times to count.

Too many times to feign modesty about something that was more genetics than anything she'd done to deserve the compliment. Too many times to have it mean something.

But hearing it from him? It meant something.

Stupid, stupid, stupid. They were just words. She didn't need them to know what she looked like, didn't want to be seduced or to let any man think he'd taken away her choice. Her power.

But Clinton was threatening to do just that with his light accent, his sure touch. Though he'd claimed not to like games, Ivy couldn't help but feel he was playing along. She had to regain her control. Before she could, he was nudging her legs apart.

"Mine," he breathed, then settled his mouth on her.

She arched into him, her head back, her hands in his hair. Maybe control was overrated.

Sensations flowed through her, her limbs growing heavy, her muscles lax as the pressure built. When her orgasm broke, she rode the waves of pleasure with a soft cry.

She floated back to earth, her breathing ragged, her skin coated in a fine sheen of sweat.

She was boneless, weightless, her body still flushed and vibrating. It took her a moment, surely longer than necessary, to focus on him. He shouldn't look so strong, so commanding, kneeling before her like that, tension emanating from his long, lean body, his hair mussed from her fingers, his face all sharp lines and angles.

She shouldn't want him this much. Not nearly this much.

She absently rubbed her hand over the odd, unwelcome catch in her heart.

And wondered if maybe he wasn't holding all the cards, after all.

IF A MAN didn't have self-control, he had nothing.

C.J. was afraid he was very close to having nothing.

Because the taste of Ivy on his tongue, the feel of her under his hands, the sight of her—all that smooth skin, all those glorious curves—threatened his resolve to keep things between them on even ground. To keep himself in charge.

She watched him, her blue eyes slowly focusing. Turning wary. Shuttered.

Mine.

He curled his fingers into his palms. She'd been pissed when he'd said it, but he didn't want her to belong to him. Didn't want to own her or control her. He just wanted her, all of her, for one night. He wouldn't let her hide from him.

But he had to be careful. Ivy was powerful. Knew how to twist a man into knots, knew how to kiss him, exactly where to touch him to make him weak. Mindless.

In the living room he'd been nothing more than

aching need. Burning desire. He'd resisted—
barely—the urge to take her like an animal, to
push his way into her lovely heat, but it had cost
him.

Scared the hell out of him.

He couldn't stop himself from touching her.
He traced light circles above her knees, and she
smiled a small, satisfied smile. He shifted onto his
hands and knees, crawled over her, loving how
her legs opened to accommodate him, how she
reached for him.

He pressed his nose against the base of her
throat and breathed her in. She was perfect. Her
beauty called to him, but it was her confidence,
her keen intelligence that drew her in. Fascinated
him.

He raised his head, slid up her body. Her hard
nipples brushed against his chest, and he bit back
a groan. Shoveled his hands into her hair above
her ears, his thumbs at her temples.

"You take my breath," he told her, not happy
about admitting it. Even less happy that it was
true.

"I'm going to do so much more than that." She
leaned up to give him a firm kiss. Gently bit his
lower lip, tugging at it before letting go again.
"I'm going to take all of you. I want you inside
me, Clinton. I want you."

Her words blew through him, and he crushed
his mouth to hers with a low growl. She answered

his kiss, the ferocity of it, the need, as she pushed against him, forcing him back until he sat on his heels. She scooted out from under him, tore off her shirt and bra and let them drop to the rumpled bed then wiggled out of her skirt. Her head lowered, she opened his belt, undid his pants.

The back of her hand brushed against his stomach, and he sucked in a breath. He stood, quickly shed his pants and underwear, stepping out of them as he reached for her.

She held up a hand, stopping him. "My turn."

He shook his head. How the hell was he supposed to think clearly when his mind was buzzing? When she knelt on the bed like a fantasy come true, her hair a mass of gold, her eyes heavy-lidded, her mouth pink and swollen from his kiss?

"Your turn?" he repeated dumbly.

"My turn to look at you." She let her gaze roam over him, taking her time—payback, he was sure, for how he'd taken his with her. "My turn to touch you."

If possible, he got even harder, his entire body stiffening as she moved toward him, not stopping until the tip of his penis brushed the soft curls at the apex of her thighs. It took all his willpower not to yank her against him, not to bury himself in her, right then and there.

She laid her hands below his chest, her palms flat against his rib cage, then smoothed them down to his waist before trailing her fingers across his lower abdomen. His cock jumped.

And smiling, she wrapped one warm, soft hand around him and squeezed gently.

His eyes nearly popped out of his head, and he couldn't stop from pulsing against her palm. Prayed he had the strength to make it through the next few minutes without embarrassing himself. Without letting her know how badly he wanted her. How much he needed to be with her.

She shifted closer, and the movement had her breasts swaying, her hair sliding over her shoulder. Then she bent her head, that hair a curtain, and licked the tip of his erection. Made a purring sound of approval before taking him in her mouth.

He went wild. The sight of her giving him such pleasure, the feel of her mouth on him was too much. He jerked her upright, cut off her delighted laughter with a rough kiss.

He couldn't get enough of her. Wanted only the feel of her on his fingers, the taste of her kiss on his lips. It was exciting and frightening as hell, but he couldn't stop himself. He cupped her breasts, kissed her throat and then moved down to take one tip into his mouth and sucked. Her hips bucked, and she dug her nails into his back.

C.J. fell onto the bed, had enough sense to support his weight on his elbows so he didn't crush her, but kept their cores aligned, her softness against his hardness, their hands giving pleasure as their kisses grew hotter, a clashing of tongues and teeth.

She grabbed his ass, pulled him against her, rubbing her curls against him. "Clinton," she gasped. "Now."

The words sounded ripped from her throat, raw and needy.

He reared up, grabbed his pants from the floor and dug into his pocket for his wallet, pulled out a condom. He sheathed himself quickly and took her in his arms, but she pushed against his shoulders, turning them until he was on his back. She straddled him, a siren here to make all his dreams come true, a woman in control of her body and her emotions.

Until you looked closer and saw the flush on her cheeks, the way her chest rose and fell quickly. Saw that her eyes were slightly dazed, her hands unsteady.

He couldn't look away as she rose onto her knees and kissed him. He wound that magnificent hair around his hands, held on as she lowered herself and took him into her body.

Her lips parted on a sound of wonder, and he clenched his fingers, tugging her head back. She was hot and tight and wet for him. She began to move, rocking slowly against him, her hands on his chest, her fingers curled as if seeking purchase. He let her set the pace until he couldn't stand it any longer.

Gripping her waist, he thrust into her, again and again, going harder, faster, deeper. Their bodies grew slick with sweat, and she made low, throaty moans that drove him crazy. She rode him, her hips pumping until she tightened around him, her back arched, her eyes closed as she came.

While Ivy was still in the throes of climax, he wrapped his arm around her and flipped her onto her back.

"Look at me," he demanded, moving inside her.

Her eyes opened and he held her gaze as he quickened his pace. His body tensed and, with a low shout, he emptied himself in her.

HE WASN'T A man to overindulge.

Hell, he wasn't a man to indulge, period.

C.J. snorted at that thought as he woke up hours later, his eyes still closed. Many would disagree, seeing as how he owned a penthouse apartment in Houston, a ranch he rarely got to outside Denver, more cars than one man needed in a lifetime and various other toys, including a boat he'd been on once and his own small airplane.

Which he fully intended to learn how to fly one day.

So, yes, one could say he indulged in material things, but he didn't indulge in risks. Couldn't afford to when he had so many people to look out for. When he had so much to lose.

But he'd indulged last night. Had given in to desire and had taken Ivy to bed.

He couldn't even regret it. Not when it had been everything he'd imagined and more.

He picked up his phone from the bedside table and glanced at the time. Not even five. He heard her moving around in the bathroom, told himself he needed to get up, get showered and shaved. He could order room service, work on the proposal sitting on the desk, make a few phone calls before his ten o'clock flight back to Houston.

But he could hardly kick Ivy out. He didn't have a lot of experience with one-night stands, but he knew better than to try to get rid of a woman before she was ready to leave. Still, he needed her gone.

If only because he wanted her to stay.

Ivy stepped out of the bathroom, the light illuminating her shape before she shut the door, enclosing the room in darkness again. He waited, hearing her move carefully, and realized she wasn't coming back to bed.

She was leaving.

He sat up and turned on the lamp. She whirled around, her shoes in her hand, and he saw a flash of uncertainty in her eyes. But then she blinked, and he wondered if he'd imagined the whole thing.

"Sorry," she said, her voice still sleep roughened. "I didn't mean to wake you."

"Obviously," he said, wondering why he was

so pissed that she'd been ready to sneak out like a thief in the night. "Not going to say goodbye?"

She studied him. She should have looked haggard—neither of them had gotten a lot of sleep last night. After they'd had sex the first time, they'd both dozed, but he'd woken up hard for her not two hours later. Still, there were no dark circles under her eyes. Her hair was a shiny mass waving softly around her shoulders, her face clean of makeup.

His groin tightened. Hell, would he ever get enough of her?

"I'm not big on goodbyes," she finally said. "And like I said, I didn't want to wake you."

"I'm up now." In more ways than one, har har. He patted the bed. "Come here."

She tipped her head. "I don't think so."

He wasn't sure he'd heard her correctly. Then again, she'd been right when she'd told the teenage waitress he wasn't used to being turned down. "Excuse me?"

Balancing on one leg, she put on her shoe, then switched sides to put on the other one. "I said I don't think so. You've got the look of a man ready for another tumble." She flipped her hair off her shoulder. "Afraid you're out of luck in that regard."

"I want you. I want to touch you again. Taste you. I want to feel your body tighten around me. I want to watch your face while I make you come."

"Your wants have been noted. They're also going to be denied."

His eyes narrowed. What kind of game was this? "We were good together."

"That we were, but it was a one-time thing. You see, I decide who touches me and when. And right now, you're not on that list."

He swung his legs off the side of the bed and stood, his movements carefully controlled. "You wanted me to touch you last night."

"Right again, but now I don't." She slid her gaze over his naked body, his erection. Then she smiled at him. "Nice meeting you, cowboy."

And she turned and sashayed out of the room.

C.J. couldn't believe it. Who the hell did she think she was? No one walked away from him.

They weren't done. Not by a long shot.

He strode into the living room as the suite door shut behind her. Fully intending to chase her out into the street if necessary, he made it halfway across the room before remembering he didn't have any clothes on.

Son of a bitch.

He rushed back to the room and grabbed his pants, was yanking them on when he went into the hall, his long, angry strides eating up the distance. But not fast enough.

She was already gone.

He jogged down to the elevator, jabbed the button repeatedly. "Come on, come on," he muttered like a curse, like a prayer. He considered taking the stairs, but that would take too much time.

Finally, the elevator pinged and the doors opened. He leaped inside, pressed the button for the lobby... and caught sight of his reflection in the mirrors.

Aw, hell.

His hair was standing on end, his chest and feet bare, his pants not even zipped, his eyes wild.

He'd lost his ever-loving mind.

The doors started to close, and he stuck his arm out, stalked back to his room only to find the door had shut behind him, locking him out.

He glared at it. Considered giving it a good kick but he'd probably just break his toes. Now he'd have to go down the hall, knock on his mother's or Oakes's door, come up with some lie about how he'd locked himself out of his room at this hour, half-dressed.

Served him right for acting like an idiot. He didn't even know Ivy's last name, and yet he'd been chasing after her, ready to beg her to stay with him, just for another hour or so.

She was right. What had happened between them was a one-time deal. Just as they both wanted.

The sooner he forgot about her, the better.

CHAPTER FIVE

Four months later

"GRACIE, WAIT UP!"

Gracie stopped and turned, held her hand up to shade her eyes from the bright, midday sun. Only to slowly lower it when she saw Luke Sapko jogging toward her. She blinked, frowning. Held her eyes shut for a moment, but when she opened them again, he was still there, except closer, thanks to the jogging and all.

She glanced behind her and then rolled her eyes when she realized she was looking around to see who he was talking to.

He was talking to her, of course. Although, it actually would be more likely that there just happened to be another Gracie—one he'd said more than two words to over the past five years—walking down Blaisdell Avenue right now.

Biting her lower lip, she considered—briefly but with much relish—turning around and just… walking away. Pretending she hadn't heard him, that she hadn't seen him trying to catch up to her. But that would be rude. And she wasn't rude.

Too bad. It would probably come in handy at times.

Such as when a girl stood in the middle of the sidewalk, the sun burning her bare shoulders, sweat running down her back while she waited to see what the heck the captain of the football team could possibly want from her.

"Hey," he said when he reached her.

She dug deep to find a way to return his smile. Nope. Not happening. "Hello, Luke."

Okay, that had sounded sort of prissy. And completely unfriendly.

Maybe she could be just the tiniest bit rude. Funny how, instead of making her feel ashamed, she was doing an internal celebratory dance.

She'd have to contemplate what that meant later.

"How's it going?" Luke asked, hands in the pockets of his khaki cargo shorts, his smile still on his face, as if he was really happy to be chatting with her.

Must be a slow day in the jock world in which he lived. No games on ESPN, weights to lift, protein shakes to make or half-witted teammates to hang out with.

She winced. Sighed so deeply she felt it all the way to her toes. Bitter? Her? Well, maybe a little.

It was all Andrew Freeman's fault. But that was no reason to take it out on Luke.

"I'm fine." Other than, you know, her head being hot—having thick, curly hair was like having your very own fur hat—and wondering why on earth Luke was talking to her. Yes, just fine and dandy. And because she hadn't liked her earlier mean thought about the half-wits, she cleared her throat and forced herself to ask, "How about you?"

"Everything's good, thanks." Well, there was a lesson in politeness right there.

Then again, Luke had always been nice. At least to her face. She had no idea what he said about her behind her back. And how egotistical was that? Luke probably never gave her a second thought.

Unless…unless Andrew mentioned her to him?

She snorted, covered it with a fake cough when Luke sent her a curious look. Why on earth would Andrew talk about her? Yes, yes, he and Luke were best friends, one of those bromances so popular in high school and cop movies, but Andrew hadn't wanted anyone to know he and Gracie hung out.

He'd been embarrassed by her.

The back of her throat ached. Her nose tingled. No. No way was she going to get all weepy over him. She was over what he'd done. All the way over it. No grudges or bad feelings.

She was bigger than that.

Even if there were times she felt small. Small, petty and totally unlike herself. Unlike the person she wanted to be.

"Great," she said, realizing it was her turn to talk. She gestured behind her. "I actually have to get to work now, so…"

But when she started walking away, he fell into step beside her.

What good was all that positive karma she'd built up over her lifetime if it left her at times like this?

She snuck a sideways glance at him. He was tall, and his green T-shirt clung to his broad shoulders, the sleeves hugging his well-defined arms. He'd gotten a haircut sometime during the three weeks since school had let out, and the shorter style accentuated the lines of his face, made him look older. Less cute and more…va-va-voom.

If you liked that sort of thing.

"How'd you do on the SATs?" he asked.

"How did you know I took the SATs?"

"I took them the same day. Remember?"

Well, of course *she* remembered. She just hadn't thought he'd noticed her there that morning.

"I did okay." Actually, she'd done better than okay. And really, was it so horrible if she casually mentioned her score? He might be good-looking, popular and athletic, but she was smart. Everyone knew the teenagers deemed geeks and nerds by their peers ended up ruling the world as adults. She couldn't wait. "I got eighteen hundred."

It wasn't bragging. It was the truth. He'd asked. She'd answered. Simple as that.

"That's great," he said, sounding as if he really meant it. Not that she'd wanted him to be envious or anything, she quickly assured herself. "Me, too. Well, eighteen forty."

She stopped, her body slamming to a halt out of pure shock—unfortunately, she'd just stepped off the corner and into the road. An approaching car beeped, quite aggressively, if you asked her, and Luke took her arm. Waved pleasantly at the driver as he tugged her across the street.

"Congratulations," she managed. "On your score." The score that was forty points higher than hers.

Guess karma was working after all, giving her a good kick in the rear for being so mean-spirited. For assuming he was some dumb jock.

He shrugged. "I did well on the math portion but just okay on the English. And I completely bombed the writing." He sent her another of those carefree, aren't-we-just-two-buddies-strolling-down-the-street grins. "Guess it's a good thing I don't plan on being a writer."

Gracie had aced the English and writing portions, but her math score was just above average. See? They were opposites, with nothing in common. She shouldn't feel bad about not wanting to walk with him.

A car went by, someone yelling Luke's name over the heavy bass of their rap song. He waved, apparently not the least bit worried to be seen with her. He sidestepped a mailbox, and she got a whiff of his cologne. It was subtle, not overpowering like Andrew's or a lot of the boys at school. What did they do? Bathe in the stuff?

Luke's was…nice…though. Soft and spicy but not perfume-y.

And why she was sniffing the boy and critiquing his stupid cologne, she had no idea.

Spying Bradford House, she picked up her pace, which he easily matched thanks to his longer legs. But it didn't matter, because in a matter of moments, she'd be going her way and he'd be going his—wherever that might be. The baseball field two blocks away or one of his friends' houses. Didn't his *Mean Girls*–clone girlfriend, Kennedy, live around here?

At the walkway leading up to the Victorian bed-and-breakfast, Gracie stopped. "Well, goodbye," she said so abruptly, so obviously wanting to get rid of him, she wondered if she'd suffered some sort of brain damage during her sleep last night. She considered softening her brusqueness by saying she'd talk to him later, but they probably wouldn't see each other until school started again, so why bother? "Have a good summer."

"Actually, I'm going in there, too," he said with a nod toward the house.

She had to tip her head back to see his face. "Why would you do that?"

He scratched the side of his jaw, and she noticed

the stubble covering his cheeks and chin. "Because I work there. Here, I mean."

The birds stopped chirping, car engines ceased to rumble, even her heart quit beating. Everything went still and silent. Except for the roaring in her head, of course. That was loud and clear. "What?"

"I work here. Today's my first day."

Impossible. *She* worked at Bradford House. Had quit at King's Crossing and taken a job here as part-time housekeeper a few months back when Ivy took over as the chef. Now that summer was here, Gracie also babysat the B and B's manager, Fay Lindemuth's, two young boys three times a week and on weekends.

Gracie whirled around and almost ran up the walk to the porch, took the steps two at a time, well aware Luke was behind her. That he probably thought she was some sort of freak. Stepping inside, she hurried down the hall, through the dining room and into the small office.

Fay sat behind her desk, her almost three-year-old son, Mitchell, on the floor playing cars. As soon as Mitch saw Gracie he jumped to his feet. "Gracie! Hi, Gracie! Hi! Want to play cars?"

"Maybe later, buddy," she said. Luckily, he was much easier going than his older brother, Elijah, who would have had a major fit at being told no.

Mitch just grinned. "Okay." And plopped down again.

Gracie went around the desk, lowered her voice

as she spoke to Fay. "Did you hire—" the sound of footsteps behind her made her turn, and she pointed at Luke "—him?"

Standing, Fay smiled her soft, serene smile. "Yes, to help with the yard work, housekeeping and to pitch in with Ivy in the kitchen."

Then she skirted around Gracie as if she wasn't trying to ruin Gracie's life and make her completely miserable.

Overly dramatic? A bit. But also apt.

"Hello, Luke," Fay said. "Welcome to Bradford House."

He shook Fay's hand. "Thank you, Mrs. Lindemuth. I'm excited to get started."

Gracie shook her head. This wasn't happening. This was not happening. She couldn't be coworkers with Luke Sapko.

She gave a mental eye roll. Okay, okay, so she could be coworkers with him. She just didn't want to be. Didn't want to be around him or anyone who reminded her of Andrew.

Who reminded her of what a fool she'd been.

"What about John?" Gracie asked of the retired man who'd been taking care of the yard.

"His wife had a hip replaced, and he's taking the rest of the summer off to help her recuperate." Fay frowned. "Didn't I tell you?"

Gracie bit back a scream. For one thing, yelling at her boss didn't seem conducive to a happy, stress-free work environment—or the chance of ever getting a raise. For another, she liked Fay. How could you not? There was no one as sweet, patient or kindhearted.

It was almost unnatural.

"No," Gracie said, grateful to have regained some semblance of composure. Even if it was cracked. "You didn't tell me."

"Hmm," Fay said, still stuck on her memory lapse. "I could have sworn I did. Oh, well, you found out for yourself." She turned to Luke. "John mowed the grass two days ago and did the weeding, and since Ivy's off today and tomorrow— oh, Ivy is our chef. You'll meet her Thursday— Gracie will take you with her while she cleans rooms. Show you the ropes."

"That sounds great," Luke said with that big old smile. Sure. Great for him. He was probably used to girls falling all over themselves, scrambling to spend even a minute with him.

For Gracie? Not so great.

Sometimes life was just completely unfair.

Guess she'd just have to deal with it.

"Do you have the housekeeping sheet?" Gracie asked. Fay kept a list of which rooms needed cleaning, updated twice a day.

Fay handed her the sheet. "Oh! I didn't even introduce you two," Fay said, sounding upset, as if this tiny oversight was a huge deal.

"I've known Gracie all my life," Luke said. "We were in the same preschool class and everything."

At least he hadn't said something stupid and untrue. Like that they were friends.

Gracie walked out without waiting to see if he followed. Headed toward the supply closet off the kitchen. She wasn't going to let his presence bother her. She may have spent way too much time thinking about his stupid best friend since last fall, but that was over now.

Stepping into the closet, she flipped on the light—and about had a heart attack when Luke touched her shoulder.

"Gracie, are you all right?" he asked quietly, his gaze direct and honest.

But then, what did she know? She'd thought Andrew was honest, too.

"I'm fine," she said, her tone brisk. "You startled me. That's all."

"No, I mean...you seem pissed at me. Did I do something to upset you?"

He hadn't, and guilt for treating him rudely filled her. Made her sick to her stomach.

God, she was acting like a walking, talking, breathing cliché—the girl with the broken heart, putting up barriers. It was ridiculous. This wasn't even close to being the same situation she'd been in with Andrew.

Even if it had been, she was different. Wiser. More experienced.

"Everything's fine," she told him, hoping to make it true.

He must have believed her because he smiled. "Here," he said when she started gathering supplies, "let me get those."

She handed them over, vowing to herself that she'd be friendlier to Luke.

But she wouldn't be as naive as she'd been with Andrew. As foolish.

She wouldn't trust Luke. Wouldn't like him. No matter what.

C.J. STEPPED INTO the elevator of his apartment building and prayed like hell it would break up the reception.

"It's not fair," his mother complained, her voice loud and clear over his cell phone.

Damn reliable service.

He jabbed the button for his floor, the headache that had started when he'd answered her call ten minutes ago worsening by the second. He watched the numbers light up as the elevator rose. Three. Four. Five.

Twenty to go. Twenty floors of listening to Gwen bitch and moan.

He slumped against the wall. Hell.

"Your father," Gwen continued, with all the venom that had poisoned her since her husband left her for another woman—close to thirty freaking years ago now, "has more money than anyone could spend in ten lifetimes, and he's refusing to give me my fair share."

Gwen could handle Senior cheating on her. She'd ignored it for years during their marriage, had figured they'd continue on in that vein. What she would not accept was her husband actually choosing another woman over her for the long haul.

Not that the long haul was all that long. Of Senior's five marriages, the longest had been to Rosalyn, Oakes's mom, at ten years. And with things between Senior and Carrie being strained since the engagement party, and getting worse, C.J. doubted the two of them would make it to their fourth anniversary.

Thinking of the engagement party only reminded C.J. of Ivy. Of her amazing face, that sinful body. Of how she moved. The sound of her voice. How she'd felt under his hands, how responsive she'd been to his touch. His kiss.

How she'd walked out on him.

"It's impossible for me to survive on such a paltry sum," Gwen insisted.

"Paltry?" He tapped the back of his head against the wall. Then again. And one more time for good measure. "Your monthly alimony is more than most people make in a year."

She sniffed. "*Normal* people, maybe. All I'm asking is that I'm given enough to continue living in the manner to which I've become accustomed. Really, if you think about it, the way your father is treating me is unethical."

Unethical? His mom was using big-girl words. Never a good sign. "Is that your opinion? Or someone else's?"

"David and I had lunch today. He thinks we have a strong case and should ask for an increase in my support."

"Of course David thinks you have a strong case." Gwen's longtime attorney loved nothing more than suing people. Except maybe billing well-off divorcees. "I don't think going after more money while Dad's still recovering from his stroke is a good idea."

"Is he getting worse?"

And that had sounded way too eager for C.J.'s peace of mind. His mother, a nipped, tucked, bleached-blonde vulture. "No."

But Senior wasn't getting better, either, even though it had been more than a year since the stroke. His father was trapped in his body with very little hope of ever being able to walk or talk or even feed himself again.

"I loved your father," Gwen said, her voice wobbly. C.J. had no doubt that she'd worked up a tear or two, even though he wasn't there to witness them. "I gave him the best years of my life. I supported him. I was there for him, by his side, through the tough times. I helped him build Bartasavich Industries into what it is today. I deserve to be fairly compensated."

Best years of her life? He wasn't touching that

one, considering she'd been younger than C.J. was now when she and Senior had divorced. "The company was already well established when you and Dad got married," he reminded her.

No, it hadn't been as big as it would become, but it had still been a top company in the state. Now it was a top contender in the country.

"You know I'd never wish any ill will on your father," Gwen said, her tone perfectly balanced between outrage and heartbreak. "Why, I forgave him for how horribly he treated me."

"Yes, and I'm sure he appreciated it," C.J. said as he left the elevator and dug his keys from his pocket. He unlocked the door and stepped inside while Gwen cranked up her crying from sniffles to out-and-out sobs.

He walked through the foyer, his footsteps echoing on the hardwood, then made his way to his bedroom. Tossed the phone on the bed, set his briefcase down and took off his jacket and tie. Undid the top buttons of his shirt while he toed off his shoes, then removed his Stetson and stabbed his fingers through his hair.

He picked up the phone. Yep. Still crying. Wrapping both hands around the device, he pretended to choke it then brought it back to his ear as she hit a particularly grating wail. He winced. Tugged at his earlobe as he picked up his briefcase and went out into the kitchen.

His steps faltered and he froze. The hair on his

arms stood on end. The tips of his fingers tingled. He smelled her first, that intoxicating scent that he hadn't been able to forget. Even as he tried to tell himself he was imagining it, he turned slowly, cautiously.

And, through the doorway to the study, saw Ivy sitting on his leather sofa. She was like a fantasy come true in a short strapless sundress the color of ripe peaches, her long tanned legs crossed, one strappy high-heeled sandal dangling from her toes. Her hair was back, a few wisps loose at her temples, silver hoops in her ears.

She'd come to him. Had sought him out.

He squashed the joy that tried to wiggle its way into his chest. Yeah, he may have thought of her once or twice or a hundred times in the past four months. May have dreamed of her. Relived their night together. May have considered making another trip to Shady Grove, to King's Crossing, to find her. But in the end, his pride had stopped him from hunting her down like some infatuated fool.

Thank God.

"Mother," he said into the phone, his eyes never leaving Ivy, "I have to go."

"But, C.J.—"

He hung up and, knowing she'd call back—and lecture him on his rudeness—turned the phone off.

"How is your mama?" Ivy asked while he stood

there staring at her as if he'd never seen a woman before. "Still dating the beefcake?"

C.J. walked toward her as though he was a trout she was reeling in, unable to resist her pull. He stopped in front of her, forcing her to tip her head back. "What are you doing here?"

Ivy shrugged her golden shoulders. Smiled. "I came to see you. Now, be honest. Did you miss me?"

The question hit him with equal parts fury and embarrassment because, damn it, while he hadn't missed her—hard to miss someone he didn't even know—he had thought of her.

And the confident gleam in her eye told him she knew it.

"Don't tell me," he managed to drawl in an even tone. "You're a mild-mannered waitress by day, a cat burglar by night." He regretted the words as soon as he said them. Mainly because he'd envisioned her, quite clearly and in great detail, in a snug black outfit. "Breaking and entering is a crime."

She laughed. He couldn't say he didn't like the sound.

Damn her.

When she finally wound down, she leaned forward, still swinging that foot. Winked at him. "I don't have to break in anywhere." She slowly uncrossed her legs and stood in one smooth motion. Looked up at him from under her lashes, a trick she'd probably learned in her crib. "Let's just say I have certain...charms...that open a lot of doors for me."

So much for his apartment building's advanced security system.

He should be pissed—rip-roaring, teeth-gnashing, hair-pulling pissed—not mildly irritated. Not wondering how, exactly, she'd managed to talk her way into his home. Not wanting to find out more about her.

Not wanting to reach out and rub one of those loose curls between his fingers. To step closer and breathe her in. Touch her.

He shoved his hands into his pockets. Stepped back. She'd really screwed him up. Had him retreating. It grated his pride, which had kept him sane and controlled all these months.

"So, you were in the neighborhood and thought you'd look me up?" he asked, wanting badly for that to be true.

She strolled over to the glass doors leading to the balcony. "Houston isn't exactly one of my regular hangouts. But for this view," she said with a nod at the twelve-acre park his suite overlooked, the city of Houston behind it, "I might have to change that."

"How did you find me?" he asked.

"I did some digging. You'd be amazed what a woman can find out with a Wi-Fi connection, a name and a few clicks of a mouse."

"What are you? Nancy Drew?"

"Not quite that innocent. As you well know." She looked around. "Not going to offer me a drink?"

This entire experience was so surreal, he almost did. "No. What are you doing here?"

"It seems I have something of yours."

He hadn't noticed anything missing from his wallet that night. He had his watch. His phone. All the personal belongings he'd brought with him to Shady Grove four months ago. "Still playing games, I see."

"Oh, but you know how much I enjoy those games," she purred, walking toward him, all sex appeal and artifice. She touched his chest, the warmth of her fingers burning him through the material of his shirt. "You didn't mind when you took me to bed."

He caged her wrists, wished her skin wasn't so soft. "I should call security. Have them toss you out."

"Do you often have women thrown out of your apartment?"

"You'd be the first. You said you had something of mine?"

She swallowed. Tugged herself free. "You could say that."

He waited, but she just stood there looking almost…nervous. Scared.

What was that about? Had she stolen from him

without him noticing? He wouldn't have thought
she was a petty thief—even if a flash of conscience had brought her here to make amends.
"Just return whatever it is, and I won't call the
authorities."

Now she frowned. "Excuse me?"

"Whatever you stole from me that night."

She bristled. "I didn't steal anything from you."

He rubbed his chin, totally confused. "Okay."

"I didn't steal anything from you," she repeated,
pacing in front of him with short, agitated strides.
"But I do have something of yours." Stopping in
front of him, she inhaled deeply and met his eyes.
"I'm pregnant."

CHAPTER SIX

Ivy WISHED SHE could take back that deep inhale. She'd gotten a nose full of Clinton's aftershave with it. Her stomach turned. The back of her neck grew cold and clammy.

Well, wouldn't throwing up on his feet take this moment from plain old bad to freaking horrible?

She breathed shallowly. Airplane travel and pregnancy didn't mix—at least not in her case. She'd battled morning sickness for more than two months but hadn't had a bout of it for the past two weeks. Until she'd been strapped in her seat, taking off from Pittsburgh.

Plus, yes, okay, she was nervous. She was dropping a bombshell on him. The night they'd spent together was supposed to be a one-time thing. Now, the child growing inside of her bound them for the rest of their lives.

But as bad as she felt, Clinton looked worse. The color had drained from his face, and he stood there, glassy-eyed, as if he was seconds from passing out, just…bam! Falling flat on his handsome face.

If that big, solid body started tipping, she wasn't

going to try to catch him. She was getting out of the way.

The last time she'd been underneath him, things hadn't quite worked out the way she'd planned.

His mouth hanging open like a six-foot-plus blond guppy, he blinked. Shook his head slowly, as if coming out of an intense dream.

"What?"

His voice was low. Calm. And very, very cold.

Good thing she wasn't intimidated by anyone, or else she'd be shaking in her sandals right now. As it was, she had to force her gaze to remain steady, herself not to back up to...oh...somewhere in Kentucky would suffice. "I'm pregnant."

"Am I to assume that you're trying to tell me I'm the father?"

She raised her eyebrows. She wasn't crazy about his snotty tone—and she preferred the term *sperm donor* over father—but he'd had a shock, so she'd give him a break. Never let it be said she couldn't be reasonable and tolerant.

At least once.

"No," she said, her tone all sorts of dry, "I internet stalked you, flew to Houston and talked my way into your apartment because I thought you might want to buy me a baby gift. I'll leave you a list of where I'm registered."

His jaw went rigid. "There's no need for sarcasm."

She snorted. "Please. That was such a stupid question it practically begged for sarcasm."

His cool gaze went to her stomach then back to her face. "You're lying."

The man was really testing her limits. "We don't know each other all that well, so I'm going to let that slide."

"Know each other *that well*?" he asked with a harsh laugh. "Lady, I don't even know your last name."

She nodded slowly. Pressed her lips together because her stomach was roiling again. "Fair enough. Let me fill you in on what you need to know. My name is Ivy Rutherford, and I'm twenty-six years old. I don't lie, cheat or steal, and I'm not big on second chances." She swallowed, but the sick taste in the back of her throat remained. "Something you might want to keep in mind before you speak again. I'm also seventeen weeks pregnant."

She turned to the side and smoothed the loose material of her dress over her stomach. She hadn't shown at all during the first trimester, but at week sixteen, as if overnight, a noticeable baby bump had appeared.

"Satisfied?" she asked, letting her hands fall back to her sides.

He didn't look satisfied. Or scared, which had been her reaction when that stick she'd peed on two months ago had flashed a positive sign. No, the only word she could find to describe the expression on Clinton Bartasavich Jr.'s face was *furious*.

And she was alone with him. Maybe she should have chosen a public place to tell him, instead of ambushing him in his apartment—if you could call what had to be over three thousand square feet of bright, open rooms, million-dollar views and the highest of high-end furnishings, counters, floors and appliances an *apartment*. She'd been half-afraid to even sit on that fancy couch.

"We used protection," hc said, his lips barely moving. "That night."

"Yes. I realize what you're referring to. Unfortunately, my eleventh-grade health teacher was right and the only foolproof way to prevent pregnancy is abstinence. We're in the small percentage of cases in which condoms are ineffective. Looks as if you have some sort of supersperm. You must be very proud."

"I don't believe you," he said as evenly as if they were discussing what to have for lunch.

Bile rose in her throat. Okay, no thinking about food, not even in general terms. "You think I have a pillow in here?" she asked, indicating her stomach.

"I don't believe I'm the father."

"Why would I lie?"

He sent her a bland look, and she replayed her words in her head. Winced. Guess he wasn't the only one who could ask a stupid question.

He was a Bartasavich. Oh, she'd heard all about Kane Bartasavich's wealthy family in Houston, but she'd assumed wealthy meant upper-middle class, like Charlotte's parents. Dr. Ellison was an ophthalmologist, and Mrs. Ellison owned a popular boutique clothing store on Main Street. Regular, well-off folk who lived in a big, tasteful home, tipped generously and vacationed in the Caribbean.

The Bartasaviches, she'd learned from her internet searches, were the kind of wealthy that defined the word *ostentatious*, donated millions to charities and politicians, and owned their own island retreat, a little place to escape the stresses of being richer than God and as beautiful as the angels above.

And she had to go and sleep with the heir apparent, get pregnant with his child.

She sighed. That was her. Never doing anything halfway.

"I'm not after your money," she told him. It'd be easier, much easier, if he'd been dirt-poor.

His mouth twisted. "You slept with me after knowing me all of what…twenty minutes?"

He was obviously a mistrusting soul, thinking the worst of people.

Not that she blamed him on that score. But he had no right to play the holier-than-thou card.

"Right back at ya," she said. "Not knowing me—and vice versa—didn't seem to bother you when you had me under you in that big old bed.

The way I figure it, we both got what we wanted that night. No need to cast blame."

"Maybe you got more than I did."

"What's that supposed to mean?" But she was afraid she knew. She just hoped he was smart enough not to actually say it.

"It means it seems very convenient that you're here, claiming to be pregnant with my child." He closed the distance between them. "You want something from me."

He didn't believe her. Well, she hadn't really expected him to, had she? Still, it stung, and she had to remind herself that he didn't know her. Didn't know she made her own way. She wasn't some gold digger looking for a rich man to take care of her.

She took care of herself. She was the only person she trusted to do so.

"All I want is for you to back up," she assured him. Before she gagged. Dear Lord, pregnancy wasn't for sissies.

Or, obviously, those with weak stomachs.

"What did you think?" he continued as if she hadn't spoken. "That if you showed up here, I'd blindly accept everything you had to say and maybe toss in a marriage proposal and a diamond ring?"

She snorted out a laugh. Saw he was completely serious. Then again, he probably didn't have much sense for the ridiculous. "The last thing I want is a marriage proposal. From what I've heard, marriages don't work out so well for your family." His father, a serial adulterer, had been married several times. "I hope things work out better for your brother and Charlotte. She's a nice person."

And weren't those the people who got hurt and screwed over the most?

Good thing no one had ever accused Ivy of being nice.

Clinton nodded once, sharply, as if coming to some grand conclusion. Jabbed a finger at her. "Don't move."

He brushed past her and disappeared through a door off the entertainment-slash-media area—or whatever fancy name rich people used for their TV room.

She did move. She went into the kitchen, if only to prove he wasn't the boss of her. But she didn't march out the door the way she should have. Oh, no, her curiosity wouldn't let her leave until she found out what he was up to. Curiosity and maybe a teeny, tiny bit of guilt. She had, technically, broken into his home and sprung the news on him that he was going to be a father.

She needed to stop being so defensive and give him the benefit of the doubt. Had to trust that he wasn't really an arrogant, judgmental ass.

Trailing her fingers over the cool marble countertop, she strolled around the oblong island. Everything about the kitchen—from the stainless-steel appliances to the glossy hardwood floor to the dark mahogany cabinets—screamed "high end." It was beautiful, she had to admit. In a cool, modern, don't-even-think-of-cooking-in-here-and-making-a-mess way.

If this room, this entire apartment with its dark colors, sleek, boxy furniture and gorgeous views didn't say all she needed to know about Clinton Bartasavich Jr., nothing would.

He was untouchable. Cold. On top of the world, looking down at everyone else.

Except…he hadn't been any of those things during the night they'd spent together. Or at least, not only those things. She'd touched him then, his skin warm under her hands, his body hard and responsive. He hadn't looked down at her but had held her gaze, as helpless as she'd been against the undeniable pull between them.

She bit her lower lip and leaned her elbows on the counter, her chin in her hands. Glanced at the doorway where he'd disappeared. Which one was the real Clinton?

More important, why did it matter so much to her?

She straightened when he came out, his expression dark. He slapped something onto the counter, his palm covering it as he slid it toward her. "I believe this is what you came here for."

"I'm almost afraid to look," she murmured, only half kidding.

He spread his legs, an immovable tree of a man. Slowly lifted his hand, then crossed his arms and waited.

Your turn to make the next move.

Here went nothing.

She lowered her gaze. As she'd suspected, it was a check. Facedown, his very own challenge to her.

Pick it up and see what I think you and your child are worth.

Nausea building again, she did just that. The room spun, and she held onto the edge of the counter for support. There went her giving him the benefit of the doubt.

He really was an arrogant, judgmental ass.

Her throat went dry, so she worked moisture back into her mouth. Managed to whistle softly under her breath. "Fifty grand. Wow. Guess I could buy my own diamond ring with this. Save myself from worrying about the husband part of that equation."

"Take it," he said, unemotional and inhuman. "Do whatever you want with it. But remember this, it's a one-time offer. You won't be getting a cent more from me."

"I'm not sure if this is a bribe," she said, waving the check in the air, "or plain old hush money."

He stiffened. "It's neither."

She studied him closely. Lowered her hand. "No, it's not a bribe, is it? It's a test. Aren't you clever?" she murmured, the check practically burning her fingertips. "If I'm lying about you being the father of my baby, I'll take the money and run—glad for a miniscule portion of the Bartasavich fortune—knowing the truth will come out with a DNA test. On the other hand, if I'm telling the truth, I'll get all defensive, tear this check apart and add a suggestion about where you can put those pieces before throwing them into your smug face."

His eyes narrowed to slits. "Smug?"

"Hmm..." She tapped the edge of the check against her mouth. Began to pace the length of the island. "Decisions, decisions."

Part of her, a big, screaming part, wanted to shove the check down his throat. Storm out of there with her pride and self-respect intact. Luckily, another part of her, the rational, pragmatic part of herself, prevailed. Fifty thousand dollars was a lot of money. Oh, maybe not to Richie Rich over there, but to the rest of the population? It was worth a dent in pride.

To her it was a godsend. Her job at Bradford House provided medical insurance, but there were still other expenses to consider with a new baby. Diapers and clothes and a crib and changing table. A stroller and car seat. Maybe one of those swing things.

Any extra could go into a savings account for the baby. Their own little nest egg for college or, more than likely, the emergencies that would no doubt pop up during the next eighteen years.

The bigger issue, though, was Clinton himself. If she took the money, they'd both be off the hook. He wouldn't have to take responsibility for the baby. And she wouldn't have to deal with having him in her and her child's life.

Win-win.

"Cowboy," she said, making a show of carefully folding the check in half, "it looks like you have yourself a deal."

C.J. STARED, HIS jaw aching, head buzzing as Ivy crossed to the sofa and picked up her purse, tucked his check inside.

The buzzing continued and he realized it was the intercom on the wall, the front desk trying to get hold of him. He ignored it.

"What the hell do you mean we have a deal?" he managed to spit out.

"I mean I'm going to take this check with me to Shady Grove and, as per your stipulation, I won't ask for another red cent." She came toward him, hips swaying, heels clicking on the hardwood. "After I walk out that door, you'll never hear from or see me again. You won."

It didn't feel like he'd won. It felt like he'd made a mistake. A big one.

Aren't you clever?

Hands fisted, he shoved them into his pockets.

He'd always thought so. Had never had trouble coming up with the right solution to a problem.

Until he'd come face-to-face with the woman claiming to be pregnant with his child. He hadn't been able to think straight, let alone figure out how to handle this situation or her.

His answer had been to pay her off. While he was used to throwing money at certain problems, he didn't make a habit of writing checks to women he'd slept with. She was right. It had been a test. And she'd failed.

Why the hell was he so disappointed?

"That's it?" he asked, the buzzing finally stopping as she brushed past him. He followed her. "You're not going to try to convince me you're telling the truth?"

Sending him an amused glance over her shoulder, she kept right on walking. "Nope. You're going to believe what you want anyway. And as I've been insulted quite enough for one day, I'll just go on my way."

Because she was lying, he assured himself.

"Did you know you were pregnant that night and think you could sleep with me, pass someone else's baby off as mine?" They turned the corner to the foyer. That night he'd hoped she was different, that she wanted him for himself, but it turned out she was like everyone else. A user. Manipulative. "Or maybe you don't even know who the father is," he said quietly.

Her shoulders snapped back, her spine going rigid. She turned, inch by slow inch, her narrowed eyes flashing. But her face was white. Her mouth trembling.

He wanted to take his ugly words back, retract the horrible accusation, but he couldn't.

"You," she said, slowly. Succinctly. "Are an ass."

"So I've been told." But he'd never agreed. Until now.

She whirled around, her hair fanning out. With a low moan, she pressed her hand against the wall next to the front door. Her head was down, her shoulders rising and falling heavily.

He winced. His gut tightened. She was crying. Because of him.

Shit.

"Maybe, we should start over," he said, edging closer.

"Back. Off."

He couldn't. He had to fix this. "Let's sit down. Talk this through." Rationally. Reasonably. Neither of which he'd been so far. He laid his hands on her shoulders. "Come on."

She yanked away. Stumbled to the other side of the hall, pressed her back against the wall. "Oh my God," she groaned, then swallowed audibly. "Don't touch me."

And now she was scared of him. Holding

his hands up as if to prove he was harmless, he stepped closer. "I won't hurt you."

"Stop right there," she snapped and raised her head. Her eyes were huge, the delicate skin around them bruised and dark, her cheeks colorless.

She wasn't crying. She was ill. "Are you all right?"

"Do I look all right?" she ground out from between her teeth. She tipped her head back, inhaled slowly through her nose. "It's your cologne."

"What?"

"Your cologne or—or aftershave." Another swallow. "It's making me sick."

"I beg your pardon?" he asked, sounding like some damn uptight prick. But it was hard not to get offended when a woman said you made her want to throw up.

"Bathroom," she gasped, pushing away from the wall, her eyes frantic, her hand covering her mouth. "Now."

Grabbing her by the elbow, he led her the few steps to the half bath off the foyer. Flipped on the lights and was debating whether or not to try to squeeze into the tiny room with her when she slammed the door in his face. He heard the lock click, then the unmistakable sound of retching.

He rubbed the back of his neck. Shut his eyes when the sounds behind the door continued. Damn it. He hated feeling this useless.

Hated that he'd made such a mess of things with her.

He hurried into the study, pulled out a bottle of ginger ale from the mini fridge below the bar and poured it into a tall glass. Considered adding ice but didn't want to take the chance of being gone too long.

If he wasn't there to stop her, she'd take off. Again. The way she had that night.

He had a right to be suspicious, he told himself, his strides long. To wonder about her motives. But he could have handled this whole situation better. He saw that now. And he would. When she came out, he'd convince her to stay.

He'd get to the truth.

But a niggling part of his brain insisted she could have already told him the truth. That the baby was his.

And he'd given her fifty thousand dollars to never see him again.

He let his head drop, blew out a heavy breath.

He was in such deep shit.

Someone knocked on the apartment door. More than likely whoever the front desk had been buzzing him about.

What the hell was the point of living in a secure building if the front desk was going to let anyone and everyone in?

The latest visitor knocked again. He glanced at

the closed bathroom door. Heard the water running. Another, harder knock. More insistent.

"Coming," he grumbled, then opened the door.

And would have slammed it shut again if Carric hadn't thrown herself into his arms, forcing him to take several steps back to regain his balance, ginger ale sloshing over the edge of the cup and onto his forearm.

"Oh, C.J.," she wailed against his neck.

He glanced up at the heavens. Mouthed the word *help* but no assistance was forthcoming, not even a well-timed lightning bolt. He'd have to get out of this on his own.

Story of his life.

Except he was usually fixing other people's mistakes. Today, the mess he needed to clean up was all his.

He kept his free hand at his side, held the glass away from them with the other. "Who the hell let you up here?"

She leaned back, looking beautiful as always, despite her trembling lower lip and the tears glistening in her eyes. "The nice gentleman at the front desk. He knew you were home and since he recognized me, he buzzed me through."

"He shouldn't have. This isn't a good time."

"I didn't know where else to go." She sniffed. "Everything is such a mess."

C.J. stepped back, keeping a decent distance

between them, in case she decided she needed to latch on to him again. "Carrie, what do you want?"

"I need a place to stay. Just for a night or two," she added quickly.

He raised one eyebrow, knew it made him resemble his father even more than usual, but maybe that's what she needed—a reminder of who he was. And who her husband was.

"Something wrong with my father's house?"

A swipe and another reminder about where she came in the pecking order of things. The mansion she'd redecorated after her marriage to Senior, the bed she slept in, the place she called home wasn't hers. Every piece of furniture, every pair of overpriced shoes in her closet, every nickel she spent came directly from Senior.

Without Clinton Bartasavich Sr., she had nothing. Was nothing.

Just as Senior wanted. As he'd planned.

She pressed a crumpled tissue to the inner corner of her eye. "I need a break. Seeing Clinton that way. Watching him suffer is just so…hard. So much work. He needs so much time and attention. What about me? What about what I need?"

"I'm sure it's very difficult for you," C.J. said flatly, "having a full-time staff and nurses taking care of his every need while you sit back and watch them. You want a break? Try a hotel."

Sending him a look from under her lashes, she sidled closer, and he realized he'd backed himself into a corner. Or, to be more specific, against the wall. She laid her hand on his chest. Lowered her voice. "Why should I stay at a cold, lonely hotel when you have all this space?"

She tipped her head back, her lips parted. She was beautiful, no doubt about it. Then again, all of his stepmothers had been beautiful. Beautiful and, as the years had gone by, younger and younger.

And this one, barely twenty-eight years old, was making him feel a hell of a lot older than thirty-six.

C.J. snagged her wrist and held her away from him. "Lonely? Guess your friend Chip is out of town."

Carrie's eyes widened. "Wha-what do you mean?"

He almost felt sorry for her. Almost. Then again, she'd brought all of this on herself. "Chip Foxworth. Your ex? The man you *visited* last weekend at his room at the St. Regis?"

With a gasp deep enough to use up half the oxygen in the hallway, she laid a hand over her heart. "Are you spying on me?"

"Save the faux outrage. No one needs to spy on you. You paid for Foxworth's room with my father's credit card. His business manager alerted me to the charges. You should be more discreet."

Then again, his father hadn't married his last three wives for their brains.

C.J. had planned on talking to his brother Oakes about what to do with the information that their invalid father's wife was cheating on him. Instead, the problem had landed on his doorstep. Literally.

"What are you going to do?" Carrie asked, sounding small. Afraid. Which was understandable. After all, she was about to lose everything. "You...you can't tell Clinton. It'll kill him."

"The old man's stronger than you think." But C.J. didn't relish the idea of sharing the news. "Be out of the house by Sunday afternoon, and I won't tell Dad. You can file for divorce, citing irreconcilable differences, and move on with your life. Or, I can hire a private investigator to find proof of your affair. Which, I believe, would mean you would no longer be eligible for the generous settlement allotted in the prenup you signed."

She blinked rapidly. "You wouldn't tell him. Not in his condition."

"I wouldn't want to," he admitted, leading her to the door. "But if it came down to telling him or letting you continue to make a fool of him, I'll choose the former." He opened the door, nudged her into the main hall. "Do yourself a favor. Take the money and run."

She made a squeaking sound, which he took for agreement, and he shut the door on her.

"Your life is a bona fide soap opera."

He couldn't argue with that. He turned, saw Ivy leaning against the wall next to the bathroom door, her face pale, her eyes huge and rimmed red. "How are you feeling?"

"Dandy." Her voice was rough.

"Here." He offered her the ginger ale. "This might calm your stomach."

"How am I to trust you didn't poison it?"

"You have a very creative imagination."

"Hey, you're the one who could give *Dallas*—the TV show, not the city—and J. R. Ewing a run for their money. For all I know, you regularly poison women and hide their bodies in a bedroom closet."

To appease her, he took a long drink. Held out the glass. She accepted it and took a tiny sip but that probably had more to do with her having just been sick and not her naturally suspicious nature.

"I want proof the baby is mine," he said, crossing his arms, feeling like an idiot for not just saying that outright when she'd first claimed to be pregnant with his child. "We'll have paternity testing done."

She took another sip. Licked her lips. "It's as if you don't trust me."

"It's a reasonable request."

"It certainly is. Reasonable. Rational. Completely understandable." Another sip. "I would have happily agreed to it had you brought it up earlier. Unfortunately, that ship has long since sailed."

She shoved the glass at him, giving him no choice but to take it.

"How am I to be sure the child you're carrying is mine?"

With a shrug she walked past him, her heels clicking, the sound loud to his ears. "Thanks to the check you wrote me, that is no longer my problem."

She opened the door. She was leaving. Walking out of his life, just like that.

Exactly what he'd wanted.

Reaching past her he slammed the door shut, and then stepped in front of her. "We're not done."

"When I'm done, I leave. And, believe me, buddy, I am done with you." He didn't move. She raised her eyebrows. "Don't make me kick you in the shin."

It wasn't the threat of violence that had him moving aside, it was the exhaustion on her face. Knowing she'd just been ill.

"In other words," he said, when she opened the door again, "you can't prove you're telling the truth."

"You don't get it. I came here because I thought it was the right thing to do. This pregnancy came as a shock to me, too, but I thought we could sit down, discuss our options and come up with some sort of plan on how to proceed. Together. Instead you treated me like dirt, accused me of being a lying, manipulative slut." She shook her head, her hand gripping the doorknob as if it were a lifeline. "You didn't have to be such an arrogant ass. You didn't have to make me feel so cheap. So beneath you. None of it had to be this way," she continued quietly. "It didn't have to end this way. I hope you remember that long after I'm gone."

CHAPTER SEVEN

IT DIDN'T HAVE to be this way.

C.J. paced the length of his apartment, Ivy's words replaying in his head.

He felt caged in, like a wild animal recently caught, forced to hide his instincts to keep control. Usually keeping control was easy for him. Emotions were messy and had never helped anyone make a good decision. No, problems needed to be solved by using one's head, by using logic and reason and looking at all the angles, by seeing the pros and cons of each decision.

Following your heart only led to suffering. Not that he'd followed his heart that night with Ivy, he thought with a sneer. That had all been his groin telling him what to do. He could admit that his arrogance hadn't helped, either. He'd had the most beautiful woman he'd ever seen come to him, flirt with him, and he'd given in to his baser needs.

It wouldn't happen again.

The edginess fled as he realized that he could handle this. He handled everything. His blood chilled and he was cool. Calm. Collected. Getting upset wouldn't solve anything, wouldn't get to the truth, and that was what he needed right now. The truth.

A knock sounded on his door and though he knew it wasn't Ivy, his heart sped up anyway, almost as if he was looking forward to seeing her again, as if he wanted to see her again.

He yanked the door open. "Took you long enough," he growled.

His brother Oakes raised his eyebrows. "I hadn't realized I was being timed." He came in, looking like the attorney he was, in a dark suit, his brown hair rumpled. "I left a very promising date to come over here because you said it was an emergency." He helped himself to a beer from the fridge and sat on the couch. "Well? What's up?"

C.J.'s mouth tightened. He didn't know how to go about this. He'd called Oakes as soon as Ivy had left. Demanding his brother drop whatever he was doing and telling him to come over here was one thing, but actually letting him know what was going on? That seemed extreme.

At least it wasn't Kane, who'd never let him hear the end of it.

"Are you going to stare at me all night?" Oakes asked. "Want me to read your mind?"

C.J. sighed. Damn it, he'd have to tell him. Would have to admit what an idiot he'd been. "I need your help."

Oakes froze in the act of lifting his beer to his mouth. Slowly lowered the bottle. "Excuse me?"

"You heard me." C.J. could have sworn his brother was enjoying this somehow.

"Yeah, I did, but I'd love to hear it again." Oakes grinned and stood. "I don't think I've ever heard you say that you needed help before. Or that you were wrong, but that's a miracle for another day." He took out his phone and snapped a picture.

"What the hell are you doing?"

"Just wanted a memento of this momentous occasion," Oakes said in his cheerful way. "Maybe you could repeat yourself? That way I can have a video of it to share?"

C.J.'s response to that was short and to the point.

Oakes put his phone back in his pocket. "I love my phone but not that much. And I don't think I have that app, but I'll look into it for those long, lonely winter nights. Now," he continued. "What do you need help with?"

"I need you to find out information about someone."

"I'm not a private detective," Oakes reminded him. "Those years in law school and all that. I can give you a name—"

"You can find out just about anything you want about someone," C.J. said, knowing Oakes could get information about people for his clients and the cases he worked on.

"So can you. All you have to do is place a few calls and—"

"I don't want anyone to know about this."

"New business venture?" his brother asked.

"No, it's...personal."

"Really? I thought you didn't do personal."

C.J. bristled. "What the hell is that supposed to mean?"

Oakes lifted a shoulder, not the least put out by C.J.'s tone or hostile glare. "You haven't dated since Dad got sick, and you focus on work. Everything all right?"

He wished he'd focused on work that night with Ivy. Leave it to Oakes, the best of them all, to worry about C.J.'s well-being. "I'm fine I just..."

Screwed up. Big-time.

Shit.

He sat on the edge of the chair, clasped his hands between his knees. "I met someone."

"You want me to run a background check on the woman you're dating? That seems a bit cold and paranoid. Even for you."

"We're not dating. We...spent the night together. The night of Kane's engagement party."

"Not that I don't love being privy to the more personal aspects of your life," Oakes said, "but I'm having a hard time following you. You slept with a woman in Shady Grove and...oh." His eyes widened and he chuckled. "Oh, I get it."

C.J. doubted that. "Got what?"

"She dumped you, but you're hooked, and now you want to convince her to give you another chance." He made a motion of a fishhook in his cheek. "Never thought I'd see it."

"That's not what happened." He wasn't hooked. But she had left him. He wouldn't forget that. Twice she'd walked out on him. That was unacceptable. "We hadn't spoken since that night, but she came here today."

"She came to Houston?" Realization dawned and Oakes shook his head. "No."

C.J. pressed his lips together. Nodded shortly. "She says she's pregnant."

Oakes went into lawyer mode, standing and pacing, and C.J. could almost see his brother's agile mind working. "Any chance it's true?"

"No."

Oakes turned, gave C.J. a look he'd never seen from his younger brother before. "No? No chance at all? So you didn't have sex with her?"

And this wasn't something he wanted to discuss. He hadn't participated in locker-room talk, bragging about his exploits and conquests, since he was thirteen and had gotten to first base with a girl two years older who'd wanted him to take her to some country-club dance and buy her jewelry.

He'd found out later that she'd only liked him for his looks and for his father's money.

"We had sex," C.J. admitted through clenched teeth. "But we used protection."

"Nothing but abstinence is one hundred percent," Oakes said, as if convincing a jury of C.J.'s guilt. Repeating Ivy's words. "You say you used protection. Was she on birth control, as well?"

"I don't know. I didn't ask."

Oakes gave him a look that was filled with disbelief and disappointment. "Just a suggestion, but if you're going to have one-night stands, you might want to make sure you're both protected from something like this."

C.J. felt like a big enough idiot already. He didn't need to hear it from his little brother. "Are you going to check into her or not?"

He didn't want to go to a stranger to handle this, but he would if he needed to.

"What do you want to know about her?" Oakes asked.

"Everything. Where she works. Where she lives. Who her friends are. Her history. Past lovers and relationships. Education. Family."

"Guess you didn't get around to discussing any of that, huh?" Oakes asked.

"Spare me the lecture. I've got enough on my mind."

"What are you going to do about the baby?"

"I'm not sure the baby is mine. This could be some scheme to give her kid the Bartasavich last name and to get enough money to set herself up for life."

But his instincts told him it wasn't.

Oakes made a note. "I know a guy—"

"You—"

"No," Oakes said. "I told you. I don't do background checks, but I know a guy who does and who is very thorough. He's discreet, too, so don't worry about that. He can be completely trusted."

"I don't know," C.J. said. This was personal, and he didn't want his personal business spread around.

"Trust me," Oakes said. "He's the best."

C.J. nodded. He did trust Oakes. "How long will it take?"

"Depends on how much you can give him to start with."

"Not much," he hated admitting. "Her name is Ivy Rutherford and she lives in Shady Grove. She grew up there," he added, remembering her saying that she'd lived in the small town her entire life. "She works at the hotel where the engagement party was held."

Oakes wrote that down. "Luckily, Shady Grove is small enough she should be easy enough to track down. Assuming, of course, that she's still living there."

C.J. had a feeling she was, that when she left Houston, she'd go back to that tiny town where his brother had decided to spend the rest of his life. "The security department here might have video surveillance of her coming and leaving the building if you need a picture to help identify her."

"That should be enough for him to get a good start. I'd say he'll have what you need within a week."

Clint nodded. "Good." That would give him enough time to tie up loose ends at the office.

Then he was tracking Ivy down.

FUNNY HOW DOING the right thing often came back to bite a person in the ass.

Lesson learned, Ivy thought late the next morning as she scraped her hair back, wrapped an elastic band around it. She'd be sure to avoid doing that again for the rest of her life.

She grabbed flour, sugar, baking powder and baking soda from the pantry at Bradford House and carried them into the kitchen. She never should have gone to Houston. Never should have told Clinton she was pregnant. Giving into her attraction to him that night had been reckless. Seeking him out to tell him she was carrying his child? That was just stupid.

Topping off her reckless, stupid behavior by throwing up in his extremely clean bathroom, well, that could only be described as humiliating. The one saving grace was that the woman who'd shown up while Ivy had been kneeling on that cold tile floor—her stomach empty, her eyes watering—hadn't realized Ivy was even there.

She supposed she should be thankful for small favors, but she just didn't have it in her at the moment.

How could she have been so foolish? Worse, why had Clinton's crappy attitude bothered her so much? She didn't need his approval. Certainly didn't care what he thought about her.

She scooped flour into a measuring cup, leveled off the excess. It bothered her, she realized. She'd wanted him to show that softer side she'd seen when he'd been with his family at King's Crossing. The humor and charm that was so attractive. That had made him seem approachable.

She'd wanted… God…she'd wanted him to show her just a bit of kindness.

Pathetic. Anyone who spends their lives relying on the kindness of others is looking to get kicked in the teeth. Again and again and again. She was smarter than that. She didn't need kindness. Couldn't count on it.

She counted on herself. Period.

She didn't need Clinton Bartasavich Jr. in her life and neither did her child. They'd be just fine on their own.

"I didn't think you were coming in today."

Ivy glanced over her shoulder as Fay, her boss at the bed-and-breakfast, walked in from the dining room. "I changed my mind."

There had been no reason to stick around Houston as she'd originally planned. So she'd canceled her hotel room and booked an earlier flight, getting into Pittsburgh at 3:00 a.m. That she still had to pay for the hotel room and had incurred over one hundred dollars in airline fees sucked. No doubt about it. Doing the right thing cost a person. In more ways than one.

But in the end, every penny had been worth it.

After her encounter with Clinton, she'd just wanted to come home. Had wanted to curl up in her bed, pull the sheet over her head and pretend the past…oh…four months had never happened.

That had worked for about two hours, after which she'd kicked off the covers and spent a good portion of her morning pacing her cramped apartment, cursing out her cat—who insisted on winding his way between her legs with every step—and muttering to herself about what an idiot she'd been to actually think any good could come of her trip to Texas.

So she'd showered, forced down a few bites of dry toast and decided keeping busy was the way to go. A way to keep her mind from replaying the things Clinton had said to her. How he'd treated her.

A way to stop from thinking about that check, now hidden in a sandwich bag in the back of her freezer.

Fay crossed to the sink to fill a cheery red teapot. "How was your day off?"

Ivy pressed her lips together until they went

numb. "Fine," she managed, dumping the flour into a large bowl.

She kept her gaze averted as Fay set the pot on the stove and lit a fire under it. Didn't want to take a chance on her boss seeing the truth in her eyes. Fay wasn't much for prodding, but she would worry if she thought something was wrong. If she thought someone was upset, she'd question—gently and with great trepidation—what had happened. Wonder what she could do to help. She was one of those fragile souls with an incessant need to please others, to make sure everyone around her was happy.

When what she needed to worry about was fixing her own life.

Talk about a mess. It almost made Ivy's situation seem like no big deal. Yes, being a divorcee with two kids and a history of depression—a history that included a suicide attempt a few years ago—sure put Ivy's own problems into perspective.

"You really didn't have to come in," Fay said, nibbling on her pinkie nail. "Gracie came in early and helped out with breakfast service."

"It's no big deal. My plans fell through." She'd thought it would take at least a few hours, if not an entire evening, for her and Clinton to discuss what they were going to do about her pregnancy. "And I wanted to get some prep work done for tomorrow."

"Are you sure?"

Ivy tossed aside the measuring cup, and it slid several inches across the Italian marble. "I said it's no big deal."

But her waspish tone made it sound like it was a big deal. Damn.

"It's just...you look tired," Fay blurted.

Ivy glared so hard, the other woman took a step back. "Why do people say that? Why don't they just say, you look like hell? It'd be honest."

"You could never look bad." Fay's quick assurance did little to make Ivy feel any better. She really was tired. And cranky with it.

She sighed. She'd have to try to steal a few hours of sleep before her shift at King's Crossing tonight.

And she needed to tell both her bosses that she was pregnant. At least she had a few days before she worked again at the River View, a restaurant across town where she often picked up a handful of shifts a week. She wasn't looking forward to letting Mr. and Mrs. Mongillo, the owners, know she was having a baby.

It wasn't as if she could keep it a secret much longer. And why should she? She wasn't ashamed of her condition or that she'd spent the night with a man she'd found attractive and interesting.

She just didn't want anyone to judge her. No, that wasn't true. She didn't care what people thought.

But maybe a small part worried about losing

Fay's good opinion of her. They weren't ready for matching BFF bracelets and sleepovers, but they got along well enough. Having another woman to talk to, to gossip with and laugh with was...nice. Weird, but nice.

Too often, other women viewed her as competition. The enemy, always ready to steal their boyfriends or husbands.

Fay, who should have viewed her only as an employee, often treated her more as a friend. Ivy didn't want to lose that.

She would, of course. No relationship lasted forever. She just hoped this fledgling one with Fay made it a few more months.

"I have to tell you something," she said, knowing she couldn't put this off forever.

Fay just waited. See? No prodding. No pushing. She simply stood by and let things happen.

Ivy preferred to *make* things happen.

"Look, what I'm about to say... I just want you to know this doesn't change anything. I'll still come in to work every day. It's not going to get in the way of my doing my job here."

A job she'd desperately needed before to help pay off the loan she'd taken out for her mother's funeral. To help pad the nest egg she was trying to build to pay for culinary school. A job that was of the utmost importance now that she'd soon have a baby to take care of.

Fay, sweeter than any woman should be, took hold of Ivy's hands. "It's okay. You can tell me."

Ivy nodded. Tugged free to wipe her palms down the sides of her dress. "I—"

"We're back," Gracie said as she walked into the kitchen, Fay's son Mitchell on her hip. "Camden's mom said she'll drop off Elijah before five…" Gracie frowned. Glanced between Fay and Ivy. "What's going on?"

"Nothing," Ivy muttered. She hadn't considered telling Gracie. What if the teenager thought having unprotected sex was a good thing? She already looked up to Ivy. What if she thought getting pregnant was a great idea? That she should try it, too?

Ugh. She wasn't even a mother yet, and already she had a supersize case of guilt.

"Actually," Fay said, "something very important is going on. I believe Ivy was just about to tell me she's pregnant."

Ivy's jaw dropped. She shut it with a snap. "What?"

"It's about time," Gracie said, setting Mitchell in a chair at the long farmhouse table and handing him a coloring book and box of crayons. "I mean, it's not as if you can wear loose dresses and tops forever and not expect people to notice."

Ivy shook her head, then looked at Fay. "You knew?"

Fay looked embarrassed. Or guilty. "I suspected. You had a few bouts of morning sickness, especially whenever you cooked meat. That, plus the way you've been dressing…"

She trailed off as if there was nothing more to say, which, Ivy supposed, there wasn't.

"So, you suspected I was pregnant and instead of asking me, you told Gracie?" And if these two knew, did that mean others did, as well?

Of course it did. This was Shady Grove. News spread. Fast.

"Please give me some credit," Gracie said, sitting down next to Mitchell. He automatically climbed onto her lap. "Molly has been pregnant five times in the past nine years. I know the signs."

"Are you all right?" Fay asked. "No problems with the baby?"

"I'm fine. The baby is fine. I went to the doctor last week."

"Then why didn't you tell us?" Fay wanted to know.

Ivy sighed. "I'm not in a relationship or anything. What happened between me and Clin… between me and the baby's father was a onetime thing. I didn't want you to think I was…"

"Easy?" Gracie asked, coloring a picture of a cartoon duck.

Ivy narrowed her eyes at the girl. "Yes. Thank you so much."

Gracie shrugged. "It's no big deal. A woman's sex life is her own business. Plus, the reason our foremothers had the whole sexual revolution was so we could make our own choices. And that includes who we sleep with."

The kid sure did have a way with words.

"I hope you know I would never think anything like that about you," Fay said, earnest and horrified. As if having a bad thought about someone was akin to kicking kittens and pinching puppies. "I don't like to judge people. No one knows what someone else is going through, so it's better to just accept them. Be there for them when they need you."

Shame filled Ivy. Hadn't she worried that Fay would look down on her? And hadn't she thought Fay was somehow weak because she was sweet natured and giving?

Ever since Fay's husband had left her a few years back, ever since Fay had ended up in the hospital after taking a bottle of sleeping pills, people had judged her. She was healthy now. At least physically.

Ivy wasn't sure she'd ever be stronger.

Still, how difficult it must be, knowing that people were saying awful things about you. Fay must have heard the ugly rumors. Must realize that some people were still talking about her.

"Gracie and I both care about you," Fay continued, able to open up and express her feelings without a qualm. A trait Ivy considered dangerous. If people knew what you thought, how you felt, they could use it against you. "We're here for you and will help in any way we can. I hope you know that."

Ivy did know that. But knowing it and trusting it were two different things.

"I'm available to babysit," Gracie said. "Nights and weekends. You just let me know."

Ivy's eyes stung. Tears. God. She blamed her whacked-out hormones. She never cried. Not when the girls in high school had called her ugly names. Not when some boy had used her. Not when she'd let some boy use her. Not when her mother had blamed her for the way her life had turned out, had wished she'd never been born. But now, two people were being nice to her and she was all weepy. It was pathetic.

She sniffed. Cleared her throat. "Thanks. Both of you. I'm just… God. I'm scared," she admitted. "I don't know what to do or what to expect."

"Bigger boobs," Gracie said, ticking items off on her fingers, "swollen ankles, hemorrhoids, mood swings, stretch marks and possibly an episiotomy if something tears while you deliver."

Ivy stared at Fay, horrified. "Please tell me she's exaggerating."

Fay looked at her with sympathy. "I wish I could. But trust me. It's all worth it in the end. And not every woman has to deal with all of those things or even any of them. But I don't think that's what you meant."

"It wasn't, but now those are all I can think about."

"Try to forget all of that," Fay said. "They're not important. The only important question is— are you happy about this baby?"

Ivy shut her eyes. "I wasn't," she admitted, not feeling guilty about it. She didn't blame or resent the baby. And really, she couldn't be expected to be held accountable for her feelings. "But I wasn't unhappy, either. At first I was just...shocked."

"And now?" Fay asked quietly.

Ivy looked at her, wondering if she'd misjudged this quiet, fragile woman. Maybe she was stronger than anyone realized. She glanced at Gracie, the girl who was almost like a little sister to her, and at Mitchell, so adorable and easygoing with his angelic grin and sweet disposition. She thought about the life inside her. Thought about how she'd be responsible for that life, caring for it, loving it always, and it didn't seem like a burden.

It seemed like an honor.

She was going to have a baby. She was going to be a mother, something she'd always wanted but had feared would never happen—that no one would ever believe she was capable of that kind of love. Though it was earlier than she'd planned, though it was with a man she didn't know, it had happened and she was going to embrace this pregnancy and this child.

"Now," she told Fay, smiling at the thought of having a child to love, having her own family, "I want this baby."

It wouldn't be easy. Despite working two—and at times, three—jobs, she barely made ends meet. She knew nothing about babies, nothing about being a mother, but she could learn. She glanced at Fay, then at Gracie.

Maybe she wasn't as alone as she thought.

CHAPTER EIGHT

SOMETIMES LIFE WAS just so unfair.

Gracie didn't want to go outside. Didn't want to have to walk across the side yard and get her brothers, but it was her responsibility to watch them. To keep them safe, yes, but when it came to the boys, it was even more important to keep other people safe from them.

How little kids could find so much trouble was beyond her.

While she was listing her complaints as she descended the front porch steps, Gracie acknowledged that she wasn't exactly thrilled to be left watching her brothers on a Saturday afternoon in the first place. She wanted to be hanging out with her friends, but since Leighann was with her on-again-off-again-freaking-on-again boyfriend and Kassandra and Chelsea were out of town, Gracie had nothing to do anyway, so she hadn't put up a fuss when her parents had asked her to babysit.

She should have, she realized as she crossed the yard, the grass warm and soft under her bare feet. Because now she was stuck at home. The baby and Chandler were napping, but the others…?

Well, they'd been quiet for way too long. She'd looked for them all over the house but no luck. She'd checked the backyard, the garage, even had one of the dogs helping, but the four of them were nowhere to be found.

Not good. The twins, all on their own, could cause mass destruction. They were the ringleaders and often got their brothers to go along with their ideas. And she really didn't feel like putting out any fires.

Literally.

They were nowhere to be found. Darn it. She stood in the bright sunshine outside her back door, twisting one of her curls around her finger. Around and around and around. They'd never taken off before, at least not down the street or anything. But they had, a few months ago when the weather had finally turned nice, ventured into the yard next door.

Andrew's yard.

She could hear people out there now. Andrew's mom didn't spend a lot of time outside, but sometimes Andrew and his buddies would be out there, tossing a football back and forth. Not that she'd been spying on him or anything. It was just that her bedroom window overlooked his yard.

Sauron, her huge, black dog, barked and took off in the direction of the voices. Leaving Gracie no choice but to follow.

She walked slowly. Maybe she was borrowing

trouble. It could be anyone out in the yard. Andrew's mom or Leo Montesano, her firefighter boyfriend. Maybe Gracie would get lucky.

She turned the corner, stepped over the invisible line that separated the properties and sighed. No. No luck for her. Not today.

Okay, so maybe she was a little lucky. Because, while Andrew was there, he wasn't alone. He was playing football with Luke and her brothers. Both Andrew and Luke had their shirts off, and she was honest enough to admit that seeing them shirtless was not a hardship.

It was purely a physiological response. She was a female in the throes of adolescence, a hormonal time and, some researchers said, the time when she was most fertile. The prime of her life. Though she would argue that time and evolution had pushed that prime back by at least ten years.

Still, seeing the boys bare chested was a pleasure. They were both tall, their muscles well defined. Andrew was darker, his skin already a golden tan, his hair flopping in his face as he caught a pass from one of her brothers. Luke tackled him. Hard. Both of them rolling onto the ground only to get up grinning, slapping each other's arms and backs, laughing, though Luke had just tried to drive Andrew's face into the grass.

Boys. So weird.

Her brothers were in on the action, and they'd

taken off their shirts, as well, their skinny bodies all arms and legs and slight ridges of their ribs.

And they were filthy. Covered in dirt and sweat.

She considered, seriously considered, leaving them there so she wouldn't have to deal with them, wouldn't have to try to convince four stinking, overexcited boys to come home and get cleaned up but they were her responsibility.

Her feet dragging, she stepped farther into the yard.

Luke noticed her first. Smiled at her. He'd only worked with her twice since starting at Bradford House Tuesday, and she'd kept her distance, hadn't said much, but he insisted on being nice to her. Friendly. As if she'd ever believe he really wanted to be her friend. "Gracie. Hi."

Andrew stopped playing and looked up. Blinked in surprise, then jumped to his feet. "Hey, Gracie."

She nodded. "Boys," she said to her brothers, who were begging Andrew to throw them the ball, "what are you doing?"

Three-year-old Caleb pressed against Luke's leg and smiled angelically at her. "Hi, Gracie. Luke plays football," he said with all the awe of someone who'd just met a member of the Steelers or something. "I caught his pass!" He glanced up at Luke. "Didn't I?"

Luke grinned and ruffled Caleb's sweaty blond hair. "You sure did, bud. It was a great catch."

Usually, whenever Caleb saw Gracie, he raced

over to her, but now he looked perfectly content to cuddle with some guy he didn't even know.

Traitor.

"You're not supposed to leave the yard," she told her brothers. Her tone, sharper than usual, had Caleb's lower lip trembling, had him edging closer to Luke.

Luke patted Caleb's shoulder as if comforting him over his mean old sister's bitchiness, which, of course, only made Gracie angrier. "They just sort of showed up," Luke said. "They're not bugging us or anything."

"That's not the point." She didn't want to be friendly with him, especially when Andrew was standing there watching her. She just wanted to get her brothers and get home.

Luke pulled a shirt on, while Andrew kept his off, tossed the ball from hand to hand in a way that made his biceps bulge. Was he doing that on purpose?

Six-year-old Christian blinked at her, all blond, blue-eyed, chubby-cheeked innocence. "We left you a note." He elbowed his identical twin, Colin.

Colin nodded like a bobblehead. Not quite pulling off the innocent look Christian did—at least that gave her hope that Colin did, indeed, have a conscience. "Yeah. Conner wrote it."

Conner, the oldest of the boys at almost eight, shoved Colin with two hands. "I thought you were going to write it."

Colin shoved back. "I can't write yet, stupid! I'm in kindergarten."

"You're in first grade now," Conner shouted with another shove, knocking Colin on his butt.

Which, of course, set Christian off. "You can't hit my brother!" he yelled with a bloodcurdling cry.

"They're both your brothers," Gracie pointed out, but Christian had already launched himself at Conner. The three of them fell to the ground with loud grunts, pointy elbows, kicking feet and fisted hands. Caleb raced around his fighting brothers, screaming his head off like a crazy person.

Gracie sighed at the lot that was her life.

"Uh, aren't you going to make them stop?" Andrew asked while Luke just stepped back from the melee, a small smile on his face.

"Molly says it's better for them to work their problems out on their own," Gracie said. "Besides, to get them to stop, I'd have to wade into that." She pointed at where the boys wrestled. "And I'm not about to do that. I made that mistake one time, and it wasn't pretty."

Mainly because she'd caught a bony knee to her stomach. She'd ended up struggling to get her breath back while they kept right on fighting.

Andrew looked at her as if she was nuts. No different from the way plenty of people looked at her, but it still stung.

Luke opened a cooler. "Want a soda?" he asked, as if they were at a wrestling match and should sit down and enjoy the show.

"Soda is just chemicals and sugar," she informed him—yes, sounding prissy, but she was out of her element here, and she rarely felt that way.

His grin widened. "You sound like Drew's mom. I had to bring this from home." And he popped the top and drank what equated to diabetes and death in a recyclable can.

Andrew glanced at the house nervously, then back at the fighting boys. Winced when Conner caught a fist to the side of his head. "You sure you shouldn't stop them?"

"They'll run out of steam eventually," she said, sounding funny—sort of stiff and offended, which wasn't like her at all. "Then they'll be best friends again."

"Boys," a sharp, female voice called. Gracie looked over to see Andrew's mom, a pretty brunette with shoulder-length hair, light brown eyes and a penchant for frowning, in the doorway. "Stop that this instant!"

The boys, of course, didn't stop. "My dad and Molly aren't big on telling us what to do," she explained because Andrew's mom looked so freaked out and none too happy about being ignored. "They prefer to let us make our own mistakes."

Gracie sent a pointed glance at Andrew, who had the decency to blush and duck his head.

"But they're fighting," Ms. Denning said with a feeble hand wave. "They'll get hurt."

"Probably."

Leo Montesano, firefighter and gorgeous human being extraordinaire, stepped onto the deck and Gracie's heart gave a happy sigh. The man was pure eye candy with tousled dark hair, tanned skin and a tall, muscular body. He glanced at his girlfriend—though Andrew's mom was way too old to be called that—then at the boys. Whistling a tune Gracie couldn't identify, he crossed to the hose, turned the water handle and tugged it forward.

Gracie considered telling him to stop, since she'd be the one to get the boys cleaned up, but they were already so filthy the water couldn't hurt. Besides, this was obviously a fight that wasn't going to end quickly or well on its own, and she really didn't want to drag all the kids to the ER because someone broke a bone.

Again.

So she stepped onto the porch as he turned the hose on full blast, dousing her brothers.

Colin broke first—jumping up with a scream. He got a mouthful of water for his efforts. The other two took more convincing, but the water must have been cold enough that it forced them apart. But then, in the ways of little boys, which

Gracie just did not understand, they started yelling joyfully and laughing, enjoying getting soaked.

"Me, too!" Caleb shouted at Leo. "Squirt me, too!"

Leo obliged, though he didn't use as much water pressure, and sent Caleb into a fit of giggles.

"Boys are so strange," Andrew's mom murmured.

Gracie could only nod in agreement.

By the time Leo turned off the hose, Gracie's brothers were soaked and running around on the wet grass, Sauron barking crazily next to them.

"Come on," Gracie said. "Let's get home. You need to put on dry clothes."

"No, we don't!" Colin shouted.

And he stripped naked. Right there in front of everyone.

From behind her, Gracie heard Andrew's mom gasp, then mutter a prayer of thanksgiving that her child wasn't an exhibitionist. By the time she went inside, Christian and Caleb were both naked, too, and the twins were chasing each other, trying to hit each other with sticks they'd picked up.

Luckily, Conner only took off his shorts, but he joined in the game.

"Take it back to our own yard," Gracie called out to them and, miracle of miracles, they actually listened and went running off toward home. "And don't you dare go inside and wake up the babies." She turned to Leo who was winding up the hose. "Thank you."

Though she wasn't sure she agreed with using force to get her brothers to listen, it was sort of nice having someone help her get them under control. She faced Andrew. "I'm sorry they bothered you."

"They didn't," he said, but then his phone buzzed and he checked it. He sent Luke a furtive glance, then muttered something about being right back. He walked away, texting as he went.

Gracie's cheeks burned at his dismissal. Well, hadn't she told him back on Valentine's Day that they weren't going to be friends? She shouldn't be disappointed that he'd taken her at her word.

Luke began picking up her brothers' clothes, and she hurried over to stop him, sending one more glance at Andrew's back. "You don't have to do that."

"It's not a problem," he said, apparently not bothered to be holding their underwear. When she tugged on them, he lifted his eyebrows. "Gracie. Really. I've got them. You might want to get your dog, though."

It was then she noticed Sauron hadn't gone with the boys but was rolling in the mud. She shut her eyes. Ugh. Why her?

"Sauron, stop it," she demanded, snapping her fingers. He sent her a look that said "Are you kidding me?" and went right back to rolling. She grabbed his collar and yanked, but all she managed to do was get him to his feet. She set her hands on her hips. "Go home." For added affect, she pointed toward their yard, where she could now hear a bloodcurdling scream that sounded like Colin's.

Just when she thought she was going to have to drag him the entire way home—and moving 150 pounds of wet, dirty and now very stinky dog when you topped off at 105 wouldn't be easy— Luke whistled.

"Sauron," he called. "Come on, boy."

Her dog lifted his head, then ran over to Luke, who gave him an affectionate pat.

They walked together through Gracie's yard, Sauron practically glued to Luke's side. When they reached her back door, which the boys had left wide open, Sauron raced inside. She could hear the boys inside as they wrestled around. It was only a matter of time before the younger two woke up. "I can take those now," she said, holding out her hands for the clothes.

"I'll help you get them into the wash."

Then Luke stepped into her house, and she wasn't sure what to do, but she realized she probably should follow him. Luckily, they were in the mudroom where two washers and a dryer were.

"Your brothers are cute," he said as if he meant it.

"They're cuter when they're clean. Do you

have younger siblings? You're very good with little kids."

"I'm the youngest, but I have an older brother and sister. My parents had me later in life, one of those surprise babies. So now I have nieces and nephews." The baby started crying, the sound coming through the monitor attached to her hip.

"There's another one?" Luke asked.

"Two more. My stepmother always wanted a big family, and my father can't say no to her. About anything. Though he did promise me that they'll only have one more and stop at an even number."

"Wow. I guess they keep you all busy." He opened the washing machine's lid and added detergent. Then he tossed all the clothes in without a thought as to running colors or anything. Just like her dad when he did the wash. Must be a Y chromosome thing.

"On the plus side," she said, wrinkling her nose at Colin's shirt, "this is the first time Colin's taken this shirt off in almost a week. At least we can get it washed. Hopefully he'll want to stay naked for a while, or else he'll have a fit about it."

Luke laughed. "Man, when I was a kid it was my *Power Rangers* costume. My mom said I wore it for weeks on end. It got so bad she had to burn it, then she felt so guilty, she went out and bought me a new one."

Her lips twitched. "I remember when you had

that orange-striped shirt in fourth grade. You wore it every other day. You looked like Charlie Brown."

"Hey, I liked that shirt." He leaned against the machine as it started.

He was so handsome, her stomach did this little flop, which was stupid because he was way out of her league. He was just like Andrew, and she didn't want to go down that road again.

Besides, Luke had a girlfriend. The beautiful Kennedy.

Gracie wondered if he knew his girlfriend was basically walking, talking evil?

She cleared her throat. The baby had settled down again, and the older boys were quiet, which meant they were either watching TV or were doing something wrong and possibly illegal. "Thanks for carrying the clothes over," she said, "and for playing with the boys."

"They really weren't bugging us or anything," he assured her. "I hope they don't get into trouble for leaving the house without telling you. I should have asked if they were allowed to be over there."

"They're not your responsibility." They were hers. At least part of the time.

"It was fun." His phone buzzed, but he didn't take it out, didn't check it like most people did— as if whatever message they'd received would disappear if they didn't look at it right away.

Still, it was awkward, having popular, handsome Luke Sapko in her laundry room, his clothes splattered with mud. "I'd better check on the baby," she said, though the monitor was quiet now. "And I have to give Sauron a bath, so…"

"Need any help?"

She blinked. "No. Thank you, though."

"Oh. All right. Well, I guess I'll go." He gave her a salute and another of those grins. "See you at work."

"Yeah. See you."

He walked away.

So what if he seemed disappointed? Why would he want to stick around? They were coworkers. Not friends. He'd just offered to help her because he was nice. Incredibly, surprisingly nice. It didn't mean anything.

Even if part of her wished it did.

"No," C.J. SAID into his phone to his assistant, Julia, "I'm not sure when I'll be back."

"You do realize we're in the middle of a merger here, don't you?" Julia asked.

His fingers tightened on the phone as he got out of the rental car. "I'm well aware of everything that goes on with the company." He opened the back door and pulled out a suitcase. "Everything's under control."

Julia made a humming sound. "Your father never would have left town with this much going on. With so much hanging in the balance."

C.J. slammed the door shut. "Senior believed in delegating when necessary. Which was why he always insisted on having the best people work for him. Roger can handle this."

"He'd better be able to," Julia said of the company's vice president—a job Senior had always hoped Oakes would take over. "I only have a few more years until I retire, and I want to make sure you don't do something stupid and cost me my pension."

She hung up. C.J. shoved the phone into his pocket. Julia had worked for Bartasavich Industries for over forty years and had been his dad's assistant. C.J. hadn't had the heart to hire his own assistant after his dad's stroke but he wished he had. He didn't mind Julia speaking her mind. Other people's opinions didn't bother him.

Not when he had final say.

But he was tired of being compared to his father. He was proud of Senior, knew how hard he'd worked to make the company what it was, but C.J. wanted to make his own mark. Leave his own legacy.

Not be known only as Senior's oldest son. His namesake.

C.J. climbed the porch steps, noted how well maintained the bed-and-breakfast was, with new siding and windows, the lawn lush and green. In the background he heard a mower, could smell the scent of freshly cut grass. The sun was warm on his head, the day bright and hot.

At least, by northern standards. This was nothing compared to the oppressive heat he'd left in Houston.

There was a plaque stating that Bradford House was listed on the historical registry of Shady Grove. He wasn't sure of the protocol, so he stepped inside the foyer, where it was cooler, the colors rich and inviting, the ceilings high, the woodwork gleaming. He could see two rooms—a library and what looked to be a living room, both comfortably furnished.

The sound of footsteps made him look up, but it wasn't Ivy coming down the wooden stairs, but a very thin, tall woman with a soft smile and a reddish tint to her hair, which was pulled back in a tidy braid.

"Hello," she said. Even her voice was soft, like the colors she wore—a pink top and light blue jeans. "May I help you?"

"This is Bradford House?" he asked, though he'd read the plaque stating it was.

"Yes. I'm the manager, Fay Lindemuth. Do you have a reservation?"

"No, ma'am," he said, giving her his most charming grin, "but I'd like one."

Her own smile stayed merely polite. "Let's see what we can do for you, then. Follow me, please."

She led him into the office, then indicated the

chair across from a small desk, while she sat behind it and booted up a computer. "How long would you like to stay with us?" she asked.

"Indefinitely."

She raised her eyebrows. "Excuse me?"

He sent her a grin, hoping to put her at ease. "I have some...unfinished business here in Shady Grove. And," he added, wondering if bringing in a local connection would help his case, "my brother lives in town."

"Your brother?"

"Kane Bartasavich."

Her expression softened. "Oh, yes. He's marrying Charlotte Ellison. We're hosting Charlotte's bridal shower this October." She typed something into the computer. "I'm afraid we've never had a guest stay more than two weeks, so you'll have to bear with me. Now, what kind of accommodations are you looking for?"

"I'd like a room with as much privacy as possible, a desk and internet access."

He could work with that.

"All rooms in Bradford House have access to free Wi-Fi," she murmured, her attention on the screen. Her desk was cluttered. Framed photos hung on the walls around it. The room itself was more homey than functional, with its brightly patterned sofa and pictures of two little boys in huge hockey jerseys. "You'd probably be most comfortable in the Back Suite. It has its own sitting room with a desk and the most privacy of all the rooms."

"I'll take it."

"Unfortunately, it's booked until tomorrow night. I can put you up in the Blue Room for now."

He nodded, and she handed him a form to fill out. He did so quickly, passed it back to her along with his driver's license and credit card. While she typed in his information, he glanced around. It had taken him five days to tie up loose ends at work, delegate responsibilities and hand over two key projects before he'd been able to leave Houston. Five days of thinking about Ivy and how he'd mishandled things.

And now that he'd temporarily put his life on hold and traveled more than one thousand miles to be here, he had no idea what his next step was. All he knew was that he needed to be in Shady Grove. He had to see Ivy again, talk to her.

He had to get to the truth.

He didn't like being this...unsettled. An unplanned pregnancy would have that effect on anyone he supposed, but he wasn't used to not having a plan. An idea of what to do next, which step to take.

"You're all set, Mr. Bartasavich," Fay said as she stood. She turned, took down a key—an actual key, not a pass card—from a locked box behind her. "If you'll follow me, we'll get you settled. Breakfast is served from 7:00 a.m. to 10:00 a.m.,

Monday through Friday. Weekends from eight to eleven. We offer free coffee and snacks in the afternoon in the library. Wine and cheese in the evenings. I can also give you suggestions on places for lunch and dinner and tourist attractions."

"I appreciate it." Though he wouldn't have time to do any sightseeing.

They stepped out into the hall. "Here," she said, "let me take your bag."

He grinned at her. "And have them kick me out of the man club? No, ma'am."

She smiled back at him shyly. She was a pretty thing with her strawberry-blond hair and those light eyes.

The door at the far end of the hall opened, and Ivy stepped out. C.J.'s heart nearly stopped—which was idiotic. He was a grown man, not some teenager in the throes of his first crush. But still, she took a man's breath. Today she was wearing light green shorts that showed miles of her toned legs and a loose tank top. Her hair was pulled back in a ponytail, and she'd wrapped a floral scarf around her head like a headband. She froze when she saw him.

He nodded. "Hello, Ivy."

For a moment he thought she was going to simply turn around and walk back into the kitchen, pretend he wasn't here.

If she really was pregnant with his baby, he wasn't going to let her ignore him.

Instead, she walked toward him, all attitude and sex appeal. "You're a long way from home, cowboy."

Fay glanced between them. "Do you two know each other?"

C.J. inclined his head. "You could say that."

"We met at Charlotte's engagement party," Ivy said quickly, shooting him a shut-it-or-die look. "What are you doing here?"

He held up his key. "Just booked a room."

Her eyes narrowed, and she crossed her arms, which only lifted her breasts up, and damn if he didn't notice. She smirked, knowing the effect she had on men. They probably dropped to their knees, either in prayer or to beg for a moment of her time, when she walked down the street.

"Now, why would you do a thing like that?" she asked.

"Because you're here," he said simply.

"Oh, no," Fay murmured, shifting to stand next to Ivy. "You're not one of those guys, are you?"

He raised his eyebrows. "Excuse me?"

She waved a hand at Ivy. "Men who book a room here just to get Ivy's attention."

He couldn't help it. He laughed. "Men actually do that?" he asked Ivy.

"Legions," she said so solemnly, he wasn't sure if she was kidding or not.

"I'm here," he told Fay, "because I didn't like how Ivy and I left things."

"Funny," Ivy said, "but I liked how we left things just fine. Mostly the part about us never seeing each other again."

"We have unfinished business," he told her.

"There is no we, cowboy. Unless you're talking about you and the little brain you have in your pants."

"I think it would be better if you found somewhere else to stay," Fay said, now shifting to stand in front of Ivy, which was funny because she looked as if a stiff wind could blow her down. As if she were afraid of her own shadow.

He held Ivy's gaze. "You going to let her kick me out, Ivy? Because that won't stop me from getting what I want. From what I came here for."

"Do you want me to call the police?" Fay asked Ivy, looking really worried now. As if C.J. was planning to add Ivy's head to his collection in a basement.

"No," Ivy said. "He's basically harmless."

But her look said she wasn't so sure. Good. He wouldn't hurt her, but no one thought he was harmless.

She turned to Fay. "Why don't I show Mr. Bartasavich to his room? Since we're such good friends and all?"

"Are you sure?" Fay asked. She lowered her

voice, sent him a glance. "He seems sort of...
dangerous. Possibly unstable."

"I'm standing right here, darlin'," he drawled.
"And dangerous or unstable, my hearing's just
fine."

They ignored him.

"He won't hurt me," Ivy assured her. She turned
to him. "Come on."

He winked at Fay to let her know he wasn't
some deranged madman with murder on his mind
and followed Ivy up the stairs.

CHAPTER NINE

DAMN IT. DAMN IT! What was he doing here? Ivy thought as she stomped up the main staircase, her hand trailing over the glossy wood rail.

She rolled her eyes. Okay, she knew what he was doing here. She just hadn't expected him to actually follow her back to Shady Grove. Especially after he'd reacted the way she should have known he would, by blaming her, ditching his responsibility and going on his merry way, letting her and the baby go on theirs.

She turned left at the top of the stairs, went to the second room and unlocked the door for him, shoving it open. "Come on."

"So gracious," Clinton murmured, brushing past her, the scent of his cologne taking her back to their night together. And the day last week when she'd been at his apartment. "No wonder you're the chef here and not hostess."

"I'm the chef here because I'm good at what I do," she said, shutting the door behind them. "Played Nancy Drew yourself, did you? Tracked me down and all that?"

"I didn't actually do the tracking down myself."

He turned, his big body looking out of place in the feminine room with its soft blue walls and floral quilt. He put his suitcase on the bed. He wore a suit, much like the ones she'd already seen him in, but this one was slate gray.

How many expensive suits did one man need?

"What do you mean, you didn't do it yourself?" she asked, her eyes narrowed.

"I had someone else find you—though I'm sure I could have managed to do so myself. Shady Grove isn't that big, after all."

No, it wasn't, and Ivy was easy enough to find. Plus, she wasn't hiding. She had no reason to hide. Nothing to be ashamed of.

"Your coworker doesn't know you're pregnant?" he asked.

"Fay is my boss and yes, she knows. She just doesn't know who the sperm donor is." As Ivy had hoped, his mouth flattened at that. "And don't think I'm going to thank you for not spitting it out about our night together."

But she was grateful to him, and she didn't want to be. If she owed him, he'd take advantage of that. Would use that against her in the future.

"Any reason you don't want her to know I'm possibly the father?"

She strolled to the dresser. Picked up the antique hand mirror that was sitting there. "Such as this all being a big ruse meant to drain you of your piles and piles of gold?" She shook her head. "Nope."

"Then why not let her know?"

"I hadn't planned on telling anyone about our... connection. Why bother? I have your check, and you have my promise not to bother you again. Though why you're here, I have no idea." She set the mirror down. Linked her hands at her waist. "So...why are you here? Really?"

"I didn't handle things well," he said, his voice gruff, his gaze steady, "when you came to Houston."

"You don't say?" she asked so drily, she was surprised puffs of sand didn't come out of her mouth.

"I was shocked. Upset. I don't think that makes me a bad guy. We don't know each other, and it seemed as if you may have planned all of this."

"Well, I must be some freaking genius," she said, sitting in the armchair next to the window and crossing her legs. "Imagine putting this plan together so flawlessly. Let's see, first of all, I had to know you were going to be at that party and I had to know you're not just some random, good-looking, smooth-talking cowboy but the heir apparent to some huge corporation. That you're worth more money than God and you'd be alone that night and in the mood for company."

Clinton sat on the corner of the bed, his lips pursed. "I guess that might be a bit far-fetched.

But you did know who I was before we slept together."

"I knew you were Charlotte's future brother-in-law. Someone I found attractive. Someone I wanted to spend the night with. That was all it was supposed to be. And if I remember correctly, you were the one who came on to me first. You paid Gracie to come fetch me like some errant puppy."

He had the grace to look abashed. "I just wanted to talk to you."

She winked at him. "Well, you talked to me all right."

"I just... It's dangerous sleeping with someone you don't know."

She raised her eyebrows. "Really? A lecture on morals? Not knowing me didn't seem to bother you when we were in your room. If I recall, you were all for it. Don't play that double standard with me. I was attracted to you. I enjoy sex. So I slept with you. Thought that would be the end of it. Instead, it's not. Now we both have to deal with it."

He blew out a breath. "I'd like to talk to your doctor."

She couldn't blame him for wanting proof of the pregnancy and of his paternity. What she blamed him for was wanting to know so he could be a part of the baby's life. She knew the score here. She had nothing. Well, except their baby growing inside of her. While he had everything. Money. Power. Enough to make her life a living hell.

Enough to take her child from her if he chose.

"I have an appointment next week," Ivy said. "But I'm not sure how far along I have to be for her to do a paternity test."

"You'd allow one?"

"I would. But not so I can lay claim to your fortune. If you want to be a part of the baby's life, I can't stop you. But I'm not about to change my life to make that happen. You'll have to play by my rules."

"If you don't want money—"

"Hey now, who said I don't want money? I have your check for fifty grand, remember? Don't think you're getting that back."

He linked his hands between his knees. "Okay, if you're not after *more* money, why did you tell me? We both know you could have easily kept this from me. As far as I know, no one knew we were together that night and the chances of us running into each other in the future were slim. You could have gone on your way, could have had the baby, and I never would have known."

"Because it was the right thing to do," she said. But maybe she owed him more of an explanation. She wasn't sure. She was so used to being on her own. Of not having to explain her actions or choices to anyone.

She hadn't wanted to seek him out. She would

have preferred to raise the baby on her own—would still prefer that. But the thought of having the conversation she'd had with her own mother time after time made her sick. Of her child asking her who her father was, where he was and her not being able to answer.

Whether Melba withheld the truth for her own selfish reasons or just to hurt Ivy, to punish her for being born, Ivy wasn't sure. But not knowing where she'd come from haunted her. She wouldn't do that to her child.

"I never knew my dad," she admitted slowly. "And I don't think he ever knew about me. I always thought that was unfair. That maybe he wouldn't have wanted anything to do with me, but he should have had the choice. So I'm giving you the choice."

He nodded. "I appreciate it."

Clinton seemed sincere, and she wondered if she'd been wrong about him. But then she remembered what he'd said about not doing the tracking down to find her. "How did you find me?" she asked. "How did you know I'm the chef here?"

"I hired a private investigator."

She froze. Everything inside her seemed to still. "You hired someone to find me?"

"Yes."

She wasn't sure she wanted to ask the next question, let alone hear the answer. "What else did you hire this professional Nancy Drew to do?"

"Actually, he's more like Magnum PI, from what I understand. Right down to the mustache. And he found out where you lived. Worked."

She had a bad feeling about this. "You looked into my past."

He lifted a shoulder as if it was nothing, instead of a huge invasion of privacy. "He ran a background check on you, yes."

She slowly got to her feet. "I see. And what did you discover?"

Now he shifted. He damn well should shift. He had no right—no *freaking* right—to investigate her that way. "He found out you've lived in Shady Grove your entire life—"

"I believe I already told you that."

"You wouldn't even tell me your last name that night," he said, climbing to his feet, also. "You weren't exactly forthcoming then or when you were in Houston. You drop a bombshell on me—oh, by the way, I'm pregnant with your child so just believe every word I say because I say it—then walk away. You didn't leave me much of a choice."

Maybe she hadn't, but a girl had a right to her secrets. To protect herself from someone she didn't know. "You're not the only one here who's not thrilled with this situation."

"What are you saying?" he asked hoarsely. He stepped closer. "You're not thinking of getting rid of the baby, are you?"

"It's too late for that. And no, I hadn't considered it. But there are other options. Adoption, for one."

He made a move as if he were about to grab her arms but held himself back. "If this baby is mine, you are not giving it away."

She sighed. "Relax. I considered adoption but ultimately decided against it. I may not be wealthy, but I can support a child, and I plan on keeping my baby. I just don't want you as part of the package."

"We're going to have to figure out how to deal with each other."

"I can't do anything with you if I don't trust you. What else did your private investigator find out about me?"

"Like I said, he found out where you live. That you're the chef here. So far, that's it. Can you really blame me for wondering if you'd set this whole thing up? If you're not being completely truthful?" he asked so calmly, all rational and hard-assed, she wanted to scratch his eyes out. "You slept with me after just meeting me, and now you say you're pregnant with my child. What the hell am I supposed to believe?"

She jabbed his chest. "That's the thing. What you believe is a choice. And you chose to believe I'm some manipulative gold digger who'd have a child just to get your money. How dare you toss the fact I slept with you that night in my face? You were there, too! You're not innocent here—

you wanted to get me into bed from the moment you saw me."

That was the problem. People saw her, and they made assumptions about her. No one took the time to get to know her. They were too busy judging her.

"How is my hiring a PI any different from you looking me up on the internet?" he asked, seemingly clueless.

"Because I didn't do a background check, which I'm assuming means digging into my childhood. I didn't look into your personal life. I found your address, where you worked. You're looking into my history, digging up dirt on me so you can judge me and my past." She jabbed him again. "Go. To. Hell."

He grabbed her hand, pulled her close to him. "Don't poke me."

She wouldn't resort to struggling to get free. "Let go of me. Now."

He hesitated but then opened his fingers. She stalked toward the door.

"What the hell else could I do?" he asked. "You walked out on me. Twice."

She yanked the door open. "This makes us three for three. And if you'd wanted to know more about me, you could have asked."

"I tried that once. Didn't work out too well."

"You accused me of getting pregnant on purpose," she reminded him. "Of being some desperate gold digger. Did you really think I was going to sip tea and spill my life story after that?" But he had a point. One she wouldn't pretend didn't exist. "Look, maybe I handled things badly, but I was nervous about telling you. After I found out who you were, I was scared to death. This is my baby. My child. And you have the power to take him or her away from me. And then you acted like a complete asshole, tossing accusations my way left and right. You want me to tell all, to be truthful, but you don't trust or believe one thing I say, so what's the point? You've already made up your mind about me." Her fingers tightened on the door handle. Her voice grew soft. "You've already made up your mind about me," she repeated, knowing it was true. "Nothing I say will change a thing. And that, cowboy, is your loss."

"BOURBON," C.J. TOLD the bartender at O'Riley's, the bar Kane owned. "Neat."

She eyed him as she poured. "You're not here to cause trouble again, are you?"

He almost grinned. "You're thinking of the wrong Bartasavich. I don't cause trouble. I fix the trouble my idiot brothers get into."

She set his drink in front of him, and that was when he recognized her as the waitress who'd tried to throw him out the last time he was in this dump. Her dark hair was a bit longer and pink on the ends, but when she brushed her hair aside, he saw the neck tattoo. "Kane doesn't cause trouble around here. So don't start on him, or you'll have to mess with me, and I'm not as nice as I seem."

He saluted her with his glass. "Yes, ma'am." To show he wasn't the least bit scared, he winked as he took a sip. He waited until she'd walked away before downing the rest of the drink.

Shit. He'd blown it with Ivy again. There should be some sort of law stating he could act like a complete ass only twice in front of the same woman. He wanted to blame her and he partly did. She brought out the worst in him, with her vague answers and smart-ass comments.

But he was a grown man, responsible for his own actions and choices.

He could have chosen to trust her. To believe her. Given her time to tell him what he wanted to know on her own.

"Slumming?"

C.J. sighed and looked up to find Kane smirking at him. He'd known he couldn't avoid his brother—it was Kane's bar, after all. But dealing with him was never easy. "I'll take another bourbon. And this time, don't be so stingy with the pour."

Kane eyed his empty glass, then his face, then shrugged. Pulled the bottle down and poured a healthy amount into C.J.'s glass. "If you're here as dad's errand boy again, the answer's still no."

The first time C.J. had come to Shady Grove

had been after Kane had wrecked his motorcycle over a year ago. He'd gotten away with some scrapes and bruises and a broken arm, but it had freaked out Estelle enough—who'd run away while her mother was on vacation—that she'd called Senior and told him she was worried about her dad. So C.J. and Senior had hightailed it to Pennsylvania to check on Kane.

C.J. had then told Kane that their father wanted to offer him a job, a cushy office job Kane hadn't earned and anyone could have told Senior he would never want. But their father was nothing if not stubborn.

It was probably what kept him alive since his stroke.

"Dad's not running things at the office anymore," C.J. reminded his brother. "I am. Don't hold your breath for any job offers from me anytime soon. You want to work for Bartasavich Industries while I'm in charge, you'll have to earn it."

"Good thing I'll never want to work there."

C.J. knew his brother meant what he said. Of Senior's four sons, C.J. was the only one who worked directly for the family company, was the only one who wanted to, who'd busted his ass to prove he belonged there and not just because his father ran the company. He'd refused to take any handouts from his father, had started at the bottom and worked his way up, proving he deserved his success.

Oakes was happy with his law practice, and Zach was off playing Marine and seemed to want to make that his career. C.J. never would have thought Kane would stick with one job for very long, especially one where he was in charge, where he was responsible for employees and customers and a building and taxes. But stick he had. So much that he was getting married and staying right here in Shady Grove.

"If Dad didn't send you to try to lure me back to Houston," Kane said, "what are you doing here?"

C.J. drained his glass. "Drinking mediocre bourbon. Seriously. You can't order anything better than this?"

Kane's eyes narrowed. His arm wasn't broken now, the way it had been the last time they'd faced off at this very bar, but C.J. wasn't worried. Kane might be all badass, with his tattoos and motorcycle and piss-poor attitude, but they'd gone around enough times in their lives for C.J. to know he could handle his own against his little brother.

He was the one who'd taught Kane how to fight, after all.

"You want some fancy drink," Kane said, "maybe with a pretty pink umbrella in it? Try the country club or King's Crossing. Now, why are you here?" He stiffened. "Is it Dad? He was fine when I called to check on him. Did something happen? Did he take a turn for the worse?"

"Dad's fine." If not being able to speak and having to learn how to use his body all over again was fine. "There's no change."

Kane's expression grew grim. "Maybe we need to consider taking him to a different doctor."

C.J. wanted to point out that there was no *we* in this situation, but Kane had stepped up after Senior's stroke. He and their old man had never gotten along, but Kane had taken care of things here when Senior had been in the hospital, their father having suffered his stroke during that trip he'd made to Pennsylvania last fall. C.J. wondered if Kane realized Senior had come to try to reconcile with his second son, to see if there was some way they could be in each other's lives.

C.J. thought his brother did know, and that was part of the reason why he'd made several trips to Texas since they'd taken Senior back home. Why he called every few days to check up on him.

"He's seeing the best specialists in Houston," C.J. pointed out. Funny but it was usually him wanting to take charge, wanting to make things happen when he felt they were moving along too slowly. "We have to be patient."

Kane shook his head. "You must be drunk. You're not patient."

"I have to be in this case." He'd realized he'd drive himself crazy if he tried to control things.

He couldn't make his father get better. He could only pray that it would happen.

"So you're not here because of Dad." Kane grinned. "What's the matter, Junior? Miss me?"

C.J.'s answer to that was to flip his brother off. "I'm in town on business." He accepted the fresh drink Kane poured for him. "Personal business."

Kane frowned, but then a light C.J. didn't like one bit entered his eyes. "Does this personal business have anything to do with a woman?"

C.J. nodded. "Ivy Rutherford. She works at King's Crossing and Bradford House."

"Never thought I'd see the day when a woman would have you so wrapped up you'd leave Houston—and your precious job—just to track her down. I hadn't realized you even knew anyone in Shady Grove other than me and Charlotte."

"I met Ivy at your engagement party."

Kane's eyebrows rose. "Must have been some introduction."

"You could say that." He sipped his drink. "She's pregnant."

C.J. didn't have to wait long for his brother's reaction.

Kane laughed. Hard.

"It's not that funny," C.J. muttered while Kane still guffawed like an idiot, so loud that several other patrons turned his way. Even his scary bartender with the neck tattoo frowned at him in concern.

"You're not standing on this side of the bar. Trust me," Kane said, still chuckling. "It's freaking hilarious."

"I don't even know if it's really mine."

"Did you sleep with her?" C.J. gave a reluctant nod. "Then I guess it's possible. Don't tell me you told her you didn't believe her."

"What was I supposed to say? 'Great? Let's get married'?"

Kane shook his head, giving him a pitying look. Kane was *pitying* him.

His life was in the toilet for sure.

"You know how we grew up," C.J. said. "We were taught to watch out for ourselves, that people always wanted something from us."

"We were taught that," Kane admitted. "And maybe there was even good reason for it, but we're adults now and can make up our own minds. We learned how to spot the users, the people who wanted to get close to us for the money or because of our last name. Is Ivy like them?"

C.J. wasn't sure, and that was the problem. "Look, I'm here to see if she really is pregnant with my child, and then she and I can decide what to do, how to proceed. If she ever talks to me again," he mumbled.

Kane grinned. Looked like C.J. was really making his brother's day all jolly and bright. "You pissed her off, didn't you? You did a Senior and got all arrogant and controlling, and she told you to kiss ass."

"Something like that."

"It must kill you," Kane said, leaning against the counter, all at ease and happy with his life while C.J. was just trying to figure a few things out. "To realize you're human. You made the same mistake I made—though I was a dumb kid when I got Meryl pregnant with Estelle."

No, what killed him was that he'd made the same mistake their father had made twice. Senior had been married to their mother when he'd had an affair and gotten his mistress pregnant with Oakes. Then, when he'd been seemingly happy in his second marriage, he'd cheated again and fathered Zach.

Worse than following in Senior's footsteps? He'd acted like him. Kane had been right. C.J. had been arrogant with Ivy. Controlling.

A chip off the old block.

Shit.

But he could still fix this. All he had to was stop reacting as though Ivy was out to get him.

Before it was too late.

CHAPTER TEN

THE NEXT MORNING, C.J. met the deliveryman at the door of Bradford House, accepted the envelope from the PI Oakes had hired. The envelope filled with information about Ivy, about her past and who she really was. He paid and tipped the deliveryman, then shut the door. His fingers tightened on the packet. He stared at it, wondering what he'd find out inside, wondering if he even wanted to know.

He looked up and felt his heart tumble when he saw Ivy walking toward him, holding hands with a little boy.

He had a flash, a premonition of her coming toward him, fingers linked with their child's, her smile soft and inviting and sexy just for him, her stomach softly rounded with their second baby.

He shook his head, dispelling the image. Crazy. He wasn't a man prone to flights of fancy or who believed in premonitions or visions of what was to come. The future was what you made happen. He didn't believe in fate or destiny; he believed in hard work and following through.

But it had been a nice daydream, one he'd never

thought he'd have pictured for himself, especially not with someone who wasn't the type of woman he'd ever thought of having a future with.

"Skulking around, trying to get a look at me?" Ivy asked with that sexy smirk. "Or are you just taking your stalking up to a new level?"

"Neither," he said, holding up the envelope. "Just had some work delivered." He glanced at the boy, who was whining and holding his arms up to Ivy. Ivy picked him up, and C.J.'s stomach turned. Would he find out from the information the PI had gathered that this kid belonged to her? "Your son?" he asked, his words tight.

Though she and the boy both had blond hair, C.J. didn't see much resemblance between them. "Would it bother you if he was?"

Hell, yes. "*Is* he yours?" he asked instead, not liking feeling so judgmental.

"Sorry to disappoint you, but I don't make a habit of getting pregnant by random men. You're the first. This is Mitchell, Fay's youngest son. She has two, both born within the bonds of holy matrimony, in case you were harboring disparaging thoughts about her."

He stepped closer. "I wasn't. Hello, Mitchell." The kid pressed his face into the side of Ivy's neck and hugged her with enough force to have her eyes bugging out. C.J. frowned at her. "Is he afraid of me?"

"He's shy." She rubbed the child's back. "He's

not used to strangers, and he's not big on men in general, are you, buddy?"

"You're good with him."

Her mouth quirked. "You sound surprised."

He was. She was so overtly sexy and not exactly maternal. "Do you have siblings?" Maybe she had younger brothers and sisters she'd helped with while growing up.

"Nope." She winked. "Only child. I figure my mom was smart enough to realize once you hit perfection, there's no point having more kids."

He grinned. "I agree. Too bad that logic didn't stop my father from having three more sons."

"Just your father?"

"He had one of them with my mother. The other two with other women."

The kid lifted his head and started playing with Ivy's hair, and C.J. almost envied him. He remembered how soft it was, how fragrant, how it had trailed across his body, branding his skin. "Maybe I should be asking if you have a habit of getting women pregnant," she said.

"You're the first."

"Good to know."

"This whole thing is a first," he admitted, following her as she carried the kid upstairs. "I'm not...used to kids. Except my niece, but she's seventeen now, and when she was that little, I didn't spend much one-on-one time with her."

"Yeah, well, this is all new to me, too. Before I

started working here I'd never been around kids. Never babysat or had friends with younger siblings." She glanced over her shoulder at him. "Guess we'll figure it out together."

"Should you be carrying him up the stairs like that?" he asked.

"As opposed to having him tossed over my shoulder or dragging him up by his feet?"

"No. I meant, is it safe for you to be carrying something so heavy at all, especially up the stairs?"

"As far as I know. Again, this is my first time. But I do know that women all over the world have kids—often times more than one—and that they probably have to carry the older one during pregnancy, so I'm guessing it's fine. My doctor says I'm perfectly healthy, and since I'm beyond the first trimester, she thinks things should go smoothly."

C.J. shoved his hands into his pockets as they reached the second floor. "Good. That's…good." And made sense. He was just so out of his element here, felt so helpless, and he hated it.

"Yes. It is." Ivy studied him, since he was just standing there. "I suppose you'll want to go to your room, get working on those papers you have there," she said with a nod at the envelope.

He stared at the envelope having forgotten about it. Now he wondered what to do. He didn't often feel guilty about his decisions, wasn't usually this indecisive. "I do have work."

He always had work. Always had responsibilities and people counting on him.

She shifted the boy to her other side and he smiled, patted her cheek. "Love you, Ivy."

She kissed the top of his head. "Love you too, buddy. You're my favorite guy, you know that?"

He nodded and went back to singing a song and playing with her hair.

Something tightened in C.J.'s chest, as if she'd reached inside and squeezed his heart when she'd smiled so softly at the little boy, when her expression had softened with so much love. Who the hell was she? Why couldn't he get a read on her?

"I'm going to call my doctor," Ivy said to C.J., drawing his thoughts back to their conversation. "See if I can get an earlier appointment, maybe even today. If I do, you can come with me. We'll have her do an ultrasound in the office. I'm not sure about the paternity stuff but you'll get to hear it straight from her how many weeks along I am."

He nodded. "I appreciate it." He wouldn't apologize for wanting proof. They didn't know each other. Every time they were together that fact was brought home yet again.

"I'll come get you when I find out what time," she said before walking away.

He stepped into his room, shut the door behind him. Stared at the envelope. Thought about how she was letting him go to the doctor with her. How she'd admitted she was new at this, too. And he tossed the sealed envelope on his bed and crossed to the desk to get some work done.

As soon as Gracie stepped out of Bradford House onto the back patio, the heat hit her, like a slap to the face. She turned right around, ready to go back inside and tell Fay she couldn't possibly take Luke a glass of lemonade. It was too hot out. And did Fay have any idea what the humidity did to hair like Gracie's?

She'd likely give Luke—used to looking at his pretty girlfriend with her smooth, shiny hair—a heart attack.

And thinking of Kennedy only reminded her of how the other girl had treated her that day in school last fall. Nothing could have shored up her resolve better. No way was she going to let Kennedy scare her off.

Especially when the redhead wasn't even here.

She shut the French door with a soft click, feeling defiant. Rebellious. Ha. Take that. She may not be popular, may not be beautiful and golden, but she wasn't a coward. And after Luke had been so nice about her brothers Saturday, after he'd walked her home from Andrew's, she'd decided there was no reason for her to continue being so standoffish. Then, at some point in the future, after they'd gotten to know each other better, if they'd discovered they had enough common interests and views on certain subjects, then they could possibly become friends.

It wouldn't be the same as it had been with Andrew, she insisted to herself as she walked across the patio, the smooth stones hot under her bare feet. She and Andrew hadn't been friends. Hadn't taken the time to get to know each other. Everything between them had happened so quickly. One day they were neighbors who'd never even spoken to each other, and a few weeks later, she'd slept with him.

She switched the sweating glass of lemonade to her other hand, wiped the moisture from her fingers on her jean shorts. Her own fault for being so needy. For falling in love with him after such a short time.

Her fault for believing it when he'd said he loved her, too.

All in the past, she assured herself. She was over it. Mistakes happened and, honestly, if you couldn't make a few during your teen years, what was the point of adolescence?

She followed the low rumble of the lawn mower around the back corner of a shed on the far side of the yard. Watched Luke push the machine, his shirt damp and clinging to his broad shoulders, the width of his back. She'd been unfair in assuming Luke was just like Andrew. Unfair and judgmental, which stung.

She hated being judged, and yet she'd done it with Luke. Had assumed, since he and Andrew were best friends, since Luke was an athlete and good-looking, that he must be a user. A liar.

Of course, she wasn't ready to swear a blood oath that he wasn't either of those things. She was just willing to give him the benefit of the doubt.

For now.

Luke turned the corner, started back toward her, nodded to let her know he'd seen her, then finished the row and shut the machine off. He went to the side of the shed, turned on the hose and took off his hat before aiming the water at himself, soaking his hair and the back of his neck. Gracie thought it was a bit strange that he left his sunglasses on, but maybe the sunlight bothered his eyes. Who was she to judge? After shutting off the water, he straightened, shook himself pretty much like Sauron had done yesterday and put his hat back on.

He walked toward her, his eyes still covered by those dark sunglasses, the upper half of his shirt now completely wet and molding itself to his muscular chest. Oh, my. Her throat went dry. Her face got hot. Well, it was over ninety in the shade today, but she doubted that was the reason for her reaction.

Stupid, fickle hormones. Always getting women into trouble.

"Hey," he said when he reached her, his brows lowered, his mouth a flat line.

No happy greeting, no asking how she was. She'd gotten used to his good moods, his affable nature and friendly personality, so his grim expression and decidedly cool greeting had her frowning.

Her eyes widened. Did he…did he suspect that she'd been ogling him, like the freshmen girls who all giggled and batted their eyelashes when he passed? Now she gave an inner eye roll. Talk about egotistical. He probably wasn't thinking about her at all. Why assume his mood had anything to do with her? Maybe he was having a bad day. Maybe he was just overheated and cranky, like Chandler after being in the sun too long.

She'd promised herself she wouldn't jump to conclusions about him anymore, that she'd give him the same chance she'd want someone to give her and that was what she would do.

"Fay thought you might like a drink," Gracie said, holding out the glass.

"Thanks." He took it and drained the liquid in four deep gulps.

"Didn't you bring a water bottle with you?"

"I forgot," he said, his voice a low grumble.

"You're going to get dehydrated. When you work in heat like this, you need to make sure you stay hydrated so you don't get heatstroke."

She took back the glass. "I'll get you some more of this."

"I'm not thirsty."

She had no idea what to say. Not when he'd sounded so...churlish.

Though his attitude did give her an excuse to use that word.

"The grass looks nice." Okay, that had been lame, but at least she was trying. Giving him that chance she'd talked herself into.

His answer? A shrug.

Had she really thought he was nice?

Maybe this wasn't such a good idea. Trying to engage him socially. She should have stuck with her instincts, the ones telling her they were from two different worlds. But something told her he had a reason for not acting like himself.

She pursed her lips. Narrowed her eyes and studied him. She was used to boys and their sulks. Her brothers' moods tended to shift dramatically from hour to hour, situation to situation. But she didn't like thinking Luke was like that. Didn't want him to pout when he was upset or throw things when he was mad.

Well, she thought in exasperation, what did she want? For the boy to be a robot, humorless and emotionless? Jeez. Talk about unfair. Why couldn't she give him the same chance she gave everyone else? No judgment. No snap decisions.

Why was she still letting Andrew and what

he'd done to her control her thoughts? Guide her choices?

"Have you started the AP English work yet?" she asked. The other day they'd talked about the reading they needed to do over the summer for their advanced-placement class.

Staring somewhere over her shoulder—she guessed, it was hard to tell with those sunglasses—Luke shook his head.

She chewed on the inside of her cheek. "Your neck is getting red," she blurted. "I'll get you some sunscreen."

"I don't want it."

She blinked. Not because he didn't want to protect himself from possible skin cancer, but because his voice had been so rough. So angry. "Late afternoon is the part of the day when the sun's rays are strongest," she told him. "You need to apply sunscreen and reapply it after swimming or sweating." Which he was doing. Profusely. "Even though we're young, we can't ignore the statistics about skin cancer and how to prevent it. At the very least, you'll be saving yourself from a painful night battling sunburn."

He clenched his jaw. "I said I don't want it."

Her head snapped back at his harsh tone. But she lifted her chin. Kept her own tone cool. "Fine. Then I'll just let you get back to work."

She turned on her heel. Heard him mutter an expletive under his breath but didn't stop, just walked in calm, measured steps back toward the house.

"Gracie," he called. "Wait."

She shouldn't. She owed him nothing. He was the one always talking to her, trying to engage her in conversation, telling jokes and asking questions. All she'd done was be nice back.

But when he caught up to her, gently touched her arm and said "please," his voice low and gruff, she couldn't do anything but stop.

He took his hat off, hit it against the side of his leg. "I'm in a rotten mood, and I'm taking it out on you, which is just stupid. I'm sorry. Really."

She wanted to believe him. Guess they were both stupid. "You don't have to say that," she told him. "I'm not going to tell Fay or anything."

He frowned. "I'm not apologizing so I don't get in trouble, Gracie," he said quietly. "I'm apologizing because I was acting like an ass."

She swallowed. "Oh. Well." She didn't know what to do with her hands. She wanted to cross her arms, but she still held the glass with the quickly melting ice. "It's okay. We all have bad days, right?"

He laughed, but the sound held no humor. "Right. Thanks. It's just…" He shook his head, took off his glasses and wiped the sweat from his forehead with the bottom of his shirt.

She was so mesmerized by the ridges of his exposed stomach that he was already putting his sunglasses back on before she noticed the bruise. "Oh my God," she breathed, tugging the hand with the sunglasses down. "Are you all right?"

"It's not as bad as it looks."

"Thank goodness, because it looks really, really bad." His eye was swollen almost shut, the skin around it a dark purple. "What happened? You don't have to tell me," she added quickly when he averted his gaze. "Unless…did your dad hit you? Because if he did, we have to tell social services and the police."

His lips twitched, as if he was fighting a smile. "My dad didn't hit me. It was nothing like that."

"Oh, well, that's good. I'm sorry if I offended you—or your dad, who I'm sure is a very nice man. It's just I watched this fascinating documentary last week about domestic violence, and most people still believe it's a problem only for those with lower incomes, so I didn't want to assume that your family could be immune to it. Not that I'm assuming your dad is the kind of person to hit his family or anything, either."

She caught her breath. Most people interrupted her, but Luke waited her out. It was nice, knowing he was listening. That he didn't want her to just be quiet already.

"My dad is a nice guy," Luke assured her. "He'd never hit me or my mom. Or anyone." He gestured to his black eye. "Drew gave me this."

"Andrew?" That didn't make sense. "It must

have been an accident. During football practice or something?"

Luke hooked his sunglasses on the collar of his T-shirt. "Not during practice and not an accident. He punched me."

"Why would he do such a thing?"

Another shrug, this one irritable. "Probably because I punched him first." As if reliving the memory, he flexed and straightened the fingers of his right hand. "Broke his nose."

"You... Why...?" She couldn't believe it. Couldn't even imagine them fighting like that. "Is he all right?"

Luke's good eye narrowed. "He's great. Why shouldn't he be? He's screwing my girlfriend, after all. I mean, my ex-girlfriend."

Gracie went cold all over. Which was so weird, considering the sweat forming between her breasts, the sun burning her forearms and shoulders. "Andrew and...Kennedy?" She shook her head. "No. No, he wouldn't do that."

"He would and he did." Luke shoved a hand through his hair, then put his hat back on. "I caught them. They were at her house last night. In her room."

"You...you caught them...having sex?"

He shook his head. "They'd just finished. He didn't have a shirt on, and her hair was all messy, and she was in shorts and her bra." He gave another of those harsh laughs. "At first they tried to tell me nothing happened, but then Drew admitted they'd been hooking up behind my back for a while now. So I punched him. He got one in, too, but his nose was bleeding so badly and Kennedy was freaking out...so I left."

Poor Luke. Gracie gave his hand a reassuring squeeze. "I'm so sorry."

Sorry his girlfriend was such a bitch. Sorry his best friend had betrayed him. Sorry he was hurting.

He turned his hand, linked his fingers with hers and squeezed back. "Thanks. I just... I feel like such an idiot, you know? For not seeing the signs sooner. For being so clueless. I had no idea. Pretty stupid, huh?"

He wasn't the only one who'd been fooled. If anyone had thought something was going on between Kennedy and Andrew, word would have gotten back to Luke. Even after Kennedy had treated Gracie so badly in front of Andrew, Gracie had never considered the other girl's meanness was due to her and Andrew hooking up behind Luke's back.

She should have, she realized now. She should have guessed that the reason Andrew had pretended they barely knew each other was that he didn't want Kennedy to find out they'd hooked up. That the reason Kennedy had been so rude to Gracie, had called her a freak, was that she was into Andrew.

"You're not stupid," she told him softly. "You trusted them."

Just as she'd trusted Andrew.

Luke's smile was small and incredibly sad. "That's why I feel so stupid." He rolled his head side to side. Sighed. "I'd better get back to work. Thanks for the lemonade. I'm sorry for acting like a jerk." He took a step away but stopped. Cleared his throat. "Do you want to hang out sometime? It's cool if you don't or if you're busy," he said, his words rushing together, color flooding his cheeks. "I just thought it'd be...you know...nice to...hang out."

She opened her mouth to say no. Why would they hang out? They barely knew each other, and she doubted they had anything in common.

Except they did. They'd both been betrayed and hurt by people they'd loved.

Besides, he needed someone to be there for him. To help him get through this. And she couldn't turn away anyone in pain.

"I'm actually not doing anything tonight."

"Yeah? Me, neither. We could watch a movie at my house. My parents will be home. I can pick you up around eight?"

Her inner voice screamed at her to take it back, tell him that she changed her mind. But he looked...well...not happy. Hard to look happy the day after discovering you were playing the part of King Arthur in the whole Arthur-Guinevere-

Lancelot love triangle, but at least he didn't look so sad. So lonely.

"Sure," she said. "Eight works for me."

She went back inside, her words to him echoing in her head.

You're not stupid. You trusted them.

She wished she'd meant them. Wished she could believe them.

IVY HAD LUCKED out and gotten an after-hours appointment with Dr. Conrad late that afternoon. Now she and Clinton were in the small exam room. Clinton, she noted, was taking everything in.

"First time in one of these?" she asked as he frowned at the table complete with stirrups.

He nodded, his hands in the pockets of his dress pants. "It's...different from how I imagined it."

Ivy hopped onto the table. Might as well do it now. In a few months, any hopping would be impossible. "Yeah? How so?"

"I thought it would look more like some sort of torture chamber. But that's only because I accidentally overheard my mother talking to one of her friends about her annual pap exam when I was a teenager. Scarred me for life."

Ivy couldn't help it. She smiled. He looked so out of place, and he winced when he told the story, as if just remembering it was painful. "It's not all that bad. And there will be no torture involved this time. The doctor will come in, squirt some gel onto my stomach and use her magic wand to bring up a picture of the baby."

"You've already had an ultrasound done?"

"My first appointment. But it was hard to tell what was what. The doctor explained where the head was and everything, but it all looked like a blob to me."

She'd felt like a failure, as if she'd gotten a big fat F on her first test as a mother, but the doctor had reassured her that she wasn't the only mother not to be able to make out her baby's head from its bottom at this early stage.

Dr. Conrad, a tiny, compact woman with silver-streaked blond hair, came in and introduced herself to Clinton. "Ready for this?" she asked Ivy.

"You bet." Ivy undid the button of her shorts, unzipped them and wiggled them down just past her hips. Clinton, she noticed, averted his eyes.

"Here we go," Dr. Conrad said as she squirted the thick gel onto Ivy's stomach.

Ivy watched the screen on the monitor. She wasn't sure why she'd brought Clinton here, except there had been something in the way he'd admitted this was all new to him that had made him seem not quite as dangerous. More human. Approachable.

As approachable as someone that wealthy could be.

But now she watched his expression as the

picture formed on the screen and Dr. Conrad pointed out what was actually baby.

Awe. Pure, unfiltered awe.

And terror.

Welcome to her world, buddy.

"Everything looks great," Dr. Conrad said, still moving that wand over Ivy's stomach. "Would you like to know the sex of the baby?"

"No," Ivy said at the same time Clinton said, "Yes."

Dr. Conrad smiled and put the wand away. "Why don't I step out for a moment, give you time to decide?"

Ivy wiped the gel off her stomach, slid to her feet and pulled her shorts back up.

"You don't want to know if you're having a boy or girl?" Clinton asked.

"Nope."

"If you find out, you can be better prepared. Clothes. Nursery colors. Names." He paced, looking too big, too masculine for the room, with its posters of pregnant women and babies. "You'll have time to adjust to having either a son or a daughter."

"I don't plan on buying many clothes beforehand, just the necessities like onesies and pajamas. They don't have to be gender specific. As far as the nursery, I live in a one-bedroom apartment. The baby will be bunking with me for the foreseeable future, and if he or she doesn't like the color, he or she will just have to live with it. And I'll come up with a name for each. As far as adjusting, I'm not sure what sort of adjustment I'll need to make. Seems to me, you have a son or daughter, and you love them just the same."

"You really don't want to know?" he asked again, looking as if she'd told him she wanted to go in for elective surgery without knowing what it was for.

"There are too few surprises in life. Why would I want to ruin one of the biggest ones I'm ever going to have?"

"Seems to me this whole pregnancy is a surprise. Should be a big enough surprise."

"Believe me, it was. But while it wasn't all that happy of one, this one will be."

He frowned. "I want to know."

"Too bad. We're not finding out. If you find out, you'll slip up and tell me. And you don't want to ruin it for me, do you?"

"Fine," he said. "We won't find out."

She blinked. Shook her head. "I'm sorry, but did you just give in to me without trying to charm me, intimidate me or buy me off?" She narrowed her eyes. "You're being nice. I don't like it."

He grinned, slow and easy and sexy enough to make her knees weak. "Darlin', I'm very nice."

"No. You're not. You're charming, yeah, but that's not being nice. I know the difference. You're only giving in to me now so you can use this against me later."

"I'm not going to use anything against you later. If it's that important to you not to find out the baby's sex, then we won't find out. I'm not a complete ass, Ivy," he said softly.

She needed him to be. It was easier to keep her distance, to not count on him when he acted all bossy and arrogant. "Thank you."

The door opened then, and Dr. Conrad came back in as if she'd known how long their conversation would take. "Have we decided?"

"We're going to wait to find out the sex," Ivy said, in case Clinton was tricking her.

"All right." Dr. Conrad sat on the stool, gestured for them to take seats on the chairs. "Ivy, you said you had some questions."

"We need a paternity test," Ivy said, refusing to feel embarrassed by it. Certainly she wasn't the first woman to ask for one in this office. "I'm not sure what our options are."

"There are several," Dr. Conrad said with absolutely no judgment in her tone or expression. "You can wait until after the baby is born and we can take a sample from the umbilical cord, swab the baby's cheek or take a blood sample from the baby's heel."

Clinton frowned. "Does that hurt the baby?"

"It's a little prick," the doctor said, "and we won't need much." She smiled reassuringly. "Trust me. The baby won't remember the pain and will be over it in a matter of seconds."

"What if we don't want to wait until after the baby is born?" Clinton asked, and Ivy tried not to get upset. She'd known he didn't want to wait until after she gave birth, but if he didn't believe he was the father, why was he in Shady Grove? Why had he come to this appointment with her?

"I don't want to do anything that jeopardizes the baby," Ivy said. "If there's no medical reason to do an amniocentesis, then I won't have one."

"What's an *amniocentesis*?" Clinton asked.

"A thin needle is inserted into the uterus through the stomach and a small amount of amniotic fluid is taken," Dr. Conrad explained.

He went so pale, Ivy worried he was going to pass out. "Are you all right?" she couldn't help but ask.

"Fine." He sounded and looked anything but. "Just…the thought of it…" He shook his head. "No. We don't want to do that." He looked at her. "I would never ask you to do that. I would never ask you to do anything that would endanger the baby or cause you pain in any way."

He sounded so sincere, she had no choice but to believe him.

"There are other options," Dr. Conrad said. "The most accurate, noninvasive way to establish paternity before birth is to take a blood sample from both of you. The lab can analyze the baby's DNA found naturally in Ivy's bloodstream."

"It's safe?" Clinton asked. "For both of them?"

"Perfectly safe," the doctor assured him. "As I said, we'll just need blood samples from both of you. And it's 99.9 percent accurate. It can be done now, since Ivy's past her first trimester."

"When can we have our blood drawn?" Ivy asked, not wanting to delay the inevitable.

"I can get the lab orders printed out within five minutes," Dr. Conrad said.

Ivy stood, not looking at Clinton. "Sounds good. The sooner this is done, the better."

The sooner she could prove to Clinton he was her baby's father, the sooner they could both move on with their own lives.

CHAPTER ELEVEN

CLINTON UNROLLED HIS sleeve as he and Ivy stepped out of the hospital's front entrance. It had gotten cloudy, the sky ominous and gray, reminding him a bit of how the storms rolled in over Houston.

They crossed the street to the parking lot. He glanced around. Hills, hills and more hills, all lush and green. He hadn't seen much of Shady Grove, but what he had seen, he had to admit, was pretty.

Ivy stopped next to an old car with rust above the wheels and dents on the bumper.

"That's not your car," he said.

"If it's not, then someone out there is driving an exact replica of my vehicle."

"It's a piece of crap." And couldn't possibly be safe.

"Yep. But it's all mine. Bought and paid for with my hard-earned money." She studied him. "Wonder if you can say that about anything you own."

He resented the accusation, though he wouldn't let her see it. He worked damn hard for what he had, and he wasn't going to apologize for being born into wealth and privilege. Not when he busted his ass every day to keep his father's company running, to keep it growing. "You can't drive that."

"I can and I do," she said, unlocking the door. She turned back to face him, the wind picking up the ends of her hair. "Since the doctor is going to let each of us know the results, I guess we're done until we hear from her."

He raised his eyebrows. "You do realize we're heading to the same place?"

She smiled. "Sorry, cowboy, but I'm not following you back to your room this time. I've got things to do, places to be and all that."

He edged closer, couldn't seem to help himself. Pregnant women shouldn't look so sexy, should they? But Ivy did, with her blowing hair and that knowing, sexy smirk. "Have a drink with me," he heard himself say before he thought better of it.

Now she laughed. "Been there. Done that. Besides, I don't think Junior here should be drinking. Not until he's a few years older at least."

"You said you didn't want to know if it was a boy or girl," C.J. said. He knew he sounded accusing, but he wasn't sure he trusted her not to have already discovered the sex of the baby and not have told him on purpose. Plus, he felt like an idiot for suggesting a drink. Of course she couldn't drink. It was as if when he was close to her, his brain shut down.

"I don't like referring to my baby as *it*," she

said, not bothering to try to contain her blowing hair, just letting it wrap around her throat, the strands tickling her cheek, "so on even days I use *he*. Odd days *she*. Although…"

"What?" he asked when she trailed off.

She shrugged. "I don't know. I just… I have a feeling I'm having a boy." She shook her head. Looked embarrassed. "But then, what do I know? I don't have any experience with pregnancy or motherhood, so I'm probably wrong."

She looked worried, as if she was nervous and unsure about being a mother. "Have dinner with me," he said, wanting to spend more time with her. He told himself it was because he should get to know her better, but he had that envelope on his bed back at Bradford House. Anything and everything he needed to know about her would be in there.

He hadn't opened it yet, though.

And he wasn't ready to let her go.

"Sorry, cowboy, but I have plans." She cocked a hip. "If you want to take me to dinner, you need to ask a lot earlier. My dance card fills up quickly."

"You have a date?" he asked, incredulous. "You can't date."

"Really?" she asked in a purr that he was smart enough to recognize wasn't as innocent as it sounded. "And why is that?"

Because she was his.

Mine.

Hadn't that been his thought the first night he met her? He'd told her he'd meant that she was his for one night. Had tried to convince himself he was speaking the truth, but he'd wondered, and worried, about how badly he'd wanted to claim her as his forever.

He fisted his hands. No. That wasn't right. He didn't believe in love at first sight. Lust. Hell yes. They'd had that in spades. But he wasn't some gullible teenager confusing his attraction to her as anything more than physical.

"You're pregnant," he pointed out. "With my baby."

"Oh, but you're not sure you're the father, re-member?" she asked, throwing his logic back at him. "So until you get proof—proof you de-manded, by the way—there's still that little bit of doubt, that little bit of hope that this is all a big scam, some elaborate plan to get your money. One that ends when you get the all-important evidence the baby isn't yours. That I'm nothing but a lying, scheming tramp."

His head snapped back as if she'd slapped him. "I don't think you're a tramp."

Her lip curled and she crossed her arms. "Just a liar, then?"

He paced. "I don't know what to think. I'm just doing the best with the information I've been given. But I don't think you're a tramp, Ivy."

He wanted her to believe that. What was wrong

with him? He was known for his ability to talk his way into any deal, his ability to charm anyone, handle any problem, but this whole situation, Ivy herself had thrown him for a loop, and he'd re-acted like...like...

He'd reacted like his father.

He stopped in front of her. "Have dinner with me. Please," he added, knowing he'd need to use every bit of charm he had to convince her. He wanted to spend more time with her, and he hated the thought of her going out with some other man, of smiling at him, flirting with him. Letting him touch her.

And he couldn't fight the fact that the possibil-ity she really was carrying his child was getting bigger and bigger. She hadn't even blinked when the doctor had said they could do the paternity test right away. If she really was trying to trick him, wouldn't she delay the test as long as possible?

But she was right, too. He needed that proof.

"Why bother?" she asked. "Why spend any time together? You're still not convinced I'm tell-ing the truth."

"The more I'm with you," he admitted, "the more I believe you."

"But you're still not convinced."

He couldn't deny it. Wouldn't lie to her. "No." He exhaled. "There are reasons for it."

He'd spent his entire life guarding against being used, making sure he was well protected. Never knowing for sure if someone was with him because of who he was or what his last name was. Or what was in his bank account.

"Poor little rich boy," she said. "I hate to break it to you, but not everyone is after your money. That wasn't why I slept with you."

A couple walked past them, did a double take at her words, but she didn't seem embarrassed or uneasy. Just kept her gaze on C.J.

He edged closer. Lowered his voice. "It may not be the main reason women sleep with me," he said, knowing what he looked like, knowing his appeal. "But it's not a deterrent, either."

She rolled her eyes. "Do you honestly think I couldn't have found myself some wealthy man to take care of me before now?" She spread her arms. "Look at me. Do you really think I've never had men of certain means proposition me, want to take care of me? We may not be Houston, but there are plenty of rich men right here in good old Pennsylvania. I didn't care about how much money you had when I went up to your room."

"Do you really want me to believe you don't care about it now?"

"I'm not going to say that, because now there's more than just me to think about. So, no, I'm not going to say it's the worst thing ever, knowing my child's father—who seems to be responsible—has the means to make his or her life more comfortable. But it also makes my life more difficult. If you decide you want the baby, I can't afford to fight you. That test we just took is going to prove you're this baby's father, and I have no idea what that's going to mean to me or to my child."

He stepped back, so shocked he couldn't even stop her when she opened the car door, got inside and, a moment later, drove away.

C.J. wasn't sure how long he stood there. The wind picked up. Rain started to come down, and he couldn't force himself to move. Ivy was scared. Terrified. Of him. His stomach turned with self-disgust. Wasn't that what part of him had wanted? For her to fear him, his power?

Jesus, he really was as bad as his father.

He didn't want to be. His entire life, all he'd wanted was to be better than his old man, to prove that the only things they had in common were their work ethic and their name, and now he was acting just like Senior.

Well, not quite as bad as that. Yes, he was protecting himself and his family, but he hadn't used Ivy. No more than she'd used him. He wasn't making her promises he had no intention of keeping. Wasn't stringing her along, holding on to her until he got bored and then tossed her aside for the next pretty face that walked by.

If the baby really was his, then he and Ivy were

going to be in each other's lives. Whether she liked it or not.

He needed to prove he trusted her. That she could trust him. There was only one way to do that.

"Is MR. BARTASAVICH the father?" Fay asked late the next morning.

Ivy, in the middle of cleaning up after breakfast service, whipped her head around so quickly, she was surprised it didn't twist off and go flying across the kitchen. "Maybe ease into a question like that," she said, rinsing the baking dish she'd just scrubbed and handing it to Gracie to dry. "Hey, Ivy, great scones this morning. And the guests loved your blueberry pancakes. Oh, by the way, is the guest in the Back Suite the father of your unborn baby?"

At the table, Fay sipped her tea, eyeing Ivy over the rim.

"Okay, okay. God, you know how I hate it when you nag," Ivy said, tossing the dishrag into the water, splattering her top with water and bubbles. "Yes. He's the father. Are you happy?"

"The cowboy from Valentine's Day?" Gracie asked, setting the dish on the counter. "I thought you weren't interested in him." She didn't sound accusing, just curious.

"More like I was attracted to him."

Gracie nodded sagely, as if she was some

eighty-year-old who'd been there, done that—
dozens of times. "Yeah. The physical stuff can
really knock the good sense out of a woman."

"I don't even want to know," Fay murmured,
holding up a hand as if to stop Gracie from ever
speaking again.

"How'd you figure it out?" Ivy asked her boss.

"It didn't take much. You tell us you're pregnant, and then a few days later Mr. Bartasavich
shows up wanting to stay here indefinitely. I may
not be a genius, but even I can put two and two
together. He's here for you. You and the baby."

Fay was smarter than she gave herself credit for.
"He's here to get proof the baby is his."

"He doesn't believe it is?" Gracie asked as the
timer buzzed.

Ivy picked up oven mitts, took the sheet of oat-
meal cookies from the oven and set them on the
counter. "He didn't." Though that attitude seemed
to have changed. At least a little bit.

Not enough for her to actually trust him.

"But he does now," Gracie said.

"I'm not sure. It doesn't matter anyway. Once
he gets the proof he needs, I'm sure he'll go back
to his life in Houston."

"You don't sound too certain about that," Fay
said softly.

Ivy dropped balls of cookie dough onto a new
sheet. "Well, it's not like he'd stay here in Shady
Grove. The man runs a multibajillion-dollar com-

pany. It's just..." She put the cookies in the oven and set the timer. "What if he wants to be a part of the baby's life? He has the power to make my life miserable. And he lives in Houston. I don't want to ship my kid halfway across the country for daddy-and-me weekends."

"I think you need to take it one day at a time," Fay said. "And understand that this might be new to him, too. Unless..." She frowned.

"Unless what?" Ivy asked.

"Unless he has other kids?"

"He doesn't. That much I do know. Well, that and I didn't find anything about him having ever been married when I looked him up online." She explained about the Bartasavich family. Their wealth and power and how Clinton, after his father's stroke, was now head of it all. Head of an empire. "It's like a horrible, low-rent version of Cinderella. Except I don't want to marry the prince."

"I'd marry him," Gracie said, taking over the dishes for Ivy.

"What about love?" Fay asked, and Ivy almost pitied her for still believing in the concept of true love after everything she'd been through.

"He's handsome and rich," Gracie pointed out. "What's not to love? I mean, it's just as easy to fall in love with a rich man as it is with a poor man, right?"

"That's what my mother always said."

At the familiar deep voice, Ivy shut her eyes and groaned. What was Clinton doing here, in her kitchen, her sanctuary?

She opened her eyes to find him in the doorway, a smile on his handsome face, his hair perfect, his clothes pressed, his shirt blindingly white. While flour covered her stomach, her hair was frizzing from the stupid humidity and she'd spilled syrup on her shorts.

"It's sound advice," Gracie said, letting the water out of the sink. "And, if you think about it, fair. You should love someone because you love them. Whether or not they have money shouldn't have any bearing on your feelings."

He winked at Gracie. "Smart girl." He tipped his head, narrowed his eyes. "Does everyone who works at King's Crossing work here, too?"

She beamed, obviously pleased he remembered her from Valentine's Day. "Ivy got me a job here. The hours are much better, and Fay's about a thousand times nicer than Wendy."

"You'd have to be an actual demon to be meaner than Wendy," Ivy pointed out. She faced Clinton. "Guests aren't really allowed in the kitchen, so unless you need something—"

"I do."

When he didn't continue, just leaned against the counter, making himself at home, a large envelope in his hand, she huffed out an exasperated breath. "What?"

"You."

She blinked. Her mouth dried. "Excuse me?"

"You asked what I needed. I need you. To see you," he corrected.

She didn't like the sound of that. Oh, who was she fooling? The problem was she did like the sound of it, of him saying he needed her. She liked it way too much.

"Gracie," Fay said, standing, "why don't you come help me finish cleaning up the dining room?" She shot a worried glance between Ivy and Clinton. "You can finish the dishes after Mr. Bartasavich and Ivy are done."

"We're done," Ivy said quickly, hating that she was so weak, such a coward that she didn't want to be alone with the man. But there was something about him today, an intensity in his gaze and the way he'd said he needed her that made her wary. Worried. "You don't have to leave."

But they were already heading toward the door, and Ivy refused to give in to the need to ask them to stay.

"I hope I didn't put you in a difficult position with your boss," Clinton said, setting the envelope on the counter.

"She's not the one you have to worry about," Ivy assured him as she shot a death glare at her boss's retreating back.

So much for thinking she and Fay might be almost friends. Friends didn't let friends have private conversations with handsome men who wreaked havoc on a girl's hormones and her resolve.

"You won't get into trouble," he asked, "breaking the rules by having a guest in here?"

"No one gets in trouble with Fay. It's why her six-year-old is on the fast track to reform school. What do you want?" she asked, hoping he'd get the hint that she was busy and not in the mood for idle chitchat. She'd never be in the mood for it with him. He put her on edge. Put her back up.

And made her feel like a complete bitch.

God, pregnancy was making her unhinged. She'd never minded being a bitch before he'd come along, before she'd known she was going to be a mother. Mothers should be held to a higher standard, shouldn't they?

C.J. helped himself to a cookie, which irritated her for some reason. "Gracie, she's about what... fifteen?"

"Seventeen."

"That's around my niece's age. Maybe the next time Estelle visits Kane and Charlotte, Gracie and Estelle could meet. Hang out."

She remembered his niece from the engagement party. Blonde, beautiful and, if she had to guess, spoiled rotten. "I doubt she and Gracie have much in common."

"They're both teenage girls," he pointed out as if being the same age and gender automatically made two people bosom buddies. "They can talk about boys and movies and music."

"Absolutely," Ivy said as she plated cookies, "because the only thing of any real interest girls have to talk about are boys."

He grinned, and damn him for being so sexy. "If teenage girls think about boys half as often as teenage boys think of girls, then Kane is in big trouble." He frowned as if suddenly realizing something. "You really think the baby's a boy? Because I just had a flash of my life in sixteen years if the baby's a girl."

His face was white, and he looked so freaked by the idea of having a daughter, she didn't have the heart to remind him that they didn't have the information he needed to prove the baby was his.

But she could poke him a bit. "Well, I did say I was new at all of this, so I'm probably way off base. And if the baby is anything like me, you won't have to wait sixteen years." She winked at him. "Let's just say I was an early bloomer."

He sat heavily on the stool. "Shit."

She smiled. She couldn't help it. When he swore, his accent came out, making him seem less wealthy playboy and more…normal. "Your niece is pretty wild, huh?"

"No. She's a good girl. And if she's not and someone knows about it, I don't ever want them to tell me."

"So you don't mind a bit of deception in certain situations?"

"Mind? It's how I can sleep at night." He took another cookie. "When Estelle went to the prom a few months ago, I almost hired someone to follow her and that college boyfriend of hers. Shouldn't he be dating girls his own age?"

"I'm sure not even college girls can compare to Estelle."

He grinned. "Yeah. She's a beauty. Takes after her mother. But don't let those angel looks fool you. She got her mean streak from her daddy."

"So, Estelle lives in Houston?"

"With her mother, about half a mile from me. I get to see her often. Well, as often as work allows, which hasn't been much since my father's stroke."

"It's nice," Ivy allowed, wiping up the counter, "that you're there for her. That you're willing to spend time with her."

"It's no hardship. She's funny and bright. Besides, it gives me a chance to keep tabs on her, since Kane is more than happy to let her run wild."

"Would you stop eating the cookies?" she asked, wishing she wasn't so disappointed that he spent time with his niece only to keep an eye on her, to make sure she was behaving properly as a Bartasavich should. "They're for the guests."

He raised an eyebrow. "I'm a guest."

"They're for later," she said, feeling flustered because he was right. She moved the rest of the cookies out of his reach. Maybe if he didn't have something to nibble on, something sweet, he'd go on his way.

"You really don't think Estelle and Gracie would like each other?" he asked. "I know Estelle loves visiting her dad and Charlotte, but I think she gets bored, not having many kids her own age to hang out with while she's here."

"Teenage girls can be tough to befriend," Ivy said, remembering how they sure hadn't wanted her to be in their groups. "They tend to congregate in packs of at least two or more, and it's tough to break in. Especially if one in the group doesn't like you or is jealous of you."

"You sound as if you speak from experience."

He sounded interested. As if he was trying to figure her out, get to some deep dark secret she kept inside her head. She smiled. "This might come as a shock to you, but I was a teenage girl at one point in my life."

"Not so hard to imagine," he murmured. "Were you a member of a group, making the rules about who could and who could not join?"

"Hardly. I was one of the girls they kept out of their inner circle. It's tough to be friends with someone you're afraid is going to steal your boyfriend."

He was watching her closely. Too closely. "Is that what you did? Steal their boyfriends?"

"Didn't matter what I did, only how I looked. They disliked me, though they never bothered to take the time to get to know me." She scrubbed the counter so hard, she was surprised she didn't leave a groove. "The boys were attracted to me. The girls were jealous or just insecure or not strong enough to go against their other friends. Some women still judge me, but I've learned not to let it bother me. I'm fine on my own."

Even if sometimes she was lonely.

"You're not alone or on your own," Clinton said. "The day I checked in here, Fay took me aside and threatened to toss me out if I upset you. And it's obvious Gracie admires you."

Ivy remembered how Fay had held her hand while Ivy had told her she was pregnant. How Gracie had jumped in with her offers to babysit. "Maybe," she said quietly, afraid to count on either of them. Wanting so badly to be able to. "But Estelle is going to have some of the same issues, people judging her based on her appearance. They're going to like her because she's blonde, beautiful and rich and only because of those things. Or they'll dislike her for the same reasons. But you might be right about her and Gracie. Gracie will give Estelle a chance. She's the fairest person I know."

"Good to know," he said, looking out of place

in his dress pants and button-down shirt. Did the man not own a pair of jeans? "What about you?"

"I'm too old to hang out with teenagers."

"I'm not talking about giving Estelle a chance. I'm talking about me." He stepped closer, and her heart picked up speed. She wanted to touch him, to see if that spark between them was still there. Stupid thought. Of course it was still there. She felt it every time they were together, like an electric current running through the air.

One that was alive and, oh, so dangerous.

"What about you?" she managed, proud her voice was even, that it didn't betray her emotions or her weakening knees.

"Are you going to give me a fair chance?" he asked, his voice low, his gaze hooded. "Or are you going to keep disliking me based on my family's name? My money?"

She smirked. "News flash, cowboy, I don't dislike you based on those reasons. I dislike you because of your personality."

"Maybe," he said, not seeming the least bit offended by the idea. "Though you seemed to like me just fine before you knew how much I'm worth."

It was true. But she didn't want him to see her that clearly. She needed to keep some parts of herself hidden from him so he couldn't use them against her. "Now, that's the difference between us. You base worth on a number. I base it on how people live their lives. What they do."

"Not on what they say?"

"Hardly. Words are too easy to twist, to manipulate."

"Fair enough." He reached back, picked up the envelope and held it out to her. "This is for you."

She eyed it warily, felt herself shrinking back from it, sensing whatever was inside, she didn't want to see. "What's that?"

"It's the report from the private investigator. The report on you."

"When did you get it?" she asked, refusing to ask what he'd found out about her.

"Yesterday."

Yesterday. The thought of him knowing about her past, about looking into her life, chilled her. "I'm sure it made for a riveting read."

"I wouldn't know. I didn't read it. I didn't even open it."

She snorted. "Right."

"I didn't open it," he repeated, his voice low and intense. "I didn't read it and I'm not going to. I've never lied to you, Ivy."

"Everyone lies."

He nodded slowly. "They do. But I won't lie to you. Ever."

It was pathetic how badly she wanted to believe him. How much she wanted to make him the same promise.

But she didn't make promises she couldn't keep. She took the envelope, flipped it over to find it was still sealed. Maybe he was telling the truth after all. "What do you want me to do with this?"

"Whatever you want. Burn it. Rip it to shreds."

"I suppose now you're going to tell me this is the only copy."

Disappointment flashed across his features. She wanted to take her words back, but she couldn't. "You don't trust anyone, do you?"

"Not without a reason."

He tossed up his hands. "What the hell do you think I'm trying to do?"

She knew. He was giving up a piece of his power—information he could have about her, about who she was—in exchange for her trust.

The least she could do was give him a small measure of it.

"Thank you," she said grudgingly. "And... thank you...for not reading it."

He smiled but it wasn't cocky as much as...relieved. "You're welcome," he told her, his solemn tone mimicking hers. He reached out and touched her hair. Her breath caught. "Have dinner with me tonight."

Oh, how she wanted to agree. When he spoke to her in that low tone, when he touched her so sweetly, she wanted to agree to anything he asked. Give him everything.

And that made him dangerous.

"Why?" she asked, when she'd meant to just say no.

"Let's call it a fresh start. No preconceived notions, nothing but you and me getting to know each other."

That was the problem. She didn't want to get to know him. But she couldn't show that sort of weakness. Not when she worried he already suspected she was nervous around him. "Fine. A fresh start."

"And dinner?"

She swallowed. "And dinner. But not tonight." She'd picked up an extra shift at the River View. "Tomorrow."

"Tomorrow, then." Lifting her free hand, he turned it and pressed a warm kiss to her palm. "I'll pick you up at seven."

She wanted to curl her fingers, wanted to hold on to the feel of his lips against her skin. She wiped her palm down the side of her shorts. Licked her lips. "You might regret this," she told him as he walked away. "I might still dislike you."

He smiled at her over his shoulder, a confident smile that did nothing for her nerves or her equilibrium. "Or you might just find out you like me, after all."

That was what she was afraid of.

CHAPTER TWELVE

C.J. HELPED IVY out of his rental car. He wasn't thrilled she'd picked his brother's bar as the scene for their dinner date, but he didn't want to argue. Not when he'd gotten her to agree to dinner in the first place.

A major feat, that. One he wasn't about to ruin by picking a fight.

"Thank you," she murmured, her husky voice washing over him as she took his hand and straightened.

"You look amazing," he told her.

She grinned. "So you mentioned when you picked me up."

"That dress warrants a repeat."

It was light purple and strapless, the material hugging every curve, showcasing the slight bump of her belly, the hem ending way above her knees. The dress, her smoky eye makeup and glossed lips, her loose hair—they all deserved a dozen compliments. Even pregnant, she was a goddess. Maybe more so, now that she was with child; there was an ethereal quality about her. One of fertility and sex and female power.

With a hand at her lower back, he led her to O'Riley's door. The parking lot was full—not bad for a Thursday night—and when they stepped inside, he wondered if he'd made a mistake in assuming they didn't need a reservation. The tables he could see were all filled, the air carrying the unmistakable aroma of tangy tomato sauce.

Did one even make reservations at a bar?

"Good thing you know the owner," Ivy murmured so innocently he was sure she was being a smart-ass.

"I'll find Kane. See about getting us a table."

He hated leaving her there. For one thing, a short, thirty-something man was already making his way toward her. Not that he worried she couldn't handle herself. He knew firsthand how well she could put a man in his place.

No, the real reason he didn't want to leave her side, even for a second, was because he was scared she'd take off.

Spotting the top of Kane's head at the far end of the bar, he made his way through a surprisingly thick crowd of people. "I need a table," he told his brother. "For two."

"Do you have a reservation?" Kane asked, exchanging a bottle of beer for cash.

"We're in a bar."

"A bar that serves lunch and dinner six days a week." Kane stepped away to take another order.

When he came back he sent C.J. a smug grin. "Tonight's pasta night."

"Is that supposed to mean something to me?"

Kane shrugged a shoulder, poured tequila into a blender. "Means you'll be waiting a good hour for a table."

C.J. pushed away from the bar and stormed back over to Ivy. Ignoring the guy trying to chat her up, he leaned close to her ear so she could hear him over the music, the noise. "Let's go into Pittsburgh."

"I like it here," she said. "Why else would I pick it?"

He knew damned well the reason she picked O'Riley's was because Kane owned it. Because it was completely different from the type of place C.J. wanted to take her. Someplace pricey and classy and as far away from any member of his family as possible.

"Besides," she added, "I'm craving pasta."

And she laid her hand on her stomach.

"Looks like I'm not the only one who can test people," he said. She inclined her head in agreement, not looking the least bit guilty about using her pregnancy to get him to stay. To get him to beg his brother to find them a table.

To see how far he'd go to make her happy.

Shit.

He whirled around, narrowly missing running into a guy carrying three drinks. "Sorry," C.J. muttered.

He could insist on going somewhere else, he thought as he marched toward Kane, but that might give her the excuse she'd been looking for to cancel the whole night.

"Is there any way you can get us seated sooner?" he asked Kane when he reached the bar.

Kane, drawing a draft beer, didn't even glance at him. "An hour."

C.J. leaned forward, hating what he was about to do. He hated asking anyone for a favor, especially his brother. Especially this brother. "Come on, Kane. Help me out here."

Kane followed his gaze to where Ivy stood, now surrounded by three men, all vying for her attention. Kane smirked. "It'll cost you."

He hadn't expected anything else. C.J. pulled a couple hundred-dollar bills from his wallet. Laid them on the glossy bar.

Kane flicked them away with the tips of his fingers. "I've got plenty of those. No, Junior, you can't buy this. What it's going to cost you is a favor."

C.J. didn't like the sound of that. "What kind of favor?"

"The kind I decide. When I'm ready. Deal?"

"Deal," he ground out.

Kane stopped a middle-aged waitress, said something to her C.J. couldn't make out. After a moment, Kane turned back to him. "Looks like you're in luck. A table for two just opened up. Gloria will seat you."

C.J. raised his hand, caught Ivy's attention. When she joined him, they followed the waitress to a table in the back corner of what C.J. guessed was the dining room. He held out Ivy's chair, then sat across from her, and they gave the waitress their drink orders.

"Did I pass?" he asked when they were alone again.

She didn't even bother pretending not to know what he was talking about. "With flying colors." She winked at him before picking up her menu.

That wink and the accompanying smile almost made whatever hell Kane would put him through worth it.

After they ordered their meals, they made small talk while they waited, discussing current events instead of anything personal. Ivy had a quick mind and strong opinions. He enjoyed debating a few points with her, and while they may not have entirely agreed about politics and certain social policies, he could see her point. And he thought she saw his.

When their salads were delivered, he switched topics to Shady Grove. The people of this town where she'd lived her entire life, where his brother had made his home, had found his future wife.

"Not much to tell," she said, sipping her water.

"There are pros and cons of living here—like anywhere else, I assume. It's small enough that everyone knows each other—"

"Is that in the plus or minus column?" he asked, shaking pepper over his salad.

"Well, now, that depends on who you ask."

He raised his eyebrows. "I'm asking you. I didn't think it was a difficult question," he said when she remained silent.

"Not difficult. More like…complicated." She stabbed a piece of lettuce, waved her fork. "It's… nice," she finally said, "knowing your neighbors. Especially, I would imagine, once I have the baby. I'll know his or her teachers, the parents of his or her friends. And they'll know me." Her mouth twisted. She shrugged as if trying to rid herself of an unwanted thought. "It's safe, too, for raising a kid. Pittsburgh's close enough that if you want city living, you can get to it easily."

"So you like living here."

She tipped her head. "I guess I've never really thought about it. I don't dislike it. It's just… it's what I'm used to. This town, these people… they're the only things I've ever known."

"You never went away to college?"

"Never wanted to. But I am looking into taking culinary courses at The Art Institute of Pittsburgh." She glanced down at her stomach. "At least, I was. I guess that'll have to be put on hold for a while."

"Does that disappoint you?" he asked, setting his empty salad plate aside. "Having to wait?"

"I've waited this long. What's another year or two?"

She took things in stride, he'd give her that. This pregnancy, soon becoming a mother. They were life-changing events—more so for her than for him, and she was handling it as if it was no big deal.

It made him realize what an ass he'd been. Made him want to do better. Be better. Because his gut was now telling him that he didn't need the proof they were waiting for—that this baby was, indeed, his.

And there was one very important question he had to know the answer to.

"Do you resent the baby?" he asked. "For messing up your plans?"

Ivy wasn't sure, but there seemed to be more to Clinton's question than mere curiosity. Almost as if he was asking if she resented *him*.

"It's not the baby's fault," she said, pushing aside a cherry tomato with her fork to get to an errant garbanzo bean. "So no, I don't resent him. Or her."

She refused to treat her child the way her mother had treated her. Refused to blame an innocent baby for her mistakes. The choices she made.

The waitress came back. "So sorry things are

a bit slow tonight," she said as she cleared their plates. "We're short-staffed."

"It's no problem," Ivy assured her. Lord knew she'd put up with her fair share of miserable customers blaming her for problems in the kitchen or front of house—she'd heard complaints about everything from the food to dirty dishes to bad lighting. "We're in no hurry."

The waitress sent her an appreciative smile. "Thanks. I'll check on your meals."

"I hadn't realized O'Riley's did this much business," Clinton said.

"Me, neither. Though I'd heard the food was really good."

His gaze narrowed slightly. "I thought you'd been here before."

Oops. Busted. She fought to hide a grin. "I never said that. I said I liked it here."

And she did. It wasn't as classy as King's Crossing, but it had a welcoming feel. She imagined that it shifted into a neighborhood bar as the night went on, but for now it was packed with families and couples and groups at the tables, a few twenty-somethings and an older gentleman at the bar.

"So you did pick this place to make me miserable," he said, but he didn't look angry. More like impressed that she'd tricked him so neatly.

She stirred the ice in her glass with her straw. "*Miserable* is such a strong word. Let's just say I wanted to see how you and your brother interacted. I've always thought you could tell a lot about someone by how they behave around their family."

"And will I get a chance to put this theory into practice with you?"

"Afraid not. Only child, remember?"

"What about your mother?"

She took her time choosing a roll from the basket between them. Broke it in half and buttered it. "She passed away two years ago," she said, careful to keep any and all inflection from her tone.

He reached out. Covered her free hand with his. "I'm sorry, Ivy."

She always hated when people gave her their condolences over Melba's death. It wasn't that she was heartless. It was just that she didn't grieve her mother the way a daughter should.

Then again, Melba hadn't been the type of mother she should have been, either.

Ivy figured they were even.

She cleared her throat. Pulled away from his touch. "You and Kane look so much alike. I take it he's your full brother?"

Clinton studied her, and she wondered if he was going to let her get away with this blatant attempt at changing the subject. She'd witnessed firsthand how stubborn the man could be, but he merely took a roll for himself and leaned back in his chair. "Kane and I have the same mother and father, yes. But I consider all my brothers my full brothers."

She hid a smile. See? He was already revealing himself to her. She was glad he didn't differentiate between his brothers, that he accepted them without the tag of *half.* "Somehow I just can't imagine your mother raising someone like Kane."

"Our nanny did the bulk of the dirty work. Mom and Dad would show up for the occasional school recital or athletic event."

"Sounds lonely."

He shrugged. "Kane and I had each other. And when Dad married Rosalyn—my brother Oakes's mother—it was better. She was a real hands-on mom, always inviting us to stay at their house, baking cookies, playing games with us." He grinned. "The complete opposite of my mother. Which is probably part of the reason Mom hates her to this day. Then again, I suppose I'd hate the person my spouse cheated on me with and then left me for."

"That does seem like a good reason."

The waitress returned with their meals. Stuffed manicotti for Ivy and linguine with clam sauce for Clinton.

Ivy shook parmesan cheese over her pasta. "But things didn't work out between your father and Rosalyn, either?"

"They would have except Rosalyn wouldn't

overlook Dad's infidelities. Especially when he got Oakes's barely legal-age nanny pregnant."

Ivy blinked. "I was right. Your life really is like the TV show *Dallas*."

He snorted. Twirled pasta onto his fork. "Not mine, but Dad lived the lifestyle for as long as he could. He told me once that Rosalyn was the only woman who kicked him to the curb. Every other time, the divorce was his decision. I think out of all his wives, she's the only one he regrets losing."

"Hard to feel sorry for a serial cheater."

"True. Maybe he got what he deserved, having the woman he wanted and maybe even loved be the one who refused to have anything to do with him."

"I take it the nanny gave birth to brother number four?" Ivy asked.

Clinton took a bite, wiped his mouth with a napkin. "Zach. He's a Marine, stationed in Iraq, the last I've heard. We're not...close."

"That must be hard on you."

He frowned. "What makes you say that?"

"It's obvious your family is very important to you." She sipped her water. "Just as it was obvious both at the engagement party and at your apartment that it's important for you to take care of them. I overheard your conversation with your current stepmother," she admitted.

"Only current until the divorce goes through.

She decided it was smarter to take what she was promised in her prenup than to fight for more."

Guess the blonde was smarter than she looked. "Is it a burden?" Ivy asked, having no point of reference for needy family members. Unable to imagine what it would be like to have a large family, to have so many people wanting your time and attention, taking your focus so often. "People relying on you that much?"

"It's my job. After Dad left, my mom turned to me to vent, to be the go-between for her and my father, to be a shoulder to cry on. When Kane and I were teenagers, he rebelled in a big way. It was up to me to try to keep him under control. Then I started working for my father, and it was just a natural progression to be the one everyone turned to."

Ivy wondered who he turned to.

It was a question she was still pondering almost two hours later when he walked her up the steep steps to her apartment. She hadn't asked, of course, and she wouldn't. It was too personal. Too close to the kind of question people who were in a relationship would ask. She knew how it worked. If she asked, if she wondered about something that intimate, he'd feel the right to invade her privacy. He'd want her to open up to him.

Yes, they'd had an enjoyable evening. And, okay, he'd been charming and funny, was intelligent and confident—all traits she admired. All traits she found incredibly attractive. But none of them meant anything. It was good, great even, that she found the father of her baby appealing. That he had qualities she wouldn't mind her child having.

But it didn't mean she wanted to tell him every thought inside her head. Every feeling going through her. Every secret she'd ever kept.

Secrets like how much she'd enjoyed herself. How she liked the feel of his hand on the small of her back. How she wished she could invite him in. Have him spend the night.

And hadn't those kinds of secrets already gotten her into enough trouble?

She dug her key out of her bag, unlocked her door before facing him. "Thanks for dinner."

"It's still early— What?" he asked with a smile when she laughed.

"Cowboy, I can read you like a large-print book. You're not coming in. I have things to do, and you are nowhere on that list."

"What kind of things?"

"Wash my hair. Feed my cat," she said with an airy wave of her hand. "The usual."

"I didn't know you had a cat."

"There's a lot you don't know about me." And she was just fine with that. "But yes, I have a cat, and Jasper gets extremely cranky when he's not fed on time." A lie, since her cat was nothing if not patient and good-natured. "So...good night."

"You could always invite me inside. For a quick drink."

She rolled her eyes. "That's what got us into this mess in the first place. And I try really hard not to make the same mistake twice."

Clinton leaned one arm against the door above her head, inclined his body toward her. Classic man-on-the-make move. "Now, I wouldn't say we're in a mess." He played with the ends of her hair, let his fingertips trail against her bare shoulder. She shivered and his gaze heated. "I like spending time with you, Ivy."

Crap. Did he have to say her name like that, all husky and entreating? It rubbed her resistance raw, like a blade sawing at a rope. "Most men like spending time with me, cowboy. All for the same reasons."

"You want me to think of you with those men," he murmured, edging closer, so close his thigh brushed hers, his hip pressed against the curve of her belly. "You want me to get pissed off, maybe start a fight. Or say something idiotic and insulting, something brought on by jealousy, by the mere idea of another man touching you when all I want to do is put my hands on you myself. My mouth."

She brought her hands up to his chest. A mistake, she realized, as soon as she felt how warm, how solid he was. Any thought of pushing him away melted. "You are not coming in."

There. That had sounded firm. Commanding, even.

He slid his hand up her arm, from her wrist to shoulder, then settled it under her jaw, his palm warm and wide, his fingers curving along the back of her neck. "Are you sure?"

"Positive." But it took her too long to work moisture back into her mouth. To force the word out.

Damn him and the cocky grin that said he'd noticed her struggle.

He slowly dragged her forward, tipping her head back. "Then I guess I'll just have to do this here."

He didn't swoop. Didn't crush his mouth to hers. It was more of a gentle seduction, the way his lips moved over hers. He took his sweet time, and that's exactly what the kiss was. Sweet. Warm. The kind of kiss that would lull her into forgetting why kissing this particular man was a bad idea.

Her hands fluttered as if looking for purchase, and she slid them to his shoulders. Held on while he coaxed her mouth open. She was all sensation. The taste of him—coffee and the tang of dark chocolate from his dessert. The rough pad of his thumb caressing her jaw. The warmth of his body against hers. His scent, now familiar and comforting.

Those sensations coalesced, like a wave building toward shore. It would be easy, so blessedly easy, to let them pull her under. To let go of her thoughts, to let down her guard.

To give up, give in and drown in her attraction to him.

Her lungs ached. Self-preservation kicked in as she struggled to focus. To breathe.

She pushed him back a full step, breaking the kiss. The hold he had on her.

They stared at each other. Her own shock and desire were mirrored in his eyes; their breathing was labored.

He reached for her and, God help her, she swayed toward him, completely under his spell before snapping herself out of it.

He curled his fingers. Slowly lowered his hand. "Ivy—"

She gave him one quick shake of her head. And bolted inside as if the hounds of hell were snapping at her heels.

Staring into the darkness of her apartment, her back pressed against the door, she felt for the door handle. Turned the lock and shut her eyes.

Jasper meowed and butted his head against her calf. She picked him up, nuzzled him against her throat.

And wondered what she was going to do now.

IT WASN'T SPYING, Gracie assured herself as she looked out her window into Andrew's backyard.

She was simply taking in the view from her bedroom. Which she was more than entitled to do anytime of the year, especially on a bright, sunny summer day.

If she just happened to have her nose pressed against the glass and was leaving a ridiculously large smudge, well, that was her right, too.

But honestly, it was hard to look away when Andrew and Kennedy were making out—*making-out* making out—right there on the deck for God and everyone to see. Including the neighbors, such as Gracie. Kennedy, in a black bikini, her red hair like a beacon against her pale, pale skin, Andrew with his shirt off.

Gracie's stomach turned. Jeez. Take it inside already.

She wasn't jealous. She sighed. Crossed her arms. Okay, so maybe there was a teeny, tiny bit of jealousy trying to work its way into her system. It stung, knowing that while Andrew had been with her, he'd really wanted to be with Kennedy.

Mostly she was disgusted, both at their current display and that they didn't care about Luke enough not to wait awhile before officially becoming a couple. God, it'd only been a week since Luke had discovered them together. The least they could have done was wait a month or so before rubbing their relationship in his face.

Poor Luke. If he saw this, it would kill him.

Something about that scenario niggled at her brain. She frowned. Luke…

Oh, no!

She turned, leaped for her phone on the bedside stand as someone knocked on her door—clear indication it wasn't any of her brothers. "Come in," she called, still hopeful she could catch Luke before he left his house.

Too late. Lukc was already following Molly into the room.

"Luke's here," Molly, queen of the obvious, said, baby Carter on her hip.

"Hey," he said, giving Gracie a grin. The swelling around his eye had gone down considerably, enough that it no longer looked as if he was squinting all the time. The skin was still black, but fading, the outer edges of the bruise bleeding into blue, then gray. He lifted thc basket of clothes in his hands. "Where do you want this?"

"Luke offered to carry it up for me," Molly said, wiggling her eyebrows at Gracie behind Luke's back, then wiping drool from Carter's chin. "Wasn't that sweet?"

Gracie blushed. Tossed her phone onto the bed. "Yes. It was very nice. Thank you," she told him.

And noticed her purple bra was there, right there, smack-dab on top of the pile.

"I'll take it," she blurted out, rushing over to grab the basket from him. He held on for a moment, sent a sly glance at the bra, then back to her, the brow over his good eye raised as if he was teasing her. Or flirting with her, which was just too crazy a thought to contemplate. She tugged until he let go. "Thanks."

"Luke!" Caleb cried from the doorway, as if discovering gold in them thar hills. Still in his pajamas, his hair sticking up, his feet bare, he rushed into the room and tackled Luke's legs. "Luke! Come see my LEGOs!"

"Luke and Gracie have to go to work." Molly laid her hand on Caleb's head while Carter babbled and reached for his brother's hair. The baby loved to pull hair. "He can look at your LEGOs another time."

"No," Caleb grunted as he pulled on Luke's hand. "Now. Come. On!"

"Do you mind?" he asked Gracie. "We have a few minutes, right?"

Did she mind getting him out of the room where he could possibly catch a glimpse of the two people who, just last week, had been his girlfriend and his best friend pawing at each other?

"Nope. I don't mind at all. Go right on ahead."

"Cute and good with kids?" Molly asked in a low murmur as Caleb dragged Luke away. "That boy is a keeper."

"We're just friends," she reminded her stepmother for what had to be the hundredth time. "Coworkers and friends."

Molly gave her a serene smile—the same one

she bestowed upon Gracie's dad whenever he tried to argue with her. The one that said "aren't you cute, in your deluded little way?" "I realize things have changed since I was seventeen, but it seems to me there's only one reason a boy spends several nights a week with a girl—two of those nights at her house surrounded by her six little brothers. And it's not because he wants to be in the friend zone."

Just because she and Luke had hung out a few times—the first being the night he'd told her about Kennedy cheating on him—didn't mean anything. Yes, she'd gone to his house twice, and okay, so he'd spent a few nights here, as well. All they did was watch movies or play with her brothers or just talk. Nothing romantic or even remotely date-like.

Gracie glanced at the window, but all she saw from this distance was the roof of Andrew's house and the endless blue sky. "Luke and his girlfriend just broke up last week. I doubt he's looking for a replacement already." And she was smart enough not to want to be his rebound. "Even if he did want another girlfriend, he wouldn't be looking at me."

Switching Carter to her other hip, Molly frowned, an unusual occurrence for someone who was always so calm and happy. "What does that mean?"

Gracie lifted a shoulder. Pretended great interest in matching a pair of socks from the basket. "Just that I'm the complete opposite of Kennedy and girls like her."

"Did you ever think," Molly asked quietly as she brushed a strand of Gracie's hair back, "that might be exactly what Luke wants?"

Gracie couldn't meet Molly's eyes. Tears clogged her throat. She wished she could throw herself into Molly's arms. Tell her about Andrew and how stupid she'd been to trust him. How afraid she was to believe that Luke could like her.

How much she was starting to like him as more than a friend.

But she couldn't say any of that. Didn't want the woman who'd been more of a mom to her than her own mother to know what she'd done. To be disappointed in her.

"Friends," Gracie said, hoping Molly wouldn't notice the unsteadiness of her voice. "Just friends."

Molly looked as if she wanted to say more, but luckily Luke came back. "One of the twins is calling for you, Mrs. Weaver. He's in the bathroom."

"Please call me Molly. Mrs. Weaver is my mother-in-law. And no one wants to be confused with that woman," Molly added under her breath, then winked at Gracie, who grinned back.

Grandma was one mean old lady.

"Hey," Luke said after Molly and Carter left, "before I forget, my sister asked me to watch my nieces Friday night. You want to come over? Babysit with me?"

Her heart beat hard and heavy in her chest, but

she forced herself to remain calm. *Just friends, remember?* "Sure."

"You don't have to," he added, wandering around her room, his hands in the pockets of his cargo shorts. "I mean, you must get tired, being around kids all the time."

"I get a little tired of it," she heard herself admit, then immediately felt guilty. "Not *tired*," she amended quickly. "More like sometimes I just want…"

"A break?"

She smiled. Nodded as she folded a tank top. "It seems selfish. Molly and Dad don't ask me to babysit every day or anything, and they make sure I have plenty of privacy when I am at home."

They'd even given her her own suite of rooms at the far end of the house—her bedroom, a front sitting room and bathroom. Trusted her enough to leave her alone in her room with a boy.

And hadn't that backfired on them? She'd brought Andrew to her room, had practically thrown herself at him, telling him he could kiss her if he wanted. Making out with him on her bed.

Not that her wanting to kiss him had given him any right to lie to her. To use her. But she couldn't deny that she held part of the blame for going too fast. He hadn't forced her to sleep with him.

She'd loved him. Enough to want to be with him. For him to be her first.

Too much to say no.

She slid a glance at Luke as he studied the pictures on her bulletin board.

Her parents gave her plenty of freedom to make her own choices. Her own mistakes.

She'd made a doozy with Andrew, and it was one she refused to repeat.

Luke turned and sent her an easy smile.

Her stomach dipped pleasantly and she had to look away. *Not going to make the same mistake twice*, she reminded herself as she crossed to the walk-in closet. No matter how much she might want to.

She was putting a pile of shirts on a shelf when Luke swore viciously.

Oh, no. She'd been so wrapped up in her discussion with Molly, she'd forgotten about Andrew and Kennedy. Sure enough, when she stepped into the room, Luke was glaring out the window.

"I'm sorry," she said. "I was hoping you wouldn't see that."

He turned to her, his mouth a thin line, but she noticed there was hurt in his eyes along with the anger.

"It's not your fault." He glanced out the window again, then moved toward her, his shoulders rigid, his gait stiff. "I guess I'm going to have to get used to seeing them together."

"It still sucks, though."

He scrubbed a hand through his short hair. "Yeah."

Her heart aching for him, she started to reach out, to do what came naturally when she was with someone in pain. Offer comfort. Give a hug. Be there for him.

And damn Andrew for making her hesitate, for making her doubt herself. For making her wonder if Luke wanted her hug or if he'd rebuff her.

Only one way to find out.

Inhaling deeply, she closed the distance between them, saw his eyes widen slightly, but then she was there, her arms around his lean waist, the top of her head barely reaching his chin. He immediately wrapped his arms around her. Lowered his head, his breath ruffling her hair.

She pressed her cheek to his chest, his heart a steady beat in her ear. "I know it's a cliché, but it really will get better with time."

He squeezed her and she felt him nod. Then he…well…it sounded as if he sniffed her hair. But then he straightened, and she told herself she'd imagined it. "Thanks. I'm okay. But do you mind if we go out through the garage?"

She knew why he asked. The garage was on the other side of the house. Far from any view of Andrew and Kennedy. What she didn't know was if Luke wanted to avoid them so he wouldn't have to see them together.

Or so they wouldn't see him with her.

No. She was giving him the benefit of the doubt, remember?

"Sure. Come on," she said, doing what she'd do with any other friend and taking his hand. Tugging him along. "We'd better get going."

He held on even after he could have let go. Yes, she thought as they went down the stairs. She was going to keep giving him the benefit of the doubt.

Until he gave her reason not to.

CHAPTER THIRTEEN

C.J. SHIFTED THE bottle of champagne he was carrying to his left hand, which already held a dozen red roses. He knocked on Ivy's door. Blew out a breath to calm his pulse. He was nervous. Like a teenager on his first date, waiting on the porch for the girl's father to answer the door, carrying a shotgun.

He thought of the phone call he'd gotten yesterday. Holy hell, he could be one of those fathers in a few years.

He really, really hoped Ivy was right and the baby was a boy.

He knocked again. Her crappy car was in the parking lot, so he figured she was home—such as it was. The building itself wasn't too bad, and it was in a nice part of town, residential, a few stores nearby. But it wasn't exactly the place he'd imagined his child being raised.

He wouldn't say anything about it to her, though. He wanted her to trust him. To think of him as a partner, not her enemy. He was making headway there, he thought. Extremely slow but steady progress. He'd had to go back to Houston for work the day after their dinner date, but he'd called her every night he'd been away to check in. To talk.

To hear the sound of her voice.

During their conversations, he hadn't pushed. Had kept the topics neutral, the tone light, in an effort to get them back on even ground. He'd risked a setback with that good-night kiss when he'd walked her to her door last week, but he hadn't been able to resist.

He wasn't a man used to denying himself. When he wanted something, he went after it. And got it. Always. But pushing Ivy, going too fast only resulted in him running headfirst into those walls she had built around herself. Her sarcasm. Her cynicism.

He was floundering, he admitted, shifting in agitation. Struggling to find a balance between his physical attraction to her and his appreciation of her humor, intelligence and strength. Fighting to think rationally and control his feelings, only to have her muddle his thoughts, to reveal some new appealing aspect of herself.

He was about to knock again when she opened the door. She stunned him. Stole his breath, even with her hair pulled back, her face clean of makeup. Her snug peach tank top showcased her full breasts, the gray yoga pants molded the slight bump of her belly, which he found alternately alluring and terrifying as hell.

"You're back," she said, sounding less than thrilled.

"I'm back." He cleared his throat. "I hope I'm not interrupting anything." he said smoothly.

She eyed him warily. Would there ever be a time when she looked at him with trust? With affection? Or even with joy?

He could only hope.

"I was just finishing up my yoga routine."

An image of her bending that amazing body of hers into certain…positions…slammed into him. He went instantly hard. Yeah. Just like a teenager.

"Is that safe for the baby?"

"I got the doctor's approval. It's good for the baby for me to exercise, and since yoga centers me, helps reduce my stress, the baby gets those benefits, too." She frowned at the flowers and champagne in his hands. "Don't tell me you just happened to be in the neighborhood."

"Not exactly. Dr. Conrad called me yesterday. I got here as soon as I could."

Ivy nodded, still blocking his entrance into her home. "Yes. She called me first, said she was going to let you know officially. That why you're here? Because I'm in no mood right now to hash out a custody or support agreement."

"I'm here to celebrate."

She blinked several times. "Excuse me?"

He liked that he could fluster her. Not that it happened often, but when it did, it proved she wasn't as immune to him as she'd like him to believe. As she probably preferred to believe herself.

"We're having a baby, Ivy," he said quietly. He held up the flowers and champagne. "That's something worth celebrating."

She studied him, her mouth pursed. He wished like hell he knew what she saw when she looked at him. What she thought.

"You're right," she finally said. "It is worth celebrating." She made a slight bow, gestured grandly. "Please. Come on in."

He stepped inside. A long, narrow living room opened into a small kitchen. An air conditioner in the window to his left hummed softly. A hallway to the right must lead to the bedroom and bathroom.

"I asked the doctor if it was okay for you to have champagne and she said a small glass wouldn't hurt the baby," he said. "But if you'd rather not take the chance, we can put it in the fridge. Open it after the baby is born."

A small smile played on her lips. "I'm sure a sip or two won't hurt the baby, as Dr. Conrad said. Besides, the baby's not due until November. Who knows what could happen between now and then?"

He bristled but kept his voice calm. "What do you mean?"

"Just that a lot can change in five months."

"You don't trust me to be around at all when the baby's born," he murmured.

"I think you believe you will be. But good intentions have a way of falling by the wayside when real life intervenes. You have a job, a life in Houston. No one expects you to drop everything and run back to Shady Grove when I go into labor. No one expects you to change your life in any way once the baby is here."

"No one?" he repeated softly. "Or you?"

Could she really have no expectations of him? Did she really think so little of him?

"Just because you have the proof you needed," she said, crossing her arms, "doesn't mean anything has to change. You can walk away now. I can raise this baby on my own."

Don't push. Do not push her. But it was tough not to do just that, especially when he wanted to make her see that he wasn't going anywhere. That he'd be there for her and their child—days, months and years from now. He wanted to demand she believe him.

Instead he had to earn that trust.

He edged closer until she had to tip her head back to maintain eye contact. "You're right," he said. "A lot can change in five months, and good intentions don't mean anything without actions to back them up. I can't force you to trust me just because I say you can. So I won't try to convince you."

Something like disappointment flashed across her face. "Can't say I blame you for giving up, but I must admit I'm surprised you folded so easily."

He grinned at how disgruntled she sounded. Try as she might to get him to believe she didn't want him around, her tone said otherwise.

"I'm not giving up. But I won't make promises, either." Promises were useless. Given in the heat of the moment and too often broken. He brushed the back of his hand along her cheek, needing to touch her. "I'm going to prove myself to you. That enough fight for you?"

She swallowed and stepped back.

"I'll put these in some water," she said, taking the roses from him but avoiding his gaze.

She went into the kitchen, and he set the champagne on the coffee table. Rocked back on his heels as his smile slid away. She'd tried to take a few giant steps back from where they'd been last week by tossing out the reminder that she didn't need him. That she didn't necessarily want him in her or their child's life.

But she hadn't kicked him out. A small victory in and of itself.

He caught sight of a long-haired black cat draped across the back of the sofa, giving him a considering look. "A man has to celebrate even the tiniest wins. Especially where women are concerned."

"Did you say something?" Ivy called.

"Just talking to your cat."

She raised her eyebrows as she came back into the room, carrying two wineglasses. "I wouldn't have pegged you for the type of man to chat up animals."

"That's because you don't know me." Hadn't she said as much the last time they'd been face-to-face? He intended to change that. He opened the champagne almost as expertly as she had that night in his hotel room. "But you will."

Their baby tied them together for the rest of their lives. There would be plenty of time for them to learn more about each other. He found himself looking forward to it.

"I like your apartment," he continued as he poured champagne into the glasses she still held.

"Now, don't ruin this special moment by telling lies, Clinton. My whole apartment could fit into that living room of yours back in Houston."

"Doesn't mean I can't appreciate what you've done with the space."

It was warm and welcoming, done in soft greens and beige, the walls cream. He'd expected her home to be…darker. Decorated in glossy blacks and reds, with shiny fabrics and bold accents. Something that screamed seduction and power. Not a place that looked like a very comfortable home.

Guess he didn't know her, either.

He raised his glass. Had to speak around the emotion tightening his throat. "To our child. May he or she be blessed with good health, my looks and your intelligence."

Her lips twitched as if she was fighting a smile. "You sure you want your kid to be that much smarter than you? Think of the teen years."

"I see your point. Better just toast to his or her health and leave the rest up to God."

She raised her glass. "Sounds good to me. To our child."

"To our child," he repeated, "and to you. To my son or daughter's beautiful mother." He touched his glass to hers, his voice a husky whisper. "Thank you for carrying my child. For telling me I'm going to be a father. But most of all, thank you for giving me a second chance."

She didn't look as if she appreciated his compliment, as if she wanted his gratitude or his honesty. Skepticism twisted her mouth. She was still suspicious of him, of his motives. Frustration simmered in his veins. He wanted to call her out on her distrust, to insist she give him the chance he was fighting so damned hard for, but the confusion and fear in her eyes stopped him. Told him he wasn't the only one trying to find their footing here.

Averting her gaze, she took a quick sip of champagne. Licking a drop off her lower lip, she hummed in appreciation, and he gulped his own drink to drown the groan that wanted to escape. "You rich and fabulous sure know how to pick a fancy wine."

"We take a course on it in elementary school," he told her straight-faced. "Wine selection is after How to Properly Order Caviar at a Five-Star Restaurant but before The Art of Looking Down on the Little People."

She rolled her eyes, then laughed, a burst of sound that went through him. Warmed him. "Just when I think I have you pegged, you do or say something that takes me by surprise. Makes me rethink everything I thought I knew about you."

Despite her laugh, he couldn't tell if that was good or bad.

"Seems only fitting," he said more gruffly than he'd intended, "seeing as how you've had me twisted up since the moment I first laid eyes on you."

Her mouth worked for a moment before she pressed her lips together. Cleared her throat. "Well, anyway…thanks. For this—" she waved a hand at the wine, her words hesitant, her gaze averted "—the flowers and champagne and for… for wanting to celebrate the baby."

"We're having a child together, Ivy. It may not have been planned. It might not have happened the way we would have preferred, but I'm not going to blame the baby or resent him or her. I'm not going to pretend it's a horrible thing when it's not. It's something worth celebrating." He stepped closer, unable to resist the temptation of sliding his hand up her arm. Of rubbing a loose wave of her hair between his fingers. "Don't you agree?"

"When you look at me like that," she said, her tone knowing and just a bit breathless, "you're not thinking about celebrating."

"There are all sorts of celebrations," he assured her as he set his glass on the table. He placed hers there, too, before wrapping his arm around her waist and pulling her to him.

He expected her to stiffen and was gratified when she went soft, her hands on his chest. He lowered his head, but she was already there, on her toes, her hands sliding behind his neck. Their lips brushed. Parted. Then met again.

He deepened the kiss, his tongue sweeping into her mouth as he smoothed his hands up and down her back. Settled them at her waist, loving the indentation there, the swell of her hips. He rubbed his thumbs over the hard points of her hip bones, curled his fingers into the upper slope of her ass. Rolled his pelvis against her.

She moaned, the sound reverberating in his own throat.

He broke the kiss, pressed his mouth to the side

of her neck. Flicked the tip of his tongue against her rapid pulse. Her head fell back.

"Let me show you," he murmured, trailing his teeth along the sensitive skin beneath her ear. "Let me touch you." Raising his head, he held her gaze. "Let me celebrate you."

IVY SWALLOWED. She could still taste Clinton, champagne and mint from his toothpaste. The feel of his body against hers was temptation itself, his hand on her stomach a warm reminder of what they'd made together. His words about celebrating had touched her. He was starting to mean something, and that made the next step much more important.

"It would be so easy for me to say yes," she admitted, her body thrumming with need, her lips tingling from his kiss, her hands wanting to touch him everywhere, to explore his body again, this time as someone who'd come to know him. "So very easy but…"

"But?" he asked quietly when she remained silent.

She sighed. "It's too important. When we take this next step—and I don't doubt we'll take it; there's too much between us not to—I want it to be right. I don't want it to be just because we're attracted to each other, because we have an itch to scratch."

"I can guarantee you that this is more than

just an itch for me." His voice was sincere, his gaze intense. "But I don't want to push you, Ivy. I don't want a repeat of our first night together." He stepped back, though it seemed to cost him, and Ivy's heart soared because she knew, could feel how much he wanted her. "So we'll slow down."

Because she was worried about what he meant by that—because she wasn't sure what she *wanted* him to mean—she linked her fingers together at her waist. "I guess I'll see you later, then. Thanks for the champagne."

He raised an eyebrow. "Are you kicking me out?" His expression darkened. "Swear to God, Ivy, if you tell me you have plans I'm going to wring your gorgeous neck."

She laughed. "Calm down, cowboy. I don't have any plans. I just figured you'd want to be on your way since you're not...since we're not..."

"Since we're not having sex, you figure I'll just skip on out? That that's the only reason I'm here?" He shook his head. "I'm not sure if I'm pissed you think so little of me. Or of yourself."

"Oh, believe me, I think quite highly of my-self, thank you very much. I've just been around enough men to know where their priorities lie."

He trailed a finger down her cheek, and it was all she could do not to lean into him. "You've ob-viously been hanging out with the wrong men."

"No argument there." He was the first man she actually wanted to hang out with.

He checked his watch and her heart sank. He probably was just saying those things to be polite. Now he'd make an excuse, an appointment he forgot about, a phone call he had to make. He smiled at her. "It's close to dinnertime. Want to go out? Get something to eat?"

She smiled, her relief way bigger than it should be. If she wasn't careful, if she wasn't smart, this man would have the power to crush her. She cleared her throat. "Actually, I picked up the ingredients for a new chicken dish I've been wanting to try. You could…stay here. I mean, we could eat dinner here. Maybe watch a movie after."

She held her breath wondering if that was a stupid thing to ask a millionaire to do. Did they even sit at home and watch DVDs? On regular televisions on regular couches, instead of some media-slash-theater room complete with professional sound system and picture?

"A homemade meal? Sounds great to me," he said with a smile. "I can't tell you the last time I had someone cook for me. Who wasn't paid to do so."

"Well, this meal won't be free. Not exactly. If you want to eat, you'll have to pull your weight in the kitchen."

He blanched, looked at the kitchen as if it was her personal torture chamber and he was next in line for water boarding. "Can't I just do the dishes?"

She took his hand. "Come on. I'll show you the ropes, and I'll even be gentle with you. I promise."

An hour later, chicken thighs were simmering in tomato sauce laced with cinnamon while a pot of rice bubbled on the back burner. Her kitchen was a disaster area. She usually preferred to clean as she cooked, but she was too busy supervising her assistant to keep her work area tidy tonight.

Clinton hadn't been kidding about being nervous in the kitchen. At first she'd thought maybe he was just against doing something as domestic and, well, blue-collar as cooking for himself. But then she'd given him the task of chopping an onion, and she'd realized he didn't think he was too good for the chore. He was just completely inept.

And embarrassed by it.

It had been sweet and had endeared him to her even more—more than was wise, that was for sure. Especially when she was still so wrapped up in his earlier words, in how he'd accepted her rejection by being so kind. So understanding. So charming. As if he cared about her, about her feelings. As if he, too, wanted to make sure the next time they were together it was right. Special.

She turned the burner down under the rice and cursed to herself. Oh, she was in so much trouble here.

"How old were you when you started cooking?" he asked from the sink, elbow deep in suds. Hey, just because she'd put him to work didn't mean she wouldn't take him up on his offer to do dishes.

She faced him. Leaned against the counter, Jasper at her feet. "I'd mastered the art of grilled cheese sandwiches and scrambled eggs by the time I was six."

"Six? Isn't it dangerous for a kid that young to be using the stove?"

"Probably. Melba—my mother—wasn't too concerned as long as I didn't burn the apartment down."

Clinton rinsed a bowl, set it in the drainer, then emptied the sink. "You must have really enjoyed cooking."

Ivy snorted. "More like, I enjoyed eating, and if I wanted to eat something that wasn't out of a can, I had to cook it."

He nodded. "Your mother didn't know how to cook?"

"For all I know, she may have been a gourmet chef, had the skills to be one, but she didn't bother making meals. She preferred to have someone else doing things for her."

He raised his eyebrows. "Sounds like my mother."

"Well, having only seen your mother that one time, I can't say for sure, but I'd guess there were plenty of similarities. Vanity, for one. Fear of ageing, of being old and no longer seductive. Of losing the power she'd held over people since she first learned how to bat her baby-blue eyes."

He stared at her, and Ivy wished she could tell what he was thinking. "You just described my mother perfectly."

Ivy nodded. Smiled. "Yeah, I figured they were cut from the same cloth."

"I'm almost glad they won't ever have a chance to meet," he muttered. "They'd probably bond, and a friendship like that could ruin the world."

"No need to worry. My mom would have hated yours. She didn't like competition. Besides, your mom has everything Melba always wanted. The wealth. The big house. Melba would have thought your mom had it made. No worries, no having to wait on drunks, no flirting for tips."

"She was a waitress?"

"Since she was old enough to serve alcohol." Ivy had taken to the trade earlier than that, having worked the breakfast shift at a local diner during high school. Having the same profession was where any similarities between Ivy and her mother ended. Melba had hated waiting on other people. But there was no shame in being a waitress. In working hard. Something her mother had never understood. "To Melba, her job wasn't a way to get ahead—it was a way to meet the man who would finally give her everything she'd ever wanted. Everything she deserved. Taking care of herself wasn't her priority."

"What about taking care of you?"

Ivy forced a smile. Took two plates from an

upper cabinet. "That, too, was a necessary evil. A burden. Don't get me wrong. She wasn't abusive or even neglectful. I was clothed and fed—though not well, until I started cooking for us. She was just...vain. Self-absorbed and focused solely on what other people could do for her. How they could help her. Focused on finding a man to take her away from her life. Give her everything."

The timer buzzed and Ivy pushed away from the counter to turn off the rice. Set the plates on the table. "My mother was beautiful. Stunning, really. One of those women people stop and stare at, the kind who turn men into slobbering idiots. She knew how much power she had, and she used it whenever she could. She loved attention and went through men like gum."

"Like...gum?"

"She chewed them up, then spit them out. She was always looking for something better. Someone better-looking, more exciting, richer." Ivy pretended great interest in folding a paper napkin, matching up the corners, getting the crease just right. Part of her was afraid to let Clinton hear about her past, about her mother. She cared what he thought, she realized, and that grated. But another part wanted him to know where she'd come from. Needed him to see her clearly. "She loved me—in her way. As much as someone so narcissistic can love anyone else. But as I got older, she viewed me less as a daughter and more as a rival. All women were competition to her, and for that competition to be her own daughter…? She hated it and began to resent me for being younger. For taking attention away from her. Things between us were tense, and as soon as I graduated high school, I moved out. We weren't close during those last few years."

That was an understatement. About the only time she and her mother spoke during that time was when they happened to run into each other.

"How did she die?" Clinton asked.

"Car accident. She'd been seeing a local businessman who was going through his midlife crisis by buying a sports car and taking on a beautiful cocktail waitress as his mistress. The roads were icy. He took a corner too fast and went off the road. She died instantly. He survived. One of those freak things where he walked away with a few bruises and scratches. He came to see me after," she heard herself admit. She'd never told anyone about her mother's lover visiting her. "And offered to pay for her funeral expenses."

"Generous of him. He must have cared about her quite a bit."

"More like he was worried if he didn't at least offer, I was going to take him to civil court, fleece him and his family of all his hard-earned money. It was payoff, pure and simple. I declined."

"You paid for your mother's funeral? She didn't have insurance?"

"When you live paycheck to paycheck, you can't afford luxuries such as life insurance or even health insurance. I paid to have her buried."

She'd used the money she had saved for culinary school. Now she was saving again.

"I take after her, you know," Ivy felt the need to point out. "In looks. In temperament. But I promise you this—I'll be a better mother."

Studying her in a way that made her nervous, Clinton slowly closed the distance between them. "I've never met your mother, but I know the type of woman you've described. As you said, your mother and mine have quite a bit in common, and I can tell you that you're nothing like them. You haven't been sitting around waiting for some man to take care of you. You're one of the smartest, hardest-working people I've ever met. I know you don't need me to take care of you or to make you happy, but I'd be damned lucky if you let me in your life."

And then, millionaire Clinton Bartasavich Jr., with his designer jeans and shirt that cost more than she made in a week, did the most wonderful thing a man had ever done. He kissed her forehead and hugged her. Just…held on.

She wanted to resist, to assert her independence. It was scary being that vulnerable, but in the end, she couldn't fight the emotions flowing through her. She relaxed, wrapped her arms around his waist and laid her head against his chest.

She wasn't sure how long they stayed that way, wrapped in that embrace, his chin resting on the top of her head, his hands making soothing circles on her back, her cheek pressed against the softness of his shirt. His warmth seeped through the material to her cheek. She could hear his heart beat strong and steady.

When she finally lifted her head, she gave him a wry smile. "And that's the story of my mother."

He laughed. "My mother doesn't seem so bad now." He frowned, scratched his cheek. "Don't get me wrong—she's a lunatic sometimes, and if she collects one more boy-toy boyfriend, I'll probably go insane, but at least she didn't blame me or Kane for her mistakes. Just our dad."

Ivy laughed, remembering his mother in that little dress at the engagement party. "I'm glad I could help you realize you don't have it so bad, after all."

"Your mother didn't know what she was missing by not being a part of your life," he said gruffly. "Don't ever think you're like her."

"I don't want to, but I have used my looks to get attention, to get certain things in life." Admitting it was hard, but somehow, making this confession to Clinton seemed like the right thing to do. "When I was younger, it was easy to charm the boys a bit to make myself feel good. Oh, look how many boys want me, want to date me, have me on their arm, but then I realized that they were using me as much as I was using them. I became cynical. I couldn't tell who was with me because they really liked me and who just wanted to use me. For a while, I couldn't even tell that about myself. I used them and told myself it was fair because they were doing the same."

Maybe Clinton had been right earlier. Lord knew she hadn't given those men or herself nearly as much credit. Especially herself.

She forced herself to face Clinton. "But I don't expect you to take care of me. Your child, yes. But I already know you'll take care of your responsibilities. I don't want you to think I'm trying to trick you into a relationship with me. If you want to go your way, I understand."

He kissed her. Hard. Just swooped right down and claimed her mouth, the kiss stealing her thoughts and her breath. When he finally broke away, he scowled at her, took hold of her upper arms as if he wanted to give her a shake. "Does that feel like I want to leave? I'm the one who came here, asking you to give me a chance. Don't push me away, Ivy."

He wanted assurances she couldn't give him, so she hugged him. But even as she held on, she knew she'd have to let him go eventually.

CHAPTER FOURTEEN

C.J. STEPPED INSIDE O'Riley's the next afternoon, tipped his hat back and scanned the bar for his brother. Pearl Jam's "Even Flow" played over the jukebox in the far corner. It wasn't nearly as crowded as it had been when he and Ivy had been there for dinner. Only a few tables had customers, while the booths lining the wall were empty.

C.J. would have thought the bar would be busier on a Friday, but maybe midafternoon was slow no matter what day it was. Then again, today was July third. Maybe people were at home, gearing up for the Fourth, getting ready for picnics, parades and fireworks. All of which he would like to share with Ivy. If he could convince her to spend the holiday with him. He thought he could. Especially after last night.

Ivy had opened up to him. Had trusted him with a piece of her past. And since he hadn't pushed for more, the rest of the evening had been relaxed and fun. They'd eaten a delicious dinner then watched the latest Tom Hanks movie. It'd all been very normal. Almost as if they were a couple.

But it wasn't enough. He wanted to spend more

time with her. And what better way than celebrating their country's independence?

He'd call her about it, maybe charm her into having dinner with him tonight, as well. Right after he figured out why his brother had texted him and invited him for a drink.

He didn't believe for one minute that the impromptu invitation was Kane's way of extending an olive branch. For one thing, Kane didn't drink. Not since becoming clean and sober over fifteen years ago. For another, Kane had never reached out to C.J. first, preferring to stay hidden. Letting his family make all the moves.

Now suddenly Kane wanted to pal around?

Something was up. Whatever it was, C.J. figured there was a good chance he wasn't going to like it.

He started walking across the room, spied Kane in the last booth. Kane looked up, caught C.J.'s eye and gave him a smug grin that set all of C.J.'s instincts humming. Had his footsteps slowing, his muscles tensing as if waiting for a blow.

A blow that landed squarely in his midsection when he reached the booth and saw Ivy sitting across from his brother.

"Look at that," Kane said. "You're right on time."

C.J. couldn't take his eyes off Ivy. "What are you doing here?"

She scowled. Then turned that glare on Kane. "Did you call him?"

Kane lifted a shoulder, all badass in his white T-shirt, with his tattoos peeking out from the sleeves. "I may have sent him a text inviting him for a drink. But only because I thought it would piss him off to find you here. I didn't think he'd actually show up."

"God save me from idiot brothers and their stupid sibling rivalry," she muttered.

"You want to avoid idiot brothers and sibling rivalry," Kane said in a slow drawl, "you'd best keep away from any and all members of the Bartasavich family."

Ivy sighed. Patted her stomach. "Hard to do that now." She stood and met C.J.'s gaze. "Did you need something?"

You.

He frowned, hoped like hell the word that had popped into his head hadn't also popped out of his mouth. But neither Ivy's nor Kane's expression changed, so he guessed it hadn't.

"What are you doing here?" he repeated. "With him?"

"He," she said with a nod at Kane, "is doing me a favor."

C.J. stepped toward her. "Anything you want from Kane," he said, his voice a low growl, "you can get from me instead."

She raised her eyebrows, her expression cunning. "I doubt that," she purred. She trailed her hand up his chest. Gave his cheek a pat. "What I want from him is a job."

C.J. blinked. Shook his head. "What?"

"He advertised for a bartender. I applied for the job, and you—" she gave him another pat, this one harder than the first "—are interrupting my job interview." She turned to Kane. "Do you want me to come back?"

"I don't mind finishing up now, if you don't." Kane stretched his arm across the back of his seat. "You can head on over to the bar, Junior. I'll join you as soon as we're done."

Ivy sent C.J. a glance, but as he was still standing there like an idiot, she just lifted a shoulder. "Okay." She retook her seat. "As I was saying before we were so rudely interrupted, I have a bit of experience behind the bar, enough to cover the basics, but I've mostly waited on tables."

Kane nodded. "I've already got enough waitresses. My future sister-in-law worked behind the bar but decided during her maternity leave she'd rather take interior design classes in Pittsburgh than come back to O'Riley's."

"I'm a quick learner," Ivy told him, sounding desperate to work at Kane's dive bar. "And I'm good with people."

"Wait a minute. Wait a minute," C.J. said, shoving Kane over so he could slide into the booth next to him. "I won't stand here and listen to you beg this moron to hire you."

"Then leave," Ivy told him in a tone so sweet, it had to be fake. "Because I need this job."

"You already have two jobs," C.J. pointed out. "At Bradford House and King's Crossing."

"Yes, I do. But since I'm no longer employed at the River View—"

"What's a River View?"

"The River View is a very nice family restaurant over on Rockland Avenue, where I used to waitress a few nights a week until I told the owners I was pregnant."

"You work three jobs?" Why hadn't he known that? Was this information in the private investigator's report? What else would he have learned if he'd read it?

"I *used* to work three jobs," she corrected. "Like I said, Mr. and Mrs. Mongillo didn't like the idea of having an unwed, pregnant woman working for them, so they let me go."

C.J.'s hands fisted. "They fired you? That can't be legal."

"Probably not," she said as if it didn't matter that her civil rights had been violated, "but it's what happened."

"You should sue them." He took his phone out. "I'll call Oakes—my brother. He's an attorney. He can—"

"Simmer down there, cowboy," she said, her tone amused, a smile playing on her lips. "I can't afford an attorney and, honestly, have no desire to fight a legal battle. I'd much rather just find another job. Which is why I'm here."

He didn't know what to do with his phone. Settled for holding on to it. "But you already have two jobs."

"Yes," she said slowly as if he wasn't all there, "that's right. One job plus one job equals two jobs. Math's not your strong suit, is it?"

"He would have failed it freshman year," Kane said, feeling the need to put his two worthless cents in, "but our father stepped in. Donated a new gymnasium to the school and Junior here suddenly got a passing grade."

"Junior," C.J. repeated, his jaw tight, "studied his ass off for the final." The seventy-five he'd gotten had been enough to save his ass. Though his father liked to take credit for it.

"I guess maybe adding isn't something those Texas schools focus on?" Ivy said. "To make it crystal clear, yes, I work two jobs and will hopefully be adding another to that. As soon as I find a third one."

"Why?" C.J. asked.

"Why what?"

"Why do you need a third job?"

"How else could I afford to buy all the pretty, sparkling things I love?" she asked.

Something wasn't adding up—and it wasn't because of his less-than-stellar math skills. "I gave you money. Fifty thousand dollars."

Had she spent it already?

"I remember the amount." Her shoulders stiff, her voice sharp, she glanced at Kane. "You really want to discuss how you paid me to take my pregnancy claims and get out of your life in front of your brother?"

He realized his mistake immediately, but it was too late.

Kane leaned back, a mean grin on his face. "Junior's a chip off the ol' block. That's for sure." He turned to Ivy. "If you still want the position, it's yours."

"She doesn't," C.J. ground out.

"She does," Ivy said. "When do you want me to start?"

Before Kane could answer, C.J. got out of the booth, took a hold of her arm and pulled her to her feet. "I'll be damned if you'll work for my brother."

She didn't try to tug free. Just smirked at him. "Then I guess you'll be damned because, in case it's escaped your notice, I'm not your property. I'm not your wife. I'm not even your girlfriend. I'm just some random woman you slept with."

"Who is carrying my child," he reminded her. "That takes the randomness out of it."

"Not really. What do you think is going to happen here, Clinton? Do you think that I'm going to suddenly roll over and do everything you want? Because I'm not. That's not how I'm made. I'm going to continue living and working here in Shady Grove while you go back to Houston and your regular life. Back to your fancy position at your father's company, back to your heiresses and country-club dates and fund-raisers and black-tie events. And I'll be here, raising my child and probably waiting on people just like you."

Her words hit him like sharp jabs and he let go of her. He hadn't thought it through, he realized. And now he had to wonder if she was right. His life was in Houston. Hers was here. That wasn't going to change because the baby was his. He wondered, though, if it should.

"I'll take care of you and the baby," he told her. "I've got the means to make sure you never have to work again."

"How nice for you," she said drily. "But while I appreciate you wanting to support your child, and I'll definitely take you up on that offer, I take care of myself. Always have."

Because she'd never been able to count on anyone to take care of her? If so, he wanted to change that. Wanted to be the one to prove to her there were still people who kept their word. People she could count on.

He edged closer. Lowered his voice. "You can count on me, Ivy. I'm not going to leave you out to dry."

Something flashed in her eyes, something that looked like hope, but then the cynical glint he was so used to returned and she shook her head. "Who are you kidding? You're not going to stick. This is just one more thing on your to-do list. I have no desire to be one of the many, many people you take care of."

Damn it, he was sticking. Why couldn't she see that? He'd thought they were getting closer, that she was finally letting him in, opening up to him the way she had at her apartment last night. If she'd needed help, she should have come to him. Instead, she tossed his offer back in his face, refusing to believe he wasn't going to abandon her or their child.

Instead of turning to him, she'd gone to his brother.

It stung. More than it should have. Somehow, he'd given her the power to hurt him.

And wasn't that what this whole episode was about? Power. Control. This was Ivy's method of pushing him away.

Kane joined them, seeming to enjoy C.J.'s pain and suffering way too much. "I have some paperwork you need to fill out," Kane said. "In my office."

"Lead the way." She turned back to C.J. "See you later, cowboy."

The hell she would. They weren't finished. Not by a long shot. Kane brushed past C.J., heading toward a set of swinging doors behind the bar. Before Ivy could follow him, C.J. snatched her wrist and pulled her through the first door he came to.

That it was the men's room and possibly not the best choice didn't occur to him until he'd slammed the door shut behind them and locked it.

Too late to go back now.

Ignoring the three urinals lined up against the wall, he widened his stance in front of the door and crossed his arms. "Now. Let's talk about this."

"YOU MUST BE wearing your cowboy hat too tight," Ivy said as she gaped at Clinton. "Because you have done some serious damage to that brain of yours."

He didn't look mentally deranged, she had to admit. He looked...well...*hot* was the only word to describe it. He was all glowering and broad-shouldered and sexy as he blocked her path to the door. The door he'd locked.

Okay, maybe she was the mentally deranged one for finding it sexy that he was taking control like this. She wasn't afraid of him. She knew he'd never hurt her, but she had to admit having him all alpha male was sexy.

Except for the part where he dragged her into the men's room, of course. That part was just disgusting.

"You are not working for my brother," he said as that brother pounded on the door.

"Damn it, Junior," Kane called. "Open the door."

But Clinton didn't even glance back, just kept advancing on her as if he was some well-groomed lion and she one of those baby gazelles or whatever it was lions stalked in the savanna. "I don't know how the hell Kane convinced Charlotte to marry him," Clinton muttered.

Ivy couldn't help it. She laughed. "Yes, that's a toughie. Let's see, your brother is extremely good-looking, completely sexy and has that dangerous, bad-boy vibe girls—especially good girls like Charlotte—can't resist. It truly is a mystery."

Clinton went still, his eyes narrowed. "You think Kane's good-looking?"

"Have I gone blind? Of course I do." She gestured to the door where the knocking had stopped. "The man is a walking fantasy."

"He's an ass," Clinton spit out. "He's irresponsible and cocky and needs a goddamn haircut."

Her eyes widened. "You're jealous."

The idea was completely crazy and absolutely wonderful.

"I've never been jealous of Kane, not once in my life." But he frowned thoughtfully, as if considering her words and his own. "All my life I've heard about how wild he was, how dangerous, how magnetic. That go-to-hell attitude and the huge chip on his shoulder has attracted women to him his entire life, but it never mattered to me because any girl I wanted wasn't interested in him.

But now, hearing you say that…" He shook his head. Lowered his voice. "It kills me, Ivy."

She blinked. Holy cow. She'd been right. Which wasn't all that horrible, but she'd also hurt him. She hadn't meant to, hadn't realized she had the power to, but seeing his reaction… Well, she didn't like knowing she could make him feel bad.

Liar, her inner voice whispered. She'd known what she was doing by coming to Kane. Knew it would upset Clinton. Wasn't that part of the reason she'd done it? To let him know, in no uncertain terms, that she was going to do what she pleased, whether he liked it or not?

"Kane is sexy, and he's exactly the type of guy I've avoided most of my life," she admitted. "Men like that, they're heartbreak waiting to happen."

Clinton edged closer, his voice a whisper. "And men like me?"

Men like him? There was no other man like him. Not to her. She'd never had this much of an attraction to a man last this long, never had it grow. "You're the most dangerous of all," she heard herself admit.

"I won't hurt you, Ivy." He touched her hair, his fingers trailing along her jawbone and down the side of her neck. "I would never take the baby from you."

"You would," she said, "if you thought I wasn't a suitable mother, and honestly, I may not be. At least by your definition."

And that was the rub. If she did something he didn't like, if she acted in a way he deemed unacceptable, he'd swoop in with his team of high-priced attorneys.

"You're never going to give me a real chance, are you?" he asked quietly.

She couldn't. It was too dangerous. There was too much at stake. Her child. Her heart.

"If you need help, financial or otherwise," he said, his voice all growly, his brows lowered, "you will come to me."

"First of all, *Junior*," she said, realizing she was backing up and she couldn't do that. She had to stand her ground. "You are not the boss of me." And, dear Lord, was that the sort of attitude she was going to have to put up with from her own kid someday? Worse, did she have to resort to acting like a teenager, just because she was out of sorts? "I do what I please. I would have thought you would have figured that out by now."

"I've figured out that you're incredibly stubborn," he said. "That you're so worried about someone taking advantage of you that you don't trust anyone."

The words stung. Possibly because they were close to the truth. "I trust people who have earned it. You are not on that list."

"What do I have to do to get on it?" he asked, frustration clear in his tone. "What, Ivy? I've apologized for my reaction when you told me you were pregnant. It was just that—a reaction. I'm here, trying to get to know you, trying to work with you so we can come up with an agreement, some sort of relationship that works for the baby and for both of us, but you insist on throwing my mistakes in my face, pushing me away in every way you can."

She went still because he was right, but she was too scared to admit it. Too scared to change. "We don't need to have a relationship of any sort as far as I'm concerned."

"Because you don't want me to have anything to do with this baby. You want me to be some asshole who's more than willing to just throw some money your way and leave you and the baby alone." He looked and sounded frustrated, his mouth a thin line, his shoulders rigid. "But that's not going to happen. I'm not going to walk away from my own child."

But when he was tired of her, when he was done with her, he'd walk away from her. And she couldn't risk getting close to a man, couldn't risk giving him that much power over her. The power to break her heart.

"If you didn't trust me to be a part of the baby's life," he asked, "if you didn't want money, why did you tell me about the baby in the first place?"

"Because I didn't want my child to grow up like I did, wondering who I came from, who my father is," she admitted starkly. "I don't even know his name. My mother refused to tell me. I was a mistake, something that ruined her life, took away all her choices, all her chances."

"That's bullshit," Clinton snapped.

Ivy nodded. "I know that, but she had all the power. While I'm left wondering what happened between her and my father. Was he an asshole? Did she love him? Did he love her? What would he do if I found him now? I didn't want my child to grow up with those questions. Good or bad, it will be better for the baby to know the truth."

"Admit it," Clinton said softly, "part of you wanted me to brush you off. That way, you wouldn't have to deal with me and you could go on being completely independent and running things all on your own. Part of you hoped I'd want nothing to do with you or the baby."

"You're right. Can you blame me? We didn't know each other. I told you because it was the right thing to do, but yes, I'd hoped you'd want nothing to do with us. That I could come back to Shady Grove knowing I'd done my best, that I'd done the right thing and leave it at that."

She wasn't proud of herself, but she couldn't apologize for it. Couldn't show any weakness.

Though she wished she could.

"Sometimes," he said, "I wonder why I even bother."

She winced, his quiet words feeling like a slap

to the face. She wanted to say something but wasn't sure what.

The door opened and Kane walked in, casual as you please, a key in one hand, papers in the other. He glanced between them. "You okay?" he asked Ivy.

Clinton's lip curled, but he didn't say anything, just watched her.

"I'm fine. Your brother and I just had a few things to discuss."

"Well, now you've had your discussion," Kane said, crossing to them. "I got the papers. You can fill them out now or at home and bring them back when you start. I'll need you here Monday night by six."

She felt Clinton watching her, waiting for her to make her choice, for her to say she'd changed her mind, that she didn't want the job, after all. That she trusted him to help her. To be there for her. To take care of her and the baby.

But she needed to take care of herself. Couldn't count on anyone else to do so for her.

So she nodded at Kane and held her hand out for the forms. "I'll fill them out now, and I'll be here tomorrow night."

Clinton's expression went stony, then he turned on his heel and walked out.

Leaving Ivy to wish she could call him back.

CHAPTER FIFTEEN

FRIDAY NIGHT GRACIE was on the couch at Luke's sister's house, a tidy one-story ranch on the outskirts of town with high ceilings and a huge yard that looked into the woods. The TV was on, some show about people doing an obstacle course for superheroes or ninjas or something.

Luke came in from the hallway, his shirt wrinkled.

She smiled. "Rough time?"

They'd tried putting his nieces to bed together, but the girls had wanted Gracie to play with them some more. So they'd had to pretend that Gracie had left before Luke could get them settled down.

He flopped onto the couch next to her with such force, she actually bounced. He leaned his head against the back. "I thought I was going to have to drug their milk or something."

"They're just excited to have you hanging out with them."

He snorted. Sent her a lazy grin that made her heart skip a beat. "They couldn't care less about me with you being here. At least they didn't act like little monsters."

Gracie tucked her knee under her other leg. "Please. Compared to my brothers, your nieces are angels. If this is what it's like to babysit girls, I'm going to suggest that if Molly wants to get pregnant again she does that gender-selection thing."

He laughed. Sat up. "Thanks again for coming."

"It was fun." That was the truth. The girls were adorable and funny and, despite a few minor pout sessions and one crying jag that lasted twenty minutes, were well-behaved.

Luke leaned forward and grabbed the remote from the coffee table. "Want to watch a movie?"

When he settled back, he was closer, his muscular thigh just an inch from hers. She shifted slightly away, masking the move by pretending to stretch. "Okay. You sure your sister doesn't mind if I'm here?"

His sister and brother-in-law had already been gone by the time Gracie had pulled up in her dad's pickup.

"Nah, she's cool with it."

Which only proved what Gracie had been telling Molly the other day, what she'd been trying to convince herself of for the past week. She and Luke were friends. Just friends. If he had…feelings…for her, there was no way his sister would let him have her over, right? His parents had to be home for him to have a girl in the house.

Gracie's parents weren't that strict. They wanted her to make her own decisions. Her own mistakes.

Sometimes she wondered if it was laziness on their part. If they'd watched her more closely, she wouldn't have made such a doozy of a mistake with Andrew.

Luke's phone buzzed, and he took it out, glanced at the message. His expression darkened as he tossed the phone onto the table.

"Is everything all right?" Gracie asked.

"Yeah. It's nothing." He flipped through channels, seemed focused solely on the shows flashing by. "What do you want to watch?"

Before she could answer, his phone buzzed again, showing a picture of a smiling Kennedy.

Gracie's throat tightened. "You can get that. If you want."

He gave one quick shake of his head. "I don't have anything to say to her." He shut his phone off. Tried to smile, but it looked forced. He turned the TV off. "Want to sit out on the porch?"

"Sure," she said as the house phone began to ring. And ring.

He jumped up and grabbed the receiver, looked at the caller ID and swore. "It's Kennedy," he said, staring at the still-ringing phone. "She must have talked to my mom and found out I was here."

The phone rang twice more, then stopped. It was silent for thirty seconds, then rang again.

"You'd better answer it," Gracie said gently. "Before it wakes up the girls."

He nodded stiffly. Clicked a button and lifted

it to his ear. "Hello?" He began to pace while, Gracie assumed, Kennedy spoke. Gracie wished he'd left the TV on. At least then she could pretend great interest in whatever was on. Without it, she was stuck on the couch while he walked around the living room, his head down, his knuckles white. "No." More silence. "*No*. Do not come over, Kennedy. I mean it."

Gracie's head snapped up. Kennedy wanted to come over? Here? Now?

She watched him, wide-eyed, while he listened to whatever Kennedy was saying. "Because I don't want to see you or talk to you." More silence. "And I don't want to hear what you have to say." He laughed harshly. "You screwed my best friend," he said flatly in a tone Gracie had never heard him use before. So angry. "As far as I'm concerned, we have nothing to say to each other. If you call here again, I'll shut off the phone and my sister will get pissed. And don't even think about coming over." He looked at Gracie. Held her gaze. "I'm not alone."

He hung up. Carefully replaced the phone. "You want a drink?" he asked, as if nothing had happened. As if he hadn't just told his ex-girlfriend he was with someone—a female someone, as even an idiot could infer.

"Uh, sure. Whatever you're having is fine."

One side of his mouth kicked up. "As long as it's not milk, right?"

He remembered she was a vegan. For some stupid reason, that meant a lot to her. "Right."

While he went into the kitchen, Gracie held her breath, but the phone remained silent. He came back a minute later with two glasses of iced tea. Handed her one, then set the other on the coffee table and retook his seat, once again sitting close to her.

"Sorry about that—" He gestured to the phone. "I don't want to drag you into my drama."

"It's okay." She sipped her drink, stared at the glass. "Has Kennedy tried to talk to you before this?"

"Yeah. She's been bugging me for days, trying to get me to see her, saying she has some of my stuff—sweatshirts and things. That we should meet up to exchange them. I told her just to drop them off at my house, and I boxed up all the shit she gave me and left it on her back patio the other day."

"If you want her to come over," Gracie said softly, setting her drink down. "I can leave."

His head whipped around. "No. I want you to stay. Unless…unless you want to go?"

He looked nervous. Sounded worried.

"I want to stay." And wasn't it her honesty that had gotten her into trouble with Andrew? She'd been too open. Had said what she thought, giving him everything she had, sharing her feelings with him, and he'd used them to his advantage.

But Luke wasn't Andrew, she reminded herself. Luke was her friend. He liked spending time with her. Wasn't embarrassed or ashamed of her.

Except they hadn't actually been seen in public, a little voice reminded her. They'd snuck out of her house the other day so no one would see them. Even now they were alone at a house at the edge of town.

"That is," she continued, worried she'd said too much, that he would see how much she was starting to like him, "if you want me to stay."

"Yeah," he said quickly. "You know I do."

She didn't. She didn't know anything. Wasn't good at these games, preferring honesty and openness. Wasn't like other teenage girls who lived for drama, who wanted the heady rush of love, the heartbreak of hurt feelings and arguments. "I'm sorry Kennedy upset you," she told him.

"I shouldn't let her get to me."

"It must be hard. You two were together for a long time."

He sighed. Scooted back. "Since the beginning of sophomore year. I feel stupid, though, because now that I look back, especially the past year, I can see the signs. Her flirting with Drew, him watching her."

"Things like that are often clear in hindsight." Hadn't she looked back and seen the signs with Andrew? How he'd treated her, how he hadn't wanted to talk to her, hadn't wanted to get to know her, even though she'd given him everything?

"That's what sucks," Luke said. "Looking back and seeing everything so clearly. I want to kick my own ass for not doing something about it, for not calling either of them on it, but especially for not saying stuff to her about all the crap she pulled during the time we were together. The head games she played, how she loved to try to make me jealous, how she'd sulk if she didn't get her way, if I wasn't showing her enough attention."

"You can't blame yourself for her and Andrew cheating."

"I don't, but I should have seen it coming. Should have broken up with her months ago. I mean, I loved her. I thought I loved her, but there were times, too many, really, where I didn't like her."

Gracie set her hand on his knee. "I'm sorry she hurt you," she whispered, hating that he, too, had suffered.

He looked at her hand, then into her face. Something in his gaze warned her, told her she needed to move back, to do or say something to remind them both that they weren't a couple. That they were too different. That she had no desire to get hurt again.

But he leaned forward, slowly, so slowly she certainly could have stopped him. But she didn't. She sat there, still as a statue as he brushed his mouth against hers. He kissed her again, moving in closer, his hands on her face. She kissed him back, her heart racing, but when he deepened the kiss, when he tried to sweep his tongue into her mouth, she jumped up.

"I—I can't do this," she blurted, then remembered the girls were sleeping and lowered her voice. "I don't want to be..." She waved a hand vaguely. "A replacement or consolation prize." She looked around, had no idea what she was looking for and crossed her arms. "I think I should go."

He was on his feet in a flash. "No...I mean... I'm sorry. I'm really sorry. I shouldn't have done that, I just..." He shook his head. Shoved his hands into his pockets. "It was a mistake. I shouldn't have done it."

She nodded but noticed he hadn't refuted her words about being nothing more than a possible rebound. "A mistake. Yes." Because he was lonely? Trying to get back at Kennedy, and Gracie was available? Because she was easy? Her stomach turned. "I really have to go."

She ran out, feeling like a fool. Wondering why he'd kissed her. Because he was using her? Or because he felt bad for her? Poor Gracie with her weird clothes and crazy hair. A pity kiss.

She wasn't sure which one was worse.

Ivy took a deep breath, then knocked on the door to Clinton's room. After the ugly scene at

O'Riley's last week, he'd returned to Houston. For work, he'd said in the voice-mail message he'd left her, though she'd known that was only partly true.

He'd wanted to get away from her.

Hadn't she known it would happen? That eventually he'd leave? He'd proved her right. She'd tried to tell herself she didn't care. Had even forced herself to attend Fay's family's Fourth of July picnic to prove how unaffected she was by anything Clinton said or did.

She'd been miserable. Had hated the merriment and smiling faces. Hated herself for pushing Clinton away. She'd thought for sure she'd never see him again, that he'd fade out of her life for good.

Until she'd arrived at work this morning and Fay had told her he was back. Back in Shady Grove and, despite being able to afford classier accommodations, back to Bradford House. Not only that, but he'd booked the room for every weekend from now until the end of the year.

Because of her.

She couldn't stay away. Not when he was this close.

Not when she'd actually missed him.

She knocked again, harder this time, anxiety and anticipation warring inside her.

He wanted her to trust him, to turn to him, and she wanted to, but she was scared. But today, now, she was making an effort.

He'd better appreciate it.

He opened the door, his cell phone to his ear, his free hand covering the mouthpiece. Seeing her, he raised his eyebrows. "Hello, Ivy."

Well, that was a cool, not-exactly-thrilled-to-see-her greeting. She reminded herself she deserved it, that she'd taken a job working for his brother, that she'd hurt his pride and made him doubt her commitment to at least trying to see where things could go between them.

"You came back," she blurted, then winced. Crap. She hadn't meant to say that.

"Is that why you're here? To state the obvious?"

"I just… I thought maybe…after our disagreement you'd…"

"Walk away and not look back?"

"Something like that." She wouldn't blame him if he had. And she hated how grateful she was that he hadn't.

The man was messing with her head, pure and simple.

Whoever was on the phone said something, drawing Clinton's attention. "Of course I'm still here." He gestured for Ivy to come in then turned and walked back into the room. She followed, shutting the door behind her.

"Now, don't jump to any conclusions," Clinton said into the phone, his back to Ivy. "For all we know this could just be a minor setback." He paused, pinched the bridge of his nose with his free hand. "Aw, darlin', don't cry." His voice was gruff, the look he shot Ivy a cross between terror and helplessness. "I'll be back in Houston Sunday night." During the pause, Ivy could hear the murmur of a female voice. "As soon as I get in. I promise. Try not to worry, okay?" Another pause. "I love you, too. Talk to you soon."

He shut the phone off and rolled his head from side to side. Sighed.

"What's wrong?" Ivy asked.

He tossed the phone onto the bed. "What makes you think anything's wrong?"

"Let's just say I have an instinct about these things. And when a man tries to soothe a crying woman, something is wrong. At least to the woman."

"That wasn't a woman. It was my niece, Estelle. She's worried about my father."

"Is he all right?"

Clinton sat heavily on the edge of the bed. "His doctor is worried that his depression is worsening. He's barely eating and he refuses to do his physical therapy. It's like he's given up and is just waiting to die."

Ivy had no idea what it was like to watch someone she loved suffer like that, but she imagined it was horrible.

She sat next to Clinton, ignored how he stiffened when she laid her hand on his arm. She kept it there anyway, wanting to give him some small measure of comfort. "I'm so sorry."

He nodded then stood. To get away from her? The thought stung, and she reminded herself that was what she'd wanted. To push him away.

She'd done the job too well.

"Estelle seems to think I can fix it," Clinton said. "Somehow force Dad to get better."

"And it's killing you that you can't," Ivy guessed.

He sent her a sharp look that let her know she was right. "Even my ego's not big enough to let me think I can save a dying man."

"I don't think it's your ego pushing you. I think it's respect, at the very least. Maybe even love for the man who raised you."

She didn't agree with Clinton butting into his family members' business, didn't like how they all turned to him to solve their problems. But she admired how he cared for them all.

She couldn't imagine being that magnanimous. Wasn't sure she wanted to be.

"Dad is a bastard," Clinton said flatly. "Egotistical, arrogant and self-centered. But he isn't all bad. And he doesn't deserve to live the way he has been for the past fourteen months. No one deserves that. And you're right. I hate that I can't talk him into getting better." He scrubbed a hand over his face. "Hell, maybe I made things worse by forcing Carrie to leave him."

"From what I overheard that day at your apartment, she was on her way out. She was looking for an excuse."

He lifted a shoulder. In agreement? Irritation? Ivy had no idea.

"If things are that bad with your father," she said, needing to ask the question that was at the forefront of her mind, "why did you come back to Shady Grove this weekend?"

Clinton edged closer so that he towered over her, his gaze intense, his expression unyielding. "You know why."

Her throat went dry. Yes, she knew.

He'd come back for her.

His words from that day at her apartment when he'd brought her champagne and flowers floated through her head.

I'm going to prove myself to you.

"The real question," he continued, "is what are you doing here?"

"Fay told me you were back, and I…"

I missed you. I wanted to see you.

Except she couldn't tell him that. Was afraid to be that open. That honest.

Was terrified he wouldn't believe her. Not after what had happened at O'Riley's.

"I need your help," she blurted.

He laughed, but the sound held little humor. "I doubt that. You seem to thrive on doing things on your own."

Ouch. But since it was true, she couldn't argue. "I need your help," she repeated, as she stood. "Fay is giving me the boys' old crib, and I need help carrying it into my apartment and putting it together."

Of course, she didn't need it quite this soon, hadn't planned on lugging it home for a few months. And she could think of about a dozen ways she'd rather spend a sunny Saturday afternoon than moving furniture. But he didn't need to know any of that.

He wasn't the only one who had something to prove. She was turning to him. Making the effort.

She just hoped it wasn't too little, too late.

He stiffened. "I'll buy you a new crib."

She rolled her eyes. "The baby doesn't care if two other babies have slept in the crib. We'll get new sheets and everything, but there's no point buying something when I have a perfectly good crib here that's ready to be reassembled in my apartment."

He studied her, his gaze wary. Questioning.

At her apartment last week, when they'd celebrated the baby, had their champagne and that amazing kiss and she'd told him about her mother, they'd grown closer. It had scared her to death. So she'd asserted her independence. He had a right to be pissed. She'd just hoped he'd be over it by now. With any other man, she wouldn't worry about it. The only reason she was making an effort with Clinton was because of the baby. Or so she told herself.

Lies. Horrible lies she forced herself to believe because the truth was so much scarier.

She'd done this to herself. Had brought on his cool attitude by going to Kane. By not accepting Clinton's help. By not trusting him when he'd said she could count on him.

She'd succeeded in putting distance between them and now she wished she hadn't. And it wasn't guilt. It was something more. Something deeper she didn't want to explore.

"Well?" she asked, frustrated and getting mildly annoyed because she was making an effort and couldn't he see that? "Are you going to help me or not?"

He straightened. "Where is it?"

She almost sagged in relief. "In the basement." Fay had an entire household worth of items down there from the house she used to share with her ex-husband.

Clinton nodded. "Let me change. I'll meet you in the foyer in five minutes."

Ivy left, quietly shutting the door behind her. In the hall, she closed her eyes and exhaled heavily.

And tried to tell herself she was making progress.

C.J. CARRIED THE last piece of the crib up the stairs and into Ivy's apartment. Was greeted by the cat with a meow. He went into Ivy's bedroom, where they'd put the rest, Ivy taking the small parts, him hauling the bigger ones.

He wiped sweat from his brow. Ivy had borrowed a pickup, so they'd been able to get it from the bed-and-breakfast to her apartment in one trip. One silent, tension-filled trip.

He wasn't going to worry about it. Wasn't going to be the one to break that tension. Not when he was still so angry with her.

"Here," she said, coming in behind him with a glass of lemonade. "You look thirsty."

"Thanks." He took it, drained the liquid in several long gulps. Handed her the glass.

She looked nervous, standing there in her shorts and another tank top, this one the color of spring grass that clung to her rounded stomach. "I didn't know you even owned regular jeans. I mean, the kind normal people buy."

He glanced at his faded jeans. He'd changed into them and a T-shirt, had put on his running shoes. "Several pairs," he said. She thought he was some snob who'd never done an honest day's worth of work.

He had. It may not have been physical work, but he knew how to put in a full day, how to work until the job was done.

"Fay found the directions," Ivy said, handing him a paper booklet opened to a diagram of parts and pieces.

He studied it. Nodded, though trepidation crept up his spine. "Got it. Tools?"

She gestured toward a pink toolbox in the corner. "Need help?"

"No, thanks," he told her coolly. "I can handle it on my own."

Her eyes narrowed, and she whirled on her heel and stormed off without a word.

A point for him, getting that last word in, but the victory felt hollow. He glanced at Jasper, who was looking at him reproachfully. "Yeah, yeah," C.J. muttered. "I know. Cheap shot. But she deserved it."

Telling himself that was the truth, he laid out the directions and went to work.

"HAVE YOU BEEN sleeping in here?" Ivy asked an hour later when she came back into the room. She frowned at him, looked at all the pieces and parts still scattered on the floor. "I thought you'd be done by now."

C.J. ground his back teeth together and slowly got to his feet. He had one side of the crib up, and it wasn't looking too steady. "You did this on purpose."

"What are you talking about?"

"This." He jabbed a finger at the half-assembled crib. "You asked me to put this damned thing together to prove I'm inept."

She laughed. "You're kidding." Her laughter

died as she took in his expression. "You're not kidding. Look, this isn't some trick or plan to make you look bad. I needed help, so I asked you."

He wanted to fling the screwdriver he was holding. Instead he set it down, then threw up his hands. "It's impossible. There's no way these pieces make a crib."

He was embarrassed and felt like an idiot for not being able to read directions, for not being able to do something as simple as assemble a bed for his baby.

"Hey," she said, her tone soothing, her hand rubbing his arm. "It's okay. We'll figure it out together."

He exhaled heavily. Nodded. "Yeah. All right." He picked up the directions. He wanted, desperately, to talk her into letting him just buy a damn crib, one already assembled that would be delivered straight to this room. But he couldn't. "Guess I fail again."

She looked at him sharply. "I told you, this isn't a game or a plan. It's not a test. Do you really think I care if you can assemble furniture? Because I can do that myself. I didn't ask you here because I *need* your help. I asked you here because I want your help."

"There's a difference?"

She huffed out a breath. "Of course. I can do most things on my own. I've had to learn to be self-reliant, and I know that's hard on you, but I can't change who I am. Not completely. But I can try to accept help, to accept the fact that I'm not alone anymore."

"Because of the baby," he said.

"Because of the baby," she agreed. "But also because of you. I'm not going to quit working at O'Riley's, and I'm sorry if that bothers you, but I need the job there. I need to take care of myself. That doesn't mean I don't trust you or that I don't want you to be a part of the baby's life." She swallowed. "It doesn't mean I don't want you to be a part of *my* life," she said softly.

He was stunned. Could only stare at her as he tried to understand what she was telling him. She wanted him in her life. She wanted to trust him.

All of the tension, the tightening in his gut, which he hadn't been able to get rid of since leaving her in Kane's bar last week, dissipated.

She was going to give him a chance. She was going to give them a chance.

Grinning, he leaned forward. Pressed a warm kiss on her mouth, one she reciprocated with such sweetness he couldn't help wrapping an arm around her and kissing her again. And again. When he broke the kiss, she was smiling.

"I take it you're done being mad at me?" she asked.

"For now. But don't worry. I'm sure you'll do something else to piss me off soon."

She laughed. "You know me so well."

He hoped that was true. Wanted it to be true. He handed her the screwdriver. "Now show me how to put together a crib."

CHAPTER SIXTEEN

"Are you mad at me?"

Gracie glanced at Luke as they walked down the sidewalk. He'd invited her to get a coffee after work, and she hadn't been able to say no. Hadn't wanted to say no. They'd barely spoken since she'd left his sister's house last week, and though she knew it was stupid of her, she'd missed him.

"No," she said. And she wasn't mad. She was confused and so scared of falling for him when she had no idea what he thought of her. "I thought you were mad at me. You didn't call or text me."

"Yeah, I thought maybe you didn't want to talk to me because of…because of the kiss."

He blushed, and she wasn't sure what he was embarrassed about.

"I do want to talk to you. I did," she said.

"Good. That's…good."

He held the door for her, and they went into the coffee shop. Though it was Saturday afternoon, there were a few empty tables. Luke excused himself to use the restroom, and she sat near a large window overlooking Main Street. Gracie fiddled with the strap of her purse.

"Can I get you something?"

Gracie looked up and frowned to see Kennedy wearing a waitress uniform, a pad in one hand, pen in the other, her long, red hair pulled back. "Oh, Gracie. Hi," she said with all the warmth and enthusiasm of someone greeting her own executioner. "I didn't realize it was you."

"Hello, Kennedy," Gracie said, refusing to be rude just because Kennedy didn't have any manners. "How are you?"

Kennedy rolled her eyes. "I'm just fine." She flicked her gaze over Gracie's hair. "I see your hair's gotten bigger this summer." She smiled, as if she was teasing, just being funny.

Gracie clenched her hands so she wouldn't touch her curls. "Yes." And Gracie saw that Kennedy was still a bitch. "I'll have an iced coffee, please. Do you have soy milk?"

She shrugged. "Anything else?"

"That's all for me, but the person I'm with will be right back."

Kennedy's eyes widened. "You're not alone? That's a surprise. Don't tell me—one of your little friends from the band is joining you?"

A few of her friends were in the marching band at school, but that was nothing to be ashamed of. Though some popular kids like Kennedy thought it was. "Actually—"

"I'm joining her," Luke said as he brushed past

Kennedy and stood there as if he wasn't sure whether he wanted to sit or not.

Kennedy's fingers turned white on the pen. "Luke. You're with…her?"

He nodded. Took his seat. Kept his gaze on the table. "I'll have a blended caramel macchiato."

"I know what your favorite drink is," Kennedy said, looking like she was about to cry. "I know everything about you," she whispered.

His hands fisted on top of the table and he kept silent until Kennedy finally left.

"I'm sorry," he said tightly to Gracie. "I didn't know she was working here."

Gracie wasn't sure she believed him, but she hated to think that he'd lie to her, especially about something like that. "It's okay. Do you…do you want to go somewhere else?"

He scrubbed a hand through his hair. "No. I'm not going to let her get to me."

But tension emanated from him, and whatever he'd wanted to talk to Gracie about would obviously have to wait. They sat in silence for ten minutes until Kennedy came back with their drinks. She set them down with more force than necessary.

"Is there anything else I can get you?" she asked, though her lips barely moved.

"No," Luke said, still not looking at her, which Gracie could have told him only made it seem as if Kennedy was more important to him than he wanted to let on.

"Oh, Gracie," Kennedy said, "I heard they're having a bag sale at the thrift store this afternoon. I'm sure you'll want to stock up on clothes."

Gracie refused to let someone so mean and ugly on the inside get to her. She smiled. "Thank you, Kennedy. I would like that, and I'll be sure to stop by there."

She always found the best deals at thrift stores, though she preferred going to one in Pittsburgh where there was a bigger selection.

Kennedy made a huffing sound and left. "God," Luke murmured, "she is such a bitch."

"She's just insecure." Gracie often wondered why that gave someone a free pass to be mean, but Molly always had excuses for people's behavior, and it had rubbed off on Gracie. "Though I can't understand why other people don't see her cattiness is really a cry for help. I mean, she's nice enough to people's faces, but behind their backs, she's constantly bad-mouthing them. I think it's because she's pretty. No one wants to believe she's not as beautiful on the inside, too."

"No," Luke said, after a moment, as if he'd been considering Gracie's words and having some sort of inner debate. "She's just a bitch." He took a sip of his drink, then sat back in agitation. "Drew cornered me in the weight room yesterday, said Kennedy came on to him months ago."

Gracie winced in sympathy. "I'm sorry, Luke."

He shrugged. "Drew could have turned her down. Could have told me about it. Instead he hooked up with her. But I think he's regretting that now."

"Oh?" Gracie asked, wondering when she'd stopped being upset over Andrew being with Kennedy and worrying about Kennedy being free again. Free to get back with Luke. "What makes you say that?"

"He apologized to me. Said he made a mistake, picking a girl over a friend. I just…got the feeling he didn't know what he was getting into with her and that he might be looking for a way out."

She stirred her drink with her straw. "How does that make you feel?"

"Doesn't matter to me," Luke said with finality, but she wondered who he was trying to convince. Her. Or himself. "I just don't want him to think we're going to be friends again, you know?"

Nodding, Gracie took a sip of her drink, only to frown. Forced herself to swallow.

"What's wrong?" Luke asked.

"Nothing." But she pushed the drink aside.

"Gracie…"

"It's no big deal," she assured him. "They used real milk in my drink. I'm sure it was an accident. I'll just get another."

But before she could even lift her hand to get

Kennedy's attention, he was on his feet, motioning Kennedy over, his expression hard.

"Yes?" Kennedy asked in a snide tone.

"Gracie's coffee has milk in it," Luke said as if Kennedy had laced it with poison.

Kennedy cocked a hip. "So?"

"She's vegan," he ground out.

"It's really not a problem," Gracie hurried to say because people were starting to stare. Because she felt as if he was using this as an excuse to get into Kennedy's face. "I'll just send it back."

He whirled on her. "Did you ask for soy milk?"

Gracie nodded. "Maybe she forgot."

"I didn't forget," Kennedy said, tossing her head. "The barista must have messed up."

Luke shook his head. "You did it on purpose."

Gracie had enough. "I think you two have some things to talk about, so I'm just going to go." And because she was miffed at him for making a big deal out of something that wasn't a big deal at all, she didn't even offer to pay for her drink. Let him buy it for her. Maybe Kennedy could drink it, since Gracie wouldn't.

He stopped her with a hand on her arm. "Wait. Don't go."

"Oh, let her leave," Kennedy said. "Can't you see what she's doing? It's so pathetic." Kennedy turned to Gracie. "Andrew told me how you threw yourself at him last fall."

Gracie went cold. No matter what she'd thought

about Andrew, she'd never expected he'd tell Kennedy about what had happened between them. "What?"

"I knew there was something weird going on when you were talking to him in school that one day," Kennedy said. "The way you were begging him to sit with you at lunch. God, it was really sad. But he told you he wasn't interested, and now you think you're going to...what? Insert yourself into the popular group by getting with Luke?"

Gracie could only shake her head. "You've been watching way too many '80s teen movies."

Kennedy turned to Luke. "Don't tell me you're falling for this dork. I mean...God...look at her."

Gracie couldn't breathe. She waited for Luke to say something. Anything. Until he did.

"Gracie and I are friends," he said, his cheeks red. He wouldn't look at her. "Just friends."

"Yes," she said, her voice unsteady, because no matter how hard she tried to tell herself not to let his words hurt her, they did. "What else would we be?" She faced him, held his gaze. "You're so much better suited for someone like Kennedy."

He winced, obviously understanding that she didn't think highly of Kennedy—or of him.

And then she walked out, her dignity wrapped around her. Her heart breaking once again.

CLINTON OPENED THE door to his room, his carry-on in one hand, laptop case in the other, only to pull up short when he found Ivy there, her hand lifted to knock.

"Hey," he said, grinning, knowing it was ridiculous to be so happy to see her when he'd just left her apartment half an hour ago but unable to deny it nonetheless. "Everything all right?"

"Fine," she said, but she was frowning slightly. "I don't want to keep you from getting to the airport but…" She shook her head. "Sorry. It's just… I could have sworn I passed Kane on my way here, riding his motorcycle."

"That was him," Clinton confirmed. He wondered how long before Charlotte put her foot down about him riding that thing.

"Kane was here?" Ivy asked.

"Surprised me, too."

The whole weekend had been one shock after another. First, Ivy had come to him for help yesterday. He'd come back to Shady Grove to prove to her that she could count on him. After putting the crib together, she'd had to work at O'Riley's. He'd gone with her, had eaten dinner there, then spent the rest of the night sitting at the bar with Charlotte, who'd had the night off.

This morning, he'd offered to take Ivy out to brunch, but she'd insisted she enjoyed cooking so they'd spent a lazy day at her place, eating, reading the paper and watching old movies on TV.

And when he'd left to pack before catching his flight back to Houston, she'd kissed him goodbye so sweetly, he'd wondered if she just might miss him while he was gone. Hoped she would.

"Kane was waiting on the porch when I got here," C.J. told her. "He came to collect the favor I owed him."

"Ooh, let me guess. He wants you to leave a horse's head in his biggest enemy's bed."

"Nothing quite that bloodthirsty. He asked me to be his best man."

"Yeah? I guess he likes you more than he lets on, huh?"

C.J. couldn't help it. He laughed. "I doubt that. Probably Charlotte forced him into it. Kane's never been the type to have many friends. I was probably the only person they could think of who would say yes."

"I don't know about that. You do have two other brothers. He could have asked either of them."

True. Though C.J. doubted Zach would even show up for the wedding, let alone agree to stand up for one of his brothers.

A family of five walked down the hall and he and Ivy stepped aside to let them pass.

"I'm not sure why he asked," C.J. said when they were alone again. "But I'm glad he did."

He and Kane still had their issues, but being asked to be part of Kane's wedding day made C.J. hopeful they could work through those issues. Eventually.

Though he knew it was going to take a hell of

a lot of work on both their parts to get past two decades of resentment.

"Ah, brotherly love," Ivy said with a cheeky grin. "There's nothing else like it. Best friends one minute, wanting to eviscerate each other the next."

"That's a brutal description. But accurate." He pulled his door shut. "Are you working tonight?"

She'd told him that she sometimes spent her nights off here doing prep work or trying new recipes.

"No. I was hoping to catch you before you left."

Shifting his briefcase to the hand holding his carry-on, he laid his other one on the small of her back. Led her toward the stairs. "Why is that?"

"I felt the baby move." She laughed. "I mean, I've felt it before, like a tiny fluttering, but I could never tell if it really was the baby or just indigestion. And this time I knew, for certain, it was the baby."

He stopped, just…slammed to a stop at the top of the stairs. "What?"

She nodded, looking thrilled and slightly ill at the same time. "It was right after you left. It was this rolling sensation. Like he was doing a somersault. Here." She took his hand and laid it against the soft swell of her stomach but C.J. didn't feel any movement. "It was wonderful and scary and just made me realize how…real…this all is. We're having a baby." She looked up, smiled into

his eyes. "I'm terrified and excited and I just...
I wanted to tell you."

She'd come to him so he could be included in
this moment. So they could share it.

Like a real couple. A real family.

His fingers curled against her stomach and he
leaned down to kiss her. "Thank you."

She returned his kiss but then stepped back.
Shrugged as if it was no big deal and cleared her
throat. "You'd better get going. You don't want to
miss your flight."

He bit back a sigh. He was coming to understand her more and more. When he got too close,
or when things got too personal between them,
she took those steps—figuratively or literally—
to maintain control.

To guard her heart.

It was annoying as hell.

But he had to be patient. He wouldn't let his
frustration get the best of him again. If he wanted
Ivy—in his life and in his bed—he had to be patient.

Even if it killed him.

Besides, he really did have a plane to catch.

"We'll have to celebrate next weekend," he said.

"We can't pop champagne for every pregnancy
milestone."

"You're right. We'll switch to sparkling cider."

"That's not what I meant. Not every little thing
needs a celebration. Look, this kid is going to have

enough to deal with just being a Bartasavich. He or she doesn't need the ego boost of you throwing a parade just for a new tooth or learning to walk."

He nodded solemnly. "Good point. We'll hold off on the parade until he or she is toilet trained."

"Ha-ha. Oh, how I hope the baby has your razor-sharp wit."

C.J. took her hand, started down the stairs, liking how her palm felt against his. "If he doesn't, we'll buy him a sense of humor."

She laughed. Squeezed his hand. "You rich people and your snooty specialty stores."

They reached the foyer, but instead of letting her go, he raised their joined hands to his lips and placed a warm kiss on her knuckles. "Have dinner with me next weekend."

"I can't. I'm working. Friday at King's Crossing and Saturday at O'Riley's."

But for the first time, she actually seemed disappointed to turn him down.

Progress. Slow and steady, but still progress.

Maybe there was something to this patience thing.

"How about lunch on Saturday?" he asked, wanting to push for more of her time but holding back.

"We have a bridal shower scheduled here Saturday so I'll be working that. I'll have a few hours free on Sunday but by the time I get up, it'll be late morning. You shouldn't even bother coming.

It's stupid for you to fly all this way to spend three or four hours with me."

"Stupid or not, I'll be here Friday night." He already had his flight booked.

She tugged free. "It's a waste of time."

"It's my time. And being with you is never a waste of it."

Before she could argue—which he knew damned well she was gearing up to do—he crushed his mouth to hers. He kissed her hungrily, wrapped his free arm around her to pull her close. She clung to him, her fingers digging into his shoulders, her breasts pressed against his torso.

By the time he tore his mouth from hers, they were both breathing hard and he was aching for her.

She licked her bottom lip and he couldn't stop himself from kissing her again. "Think of me," he whispered against her mouth. A demand. A plea.

He stepped out into the warm summer evening. And wondered if it was ever going to get easier to let her go.

THE BACK OF Gracie's neck tingled, like her very own Spidey sense warning her that trouble was nearby.

Her fingers tightening on the toilet brush, she turned her head toward the bathroom door only to find Luke there watching her.

Obviously her sixth sense was defective. If it

had been working properly, she would have known he was close by and could have slipped away before he'd trapped her in the Yellow Room's bathroom.

"Gracie," he said, then cleared his throat. Shoved his hands into his pockets. "Can we talk?"

"I'm sort of busy right now." Okay, so maybe she didn't have to sound that bitchy, but she'd managed to avoid him for the past few days—mainly because she hadn't been scheduled to work—and she didn't want that streak to end.

Plus, she really didn't want to chat with him while she scrubbed a toilet. She did have some pride.

"I can wait until you're done," he said, but not in a patient way. He was more like…determined. And when she glanced at him, she easily recognized the stubborn "I'm not going anywhere and you can't make me" look on his face.

Lord knew she'd seen that exact same expression on her brothers' faces often enough.

"Fine," she said, setting the toilet brush in the caddy along with the other cleaning supplies. She straightened, pulled off her rubber gloves and tossed them down before crossing her arms. "What shall we talk about?"

He frowned as if trying to figure out if she was serious. "We could start with you telling me why you're so pissed at me."

"Who says I'm pissed?"

He sent her a *duh* look. "You left me at the coffee shop and you haven't returned any of my texts or phone calls for four days." He edged closer, and the bathroom seemed to shrink. "Just...tell me what I did," he said quietly, "so I can fix this."

Seriously? How could he not know? "How's Kennedy?"

He opened his mouth. Shut it and shook his head. "I wouldn't know."

"So you two aren't back together?"

"No."

Gracie released the breath she'd been holding. "Oh. Well, don't worry. I'm sure you'll work things out soon."

She tried to go around him but he shifted, blocking her escape. "I don't want to get back together with her. Wait. Is that what this is about? You think I'm still into Kennedy? Are you...are you jealous?"

"Of course not," Gracie said quickly. She'd meant to sound adamant. Instead she'd come across as desperate.

And dishonest.

She'd never, not once, been envious of another girl. Had always believed everyone was special in their own way and the only way to happiness was to be true to yourself.

She knew perfectly well who she was. A cute girl with a unique sense of style, wild hair and a quick, inquisitive mind. Not a bad combination, all in all.

But at the coffee shop, standing next to Kennedy she'd felt...inferior. As if she was somehow lacking.

And though she knew it wasn't fair, she blamed Luke.

"Then what is it?" Luke asked, clearly frustrated. "What did I do?"

You kissed me, then told your ex-girlfriend we were just friends. You made me like you, made me think you were different.

"You used me," she told him, linking her hands together.

"What?"

"You. Used. Me. You knew Kennedy worked at the coffee shop, so you brought me there to...I don't know...upset her. Get under her skin." No way would Gracie believe he'd thought seeing them together would make Kennedy jealous. "Or at least so you could *accidentally* run into her."

"I didn't. I swear. I didn't even know she worked there. I took you there because I thought maybe if we were somewhere public, it would be easier to, you know, talk about what happened at my sister's, talk about our...our friendship, if there were other people around."

He sounded so sincere. His gaze was earnest and a blush climbed his cheeks. She wanted to believe him but was afraid to. "Even if that's true, it doesn't matter. As soon as you saw Kennedy, it was like a switch flipped and you became someone else. Then you went completely overboard about my mixed-up coffee order and it was so obvious you still have feelings for her and I was just…" *Hurt. Alone, yet again.* "…caught in the middle." Gracie lifted her chin. "I didn't like being put in that position so I left."

"I never meant to make you feel uncomfortable. Can you forgive me?"

It scared her how much she wanted to. But she still had some pride. Not as much as she should, perhaps, but enough to protect herself. "It doesn't matter."

He stepped closer, his voice low. "It matters to me."

She sighed. Looked as if that little bit of pride wasn't going to be enough after all. She nodded. "I forgive you."

He grinned, his shoulders relaxing. "Thank you. Hey, are you busy after work? We could get a bite to eat. Somewhere far away from the coffee shop."

She turned and picked up the tub cleaner. "I can't. Conner has a T-ball game tonight."

"Oh. Well, I could go with you and we could do something after."

She tapped the cleaner against her thigh. "I don't think that's a good idea."

"Why not?"

Because she didn't want to be his friend. Couldn't go on pretending she thought of him as a buddy. It was too hard. Too confusing. She knew how this scenario would play out. He'd eventually go out with some other girl or get back with Kennedy, leaving Gracie feeling like a fool for hoping he'd fall for her.

For waiting for him.

"I don't think we should hang out anymore," she said, almost wishing she was the type of person who could lie easily and well.

His eyes narrowed. "I said I was sorry, Gracie."

"That has nothing to do with—"

"Is this some game? Because I had enough of those with Kennedy."

"This isn't a game." She was proud of how calm she sounded. How mature. "I've just realized that it's not in my best interest to be your friend."

"Look, I screwed up," he said. "It won't happen again."

"It's not that. It's everything. We're too different." Hadn't she known that from the beginning? She should have listened to her instincts. "And you're going through a lot of…stuff right now… with the breakup and everything—"

"Which is exactly why I could use a good friend," he said taking her hand.

With tears clogging her throat, she tugged herself free. "I understand that. I do. But I…I just can't be that person for you. I'm sorry."

He studied her, his mouth flat, his gaze hooded. Then he shook his head. "Whatever." He turned and walked away but stopped in the hall, his voice soft. "I thought you were different."

She wanted to call him back. To explain all her doubts and fears. But in order to do that, she'd have to tell him her doubts. Her fears. She'd have to lay her soul bare and tell him how she really felt.

And she wasn't brave enough to do that. Not after what Andrew had done to her.

Maybe not ever again.

CHAPTER SEVENTEEN

SO FAR, SO GOOD.

It had been over three weeks since the weekend Ivy had asked Clinton to help her with the crib and told him about feeling the baby move. He came to Shady Grove every Friday night, stayed until Sunday evening. And while it was impossible to spend every moment together—she did have to work—they managed to have plenty of time together. More, certainly, than she'd ever spent with any other man.

And still, she never got tired of him. Always looked forward to seeing him again. To talking to him every night when he was in Houston. Getting to know each other while living in two different states took a hell of a lot of effort, but it had been worth it. She hadn't thought it possible, given the initial mistrust between her and Clinton, but things were now going well. Really, really well.

And they hadn't even slept together again.

Wiping down the kitchen counters at Bradford House, Ivy found herself humming. Good Lord, she was happy. The baby moved, a rolling sensation that never ceased to thrill and amaze her, and she rubbed her swollen stomach. "Yeah, I know. You're happy, too. I'm glad."

Things were going so well, she knew it was only a matter of time before it ended. At some point it was all going to come crashing down. Such was life. But until that moment, she would enjoy this. Enjoy spending time with a handsome, smart, interesting man. Enjoy the illusion that, for the first time in her life, she wasn't alone.

She turned to rinse the dishcloth and saw Gracie standing in the doorway. Ivy jumped and slapped her hand over her heart. "You scared the crap out of me!"

"Sorry," Gracie said, her small smile a pale imitation of her usual sunny grin. "I didn't want to disturb you. You looked so happy. Though I'm not sure you should ever hum like that or, God forbid, sing out loud to the baby. It could scar the poor thing for life. Unless, of course, you meant to sound flat and out of key?"

"Why would anyone try to sound bad?"

"Beats me. I just didn't want to assume you're really that horrible at something as simple as humming. No offense."

Ivy set the dishcloth aside to be put in the laundry later. "Saying *no offense* doesn't actually stop someone from being offended after they've been insulted. You know that, right?"

"Is it really an insult if it's the truth?"

"You bet." But Ivy wasn't really upset. She

already knew she couldn't carry a tune. Even her grade school music teacher had asked her to please lip sync along to their songs so as not to upset the rest of the kids. "Was there a reason you're sneaking up on me, besides trying to send me to an early grave?"

"I finished the housekeeping. Could you tell Fay I'm leaving a little early today? I'm going to Pittsburgh to see a Pirates game."

"I hadn't realized you were a baseball fan."

"I'm not, but my brothers are, and Dad and Molly need all the help they can get, taking five kids to the ballpark."

"Just five?"

"My grandma's watching the baby."

"You should ask Luke to go with you."

Gracie stiffened, her smile now seeming forced. "Why would I do that?"

"Because he's hot," Ivy said, ticking the reasons off on her fingers, "he's sweet and funny, and you're into him."

"I have no idea what that's supposed to mean."

"No need for the snooty tone, kiddo. I have eyes. And yours follow him whenever you're in the same room."

"It's purely physical," Gracie said, her face red. "He's very good-looking, so of course I look. But I don't want to...to date him or anything."

"Why not?" Ivy had worked with Luke quite a few times this summer. The teen was smart, polite and reliable. Gracie could do much worse. And Luke would be lucky to be with a girl like her.

Gracie rubbed her thumbnail along the edge of the counter. "I'm just...not interested in him that way. That's all."

"Okay," Ivy said, drawing the word out. Not for the first time, she thought something was off about Gracie. There had been for the past few weeks or so, but every time Ivy broached the subject, the teen clammed up. "Did something happen between you and Luke?"

"No."

And that had been said too quickly, too loudly for Ivy to believe it. "Are you sure? Because when he first started working here, it seemed as if you two were friends. Now you barely speak to him."

"Nothing happened," Gracie snapped, which was so unlike her that Ivy could only stare. "Could you please just tell Fay I'm leaving?"

"Sure. But I doubt she'll care. She's gone already." Fay and the boys were spending a week in the Caribbean with her parents, her older brother, Neil Pettit, his fiancée, Maddie Montesano, and their thirteen-year-old daughter, Bree. Neil, a professional hockey player and Bradford House's owner, was footing the entire bill.

Ivy might consider being envious that Fay had a relative ready, willing and able to provide luxurious vacations if she weren't in a relationship with a man wealthy enough to buy his own island.

She frowned. No. She and Clinton weren't in a relationship. They were seeing where things went between them. Taking things one day at a time. That was all. No labels. No promises.

From either of them.

"They left already?" Gracie asked. "I didn't even get a chance to say goodbye."

"Fay was a bit frazzled trying to get the boys to cooperate and pack for all three of them. I'm sure she meant to see you before she left but just ran out of time."

Gracie gave an irritable shrug. "Whatever."

Ivy did a double take. "Did you just *whatever* me?"

"Of course not." Gracie frowned thoughtfully. "Did I?"

"I'm afraid so." She wished Gracie would open up to her, but maybe that wasn't her place. "Look, whatever's bothering you—"

"Nothing's bothering me."

"Whatever it is," Ivy repeated, crossing to take Gracie's hands, "I just want to let you know that if you ever want someone to talk to, I'm here for you. You just… You haven't been yourself lately," she continued quietly. "I'm worried about you."

Gracie's lower lip trembled and she swallowed visibly. "I'm sorry."

Ivy hugged her. "Don't be sorry. I want to help."

"I appreciate that," Gracie said with a sniff,

hugging Ivy back. "I do. But I think I need to figure this out on my own."

Ivy leaned back. "Are you sure?"

Gracie nodded, her eyes bright with tears. "I am. But thanks. And thanks for being such a good friend."

Ivy smiled. Tugged playfully on one of Gracie's curls. "Thank you for giving me a chance to be one."

Gracie had been the first person to do so. But Ivy was honest enough to realize she shouldered part of the blame for that. She'd put up barriers to keep herself from ever getting hurt. And now, thanks to Gracie and Fay and especially Clinton, those barriers were starting to crumble.

Ivy just hoped they didn't crush her as they fell.

YOU HAVEN'T BEEN YOURSELF.

Gracie's hands tightened on the steering wheel of her dad's truck as she drove down Brookline Drive. As much as she had wanted to ignore Ivy's concerns and her words, she hadn't been able to. On the contrary, she'd thought of little else over the past two days.

She'd always prided herself on being true to who she was, no matter what other people thought. Had, at times, taken too much satisfaction in being different. Had felt so superior to other girls her age because she hadn't fallen prey to teenage stereotypes. No moodiness or jealousy. No cattiness or angst.

She snorted. So much for that.

Flicking on her indicator, she turned right onto Orchard Park Place, then pulled into Luke's driveway, relieved to see him shooting hoops there. At least she didn't have to worry about knocking on the door and having his mother answer.

He tucked the ball under his arm and watched as she turned off the ignition and slowly got out.

Gracie's heart raced. Her palms were damp, but she forced her feet to keep moving, to take her closer and closer to him. She wished Bradford House wasn't closed for a week while Fay was away. This would be so much easier to do on neutral territory. And while she could wait until both she and Luke returned to work, she didn't want to.

It was past time she got back to herself.

"Hi," she said, when it was obvious he wasn't going to speak first.

"Hey."

She cleared her throat. A cloud drifted in front of the bright late-afternoon sun. "Can I…can I talk to you a minute?"

"Sure." He bounced the ball. *Bounce. Bounce. Bounce.* "Everything okay?"

Some of her nervousness eased at his concern. "No. Yes. I mean…I'm fine, I just… I wanted to apologize." She swallowed, but it felt as if there was a peach pit lodged in her throat. "For not being fair to you. For getting so angry about what happened with Kennedy at the coffee shop. And for…for lying to you."

He caught the ball. Tossed it onto the grass. "You lied to me?"

"Well, it wasn't a lie exactly. More like I…I wasn't honest with you about…about my feelings," she said in a rush. "About why I didn't want to be your friend."

His eyes narrowed. "You said we were too different. That you didn't want to deal with my drama."

She winced. Hearing him repeat her excuses made them sound even worse. And they'd been pretty horrible to begin with. "I just said those things because I was afraid."

"Afraid of what?"

"That you'd get back with Kennedy. And that was wrong of me," she said quickly. "Even though I think it would be a mistake, I have no right to judge you. Especially when the main reason I hate the thought of you and Kennedy being together is that I…I like you." The last part came out so soft, she doubted he heard her. So she inhaled deeply and forced herself to hold his gaze and tell him the truth. "I like you."

Saying it should have been hard. Should have made her uneasy. Scared. But it wasn't. Somehow, standing there in his driveway, looking into his eyes, telling him how she felt about him was the easiest thing in the world.

"I like you," she repeated because he looked sort of stunned and very confused. "As more than a friend. And I didn't want to put myself in the position of having feelings for someone who was never going to feel the same way."

Been there. Done that.

"Gracie, I…" He shook his head. "I don't know what to say. I like you, too. A lot. It's just that Kennedy and I have been talking and…I'm not saying we're getting back together or anything. But we do have a history and…damn it!" He exhaled heavily. "I don't even know anymore."

"It's okay," she told him gently. Though it hurt to know he might get back together with Kennedy, Gracie wasn't going to let that stop her from being true to herself. Nothing would stop her from doing that ever again.

"I don't want you to feel bad for not returning my feelings," she continued. "I don't want you to feel bad about anything. I just wanted to tell you how sorry I am for not being honest with you. I'm not going to suggest we try to be friends again. At least, not right away. You're obviously confused and I don't want you to be uncomfortable around me."

"I'm not," he insisted, shifting as if he was about to take a step toward her, only to rock back on his heels. "I never could be."

"Thanks for saying that. I just think it's too soon for that. For both of us."

"You're probably right." But he scowled. Sounded disappointed. "I guess I'll see you at school."

She smiled. "And at work."

He blushed. Looked so adorable, her chest ached. "Right."

"Goodbye, Luke."

He nodded and she turned, walked away from yet another boy she'd fallen too hard, too fast for.

And couldn't help feeling as if she was walking back to the girl she used to be.

IT WAS LATE by the time C.J. pulled to a stop in front of Bradford House Friday night, later than he'd expected thanks to a delay at the Houston airport due to thunderstorms. When he'd landed in Pittsburgh, though, the sky had been bright and clear. Now it was dark, but the porch light was on as were others inside. He grabbed his bag from the backseat and locked the rental car behind him.

He was beat. He'd been flying to and from Shady Grove for the past month, coming back to town every weekend. He wished he could stay—or convince Ivy to go to Houston with him—but she was still skittish, and he didn't want to push her away. Still, things between them were going well enough that he had high hopes he could talk her into it before the baby was born.

He stepped inside, frowning at how quiet it was. Usually there were guests in the library, having wine and cheese or coming and going, but tonight it was empty. Silent. Where was Ivy? She'd told him she'd wait for him here. Was he too late? Had she gotten tired of waiting and gone back to her apartment?

He'd pulled out his cell phone when he noticed a piece of paper on the banister with his name on it. He unfolded it to find a key and a note telling him his room was ready. He went upstairs, the second floor eerily empty as he made his way to the Back Suite, and opened the door to find the room lit by the glow from dozens of candles.

And Ivy reclining on his bed, the covers pulled back, the pillows stacked behind her. His breath caught. His heart jumped.

She smiled, like an angel. Or like the devil, tempting him. "Hello, cowboy," she said, her voice a purr. "Glad you could make it."

He stepped inside, shut the door behind him. He couldn't speak, couldn't find words because she was so beautiful. Her hair fell in soft waves to her shoulders, and she wore a sheer white nightgown that cupped her breasts, hugged her protruding stomach. Her legs were long, toned and tanned.

"Have I died and gone to heaven?" he asked, his voice gruff, his hands trembling with the need to touch her. To take her. To make her his.

She laughed, the sound incredibly sexy. "Not

yet." She slid to her feet, all graceful lines and curves. Walked to him in a sensuous sway that not even pregnancy could diminish. When she reached him, she wrapped her arms around his neck and gave him a kiss that had his heart thumping, his body thrumming with desire. "But soon," she whispered against his mouth. "Very, very soon."

His bags fell from his hands with a loud thump and he threaded his fingers into her hair, held her face for his kiss. When they finally broke apart, they were both breathing hard.

"Are you sure about this?" he asked.

Her smile gave him her answer before she even spoke. "I didn't go to all this trouble for nothing."

She had gone to trouble for him. The candles, the nightgown and—he noticed now that his head had stopped ringing—soft, smoky jazz playing on the stereo.

"Thank you," he said gruffly. He'd had people do things for him before. Countless people trying to get on his good side, trying to earn his favor. But Ivy had done this for no other reason than to make this moment, this night, special.

He was humbled. Grateful. To show her, he kissed her deeply, gently, letting the hunger between them build again, a slow burn that grew hotter and hotter.

Breaking the kiss, he leaned back. Slid his hands down the sides of her body, the silk cool beneath his palms. Lifting the hem, he pulled it up, exposing her upper thighs, her stomach and breasts, before pulling it over her head.

His fingers flexed on the nightgown still in his hand. He felt as if he'd been punched in the stomach. "You are so damned beautiful."

Her skin was golden, her breasts were fuller than before, the pink tips jutting out as if begging him to taste. Dropping the nightgown to the ground, he fell to his knees and laid his palms on either side of her stomach. It was so hard, the skin stretched taut. He kissed her, just above her belly button. Felt his child move beneath his hands.

Smiling, C.J. straightened. Led Ivy to the bed. He cherished her with his hands and his mouth. His only thought was to bring her pleasure. To finally make her his. He reveled in each and every sigh, his excitement building with each moan. And when she climaxed, he watched her, knowing he'd never see anything as beautiful.

He hurriedly undressed and when he joined her again, she reached for him, her breathing ragged, her skin flushed. He made love to her slowly. Carefully. Every movement, every kiss, meant to show her how much she meant to him. She tightened around him with a soft cry and he emptied himself in her. Gave her everything he had.

Gave her his heart and soul.

IVY PURRED AND rolled over, her hands seeking Clinton's skin. They'd made love—twice—and he had, indeed, kept his promise all those months ago to worship her. Her body was lax and loose and very, very satisfied.

In between their lovemaking, Ivy had explained they had the entire B and B to themselves. Taking advantage of their seclusion, they'd gone down to the kitchen—Clinton in just his pants, her in her nightgown—where she'd made them French toast with fresh berries and whipped cream. It had been fun, cooking for him, feeling his heated gaze on her bare legs while he sipped the chilled champagne she'd put in the fridge.

By the time they'd finished eating, their hunger for each other had returned. She smiled, remembering how he'd made her come in front of the kitchen sink.

She grinned. She was never going to be able to do dishes there again without thinking about it.

Outside the sky was cloudy and gray, the rising sun doing little to dispel the gloominess.

But inside, in bed with Clinton warm and solid beside her, Ivy had never felt happier.

"That," she murmured, "went well."

He chuckled and pulled her against him so she could lay her head on his chest. "I'd have to agree." He rubbed her back, his touch sending tingles of pleasure through her body. "You put a lot of effort into it."

"Some," she admitted lightly, trying to brush off what had actually taken planning and work.

Yes, she'd set the mood, had tried to create a romantic atmosphere, but she hadn't done it just for him. She'd wanted to make this moment memorable.

Special.

Her throat tightened. It didn't mean anything. It certainly didn't mean she'd become one of those women who confused lust with love. Whatever this was between her and Clinton, it was still too new. Too fragile to try and make it more than what it was.

He sniffed the curve of her neck. "You smell delicious."

She'd rubbed scented lotion all over her body, and he'd shown his appreciation by loving each and every inch.

He'd been enthralled by her stomach, had rubbed it and kissed it and talked to the baby, making her laugh, making her, for some crazy reason, want to cry. And the way he'd made love to her, so gently, so carefully, their fingers entwined, had threatened to break her heart. She hadn't been able to think at all, could only feel.

She snuggled against him, felt his heart beat against her cheek.

"Thank you," he said, playing with her hair. "For going to that much trouble. For letting me love you."

His words caused a shiver of panic to climb her spine. She tried to ignore it. "You're the one who did most of the work," she teased. "And believe me, I got much more than I gave. As a matter of fact, one of us is ahead, five to two. Not that we're keeping score."

She lifted her head to grin at him, but he was watching her seriously, not smiling, his gaze unwavering. "No, I mean...I'm falling in love with you, Ivy."

She froze. Shook her head at the quiet, intense words, at the look on his face, the truth. Denial flowed through her. No. She didn't want this.

She would have gotten up, would have gotten out of the bed, but he must have sensed her intent, because he held her arms, forcing her to look at him. "Aren't you going to say anything?" he asked quietly.

She forced a laugh. "Well, now, you're not the first man to tell me that after sleeping with me."

"Don't joke," he ordered, his accent heavy despite his soft tone. "Not about this. Not with me."

She swallowed. "Clinton, let's just... Let's go downstairs. I'll make us some coffee, maybe something to eat. Then we can come back to bed, make love again. Just let's...let's not ruin this."

She thought for sure he'd agree, that he'd want to get past this moment as quickly as possible, that he'd want to go back to the way things were between them, the way she needed them to stay, at least for a little while. But he sat up, shaking his head.

"I think you should move to Houston. I think you should move in with me."

She yanked her arms free. "What?"

One side of his mouth kicked up, but she saw the nervousness in his eyes, the fear and the hope. "I care about you. You're having my baby. I want you to move to Houston. I want you to live with me."

She put both hands in her hair. Pulled. Hard. "God. Would you please stop saying that?"

He didn't mean it. Couldn't. Didn't all men say those things to get what they wanted, because the words were what they thought women wanted to hear? Except she'd already given him what they'd both wanted, and he kept right on saying them.

"Don't say what?" he asked, his tone warning her that their perfect moment, their perfect night was over. "Don't say that I have feelings for you? That I want to be with you?"

"Yes," she snapped, sliding off the bed and grabbing his shirt, since her clothes were in the bathroom. She shoved her arms into the sleeves, ignoring how it smelled of him. She buttoned it at her breasts, but they wouldn't reach over her stomach. She scooped up her panties and pulled them on. "Quit saying all of it. You are not falling in love with me, I am not moving to Houston and we are not going to live together."

He got to his feet, unconcerned with his own nudity. Why should he be, when he was so glorious? "I think I'm smart enough to know my own feelings. I started falling for you the moment I first laid eyes on you."

She was shaking. Cold and scared and so terrified of losing what they had. But she wasn't strong enough or brave enough to reach for what she really wanted. It was safer to pretend she didn't want it. That she didn't want him. Better to lose him now, like this, than to think they could have had it all.

"You don't have to say that. You don't have to offer me a commitment. I'm not going to fight you over seeing the baby. You can spend as much time with our child as you want. You know that," she told him, desperation coloring her voice.

"I'm not saying it because of the baby. Hell, even if there wasn't a baby, even if that baby wasn't mine, I'd be saying it because it's what I want. I think about you all the time and I…hell… I miss you when you're not with me. Why should we continue living in different states, why should we be separated when the answer is so clear?" His voice dropped, grew rough with emotion. "I want to be with you, Ivy. I want to live with you and raise our baby together. As a family."

"It wouldn't work. I don't want to play house with you. I live here. In Shady Grove."

"We wouldn't be playing," he growled. "This isn't one of your games. This is the way it's supposed to be. When two people care about each other, there are certain steps they take. Granted, we've done a few out of order and skipped a couple entirely, but that doesn't mean we can't get back on track."

"Steps? Back on track? Is that what this is? You're going down some sort of checklist and marking things off?" She began to pace, her steps jerky. "I'm guessing the step after Move In Together is Marriage."

His jaw was tight, his hands fisted. He stood there, naked and so handsome it hurt her to look at him. "Eventually," he said, the word almost a challenge. "Yes."

Married. To Clinton. It was crazy. It would never work. Not for the long-term.

But she could picture what their life would be like. How it would be to live in that huge apartment, to see Clinton every day, spend each night with him. It was all too easy to imagine.

"I am not moving to Houston," she repeated, sounding desperate when she wanted to come across as firm.

"Okay, okay." He held his hands out but instead of coming across as beseeching, he still looked powerful. In control. "Just spend some time with me there. A few days. I want you in my home, Ivy. I want to show you my city. To have you be a part of my life."

"I…I have to work…"

"You said the B and B is closed until Wednesday. We could fly to Houston today—"

"I'm scheduled to work at O'Riley's tonight and Tuesday. And King's Crossing Monday."

"You could call off," he said.

She could. Of course she could. Or she could find someone to cover for her. It was only a few days. A compromise. One that would show she was willing to meet Clinton halfway. That she wanted to make this work between them.

But she couldn't give in. Not even on something so small. She had to be strong. To keep control.

If she gave it up for one second, she'd never get it back.

She tucked her hands behind her back to hide their trembling and had to force the word out, the one word she knew would cost her Clinton. "No."

CHAPTER EIGHTEEN

C.J. WAS FREEZING his ass off. It didn't help that his ass was bare, that he was practically begging a woman to give him a chance, to give them a real chance at being together. Being happy.

Being a real couple.

"No."

That one word went right through him, cutting him like a knife. "What?" he asked, because there had to be some mistake. When he asked a woman for anything, when he asked anyone for anything, they always said yes.

There was no way he could ask a woman to spend a few lousy days with him—to basically take a mini vacation—and have her say no. To tell her he was falling in love with her and hear her beg him not to say it again.

"I can't," Ivy said.

He wanted to swipe the lamp off the bedside table, to rant and rave and demand she stop being so damned stubborn.

Demand that she feel the way about him, that he felt about her.

He'd opened up to her. Had given her the key to his heart.

And she didn't want it. Didn't want him. He pulled on his pants before facing her again.

"You mean you won't," he said, the words ripped from his throat.

She stepped toward him, her hand reaching for him, but he backed up. He couldn't handle her touching him. Not now. Not after what had happened between them last night, not when he was so raw now. "You want things I don't. Marriage will never be in the cards for me. I've always known that. But that doesn't mean anything has to change between us."

She sounded so hopeful, looked a wreck, as if this was tearing her up inside as much as it was him, but that couldn't be true. If it was, she'd see that they were meant to be together, that they should raise their child together.

Unless...

"Do you love me?" he asked, never having asked the question before, ever. He'd always known where he stood with people, from his family to his friends to his lovers to people he worked with and people who worked for him. But now... this...he had to know.

"Clinton, I..." She pressed her lips together. "I care about you."

"That's a start." A good one, if not exactly a declaration of her undying affection. As a matter of fact, she didn't look very happy to be admitting it at all. "Do you think the feelings you have for me now could grow into love?"

"How am I supposed to know that?" she cried, throwing her hands up. "I have no idea what the future will bring."

He shouldn't push her but he had to know. "It's not that hard a question, Ivy," he said, unable to stand there and listen to her placate him with useless, meaningless words. "Do you want to be with me? Do you see yourself building a future with me? A family? Yes or no. Damn it," he snapped when she hesitated. "They're simple questions, ones that deserve an answer. *I* deserve an answer."

She swallowed. Stared over his right shoulder, then met his eyes. Sighed. "I don't know."

And just like that, with one simple whispered confession, it didn't matter how much money he had, how much power, how he lived like a freaking king. He didn't have Ivy and would never have her. He had nothing.

"Then I guess there's nothing else to say." He wasn't about to take his shirt from her, so he grabbed his keys and the suitcase he'd brought upstairs with him last night. "I'll have my attorney get in touch with you about child support. We can work out a custody agreement later. I'd appreciate it if you'd let me be present for the birth."

"Of course. Clinton," she said, walking toward him, so beautiful it hurt to look at her. "Don't go.

We can go back to the way things were. How they have been."

"Go back to seeing each other only on weekends? To me giving and giving, constantly trying to prove myself to you? To prove you can trust me?" He shook his head. "No. I won't go back. And you won't move forward, at least not with me, so I'll move forward on my own." He went to the door. Opened it but didn't dare look back, not when everything inside him screamed at him not to go. Not to let her go. "Goodbye, Ivy."

And he walked out before he lost the last of his pride and accepted whatever small scraps of emotion she tossed his way.

THOUGH IT HAD been over three weeks since Clinton had walked out of her life, Ivy could still remember that moment as if it had happened yesterday. She'd never forget how he'd looked, so crushed, so angry. Just as she'd never forget how it had felt as if her heart was breaking to watch him go. How she'd curled up on the bed, inhaling his scent from his shirt and cried, wishing things could have been different.

Wishing she could be different.

She'd thought...had hoped...he'd come back. That he'd change his mind. That he'd realize what they had was good enough. There was no reason to risk it by tossing around I love yous and moving in together with the ultimate goal of getting married. No, she'd done the right thing. He was probably just being noble, thinking he had to offer her a commitment because he'd gotten her pregnant.

She carried a serving tray of blueberry scones into Bradford House's dining room. Smiled at the elderly couple staying in the Blue Room as she set the tray down.

She missed Clinton like crazy, and he hadn't even called. Had just had his attorney contact her to set up child support payments. The amount was more than fair, and she wouldn't have to work should she choose not to.

She wanted to work, needed it, which was why she was glad she had a shift at O'Riley's tonight. Luckily, Kane hadn't treated her any differently since she and Clinton had stopped seeing each other, but she knew he wondered what was going on. He might act as if he didn't care about his brother, but she didn't believe it.

He had asked Clinton to be his best man. She couldn't help but think that had been an overture on Kane's part. The first step at a possible reconciliation between them. She hoped she was right and that they would be able to mend the rift between them. She knew how important Clinton's family was to him. Even Kane.

She pushed the door open and stepped inside the kitchen, went directly to the sink and stared out the window. Summer was over and school had started last week. It wouldn't be long before the nip of fall entered the air and the leaves started changing. The baby kicked. Hard. Ivy smiled. She was now seven months along but she hadn't done much to get ready for the baby, a part of her still hoping Clinton would come back. She hated that he was missing it, that he wasn't able to enjoy the preparations.

"Did you hear?" Fay asked breathlessly as she came into the room followed by Gracie holding Mitch's hand.

Ivy turned. Frowned to see Fay so obviously upset. "Hear what?"

"Charlotte Ellison just called to postpone her bridal shower," Fay said. "One of Kane's brothers has been hurt, and she's not sure if they'll be traveling to see him soon or not."

Everything inside Ivy stilled. A roaring filled her head.

"What happened?" Ivy demanded. "Which brother? How hurt is he?"

"Not Clinton," Fay said, rushing over to take both of Ivy's hands in hers. "I'm so sorry. I should have told you that right away."

Ivy was shaking and had to sit down. She almost dropped right to the floor, but Fay helped her around the island and onto a stool, got her a glass of water while Gracie made Mitchell a peanut-butter sandwich.

"It wasn't Clinton?" Ivy asked, needing to know for sure. "You're sure?"

"I'm positive. It's the one in the marines."

"Zach," Ivy breathed, relieved beyond measure that Clinton was safe and whole. "Is he going to be all right?"

"I don't know," Fay said. "From what little Charlotte told me, it's really bad. The Humvee he was driving triggered a roadside bomb. Two of the men with him were killed instantly and he was severely injured."

Oh, no. Poor Zach. And poor Clinton. He must be terrified. And going crazy that there was nothing he could do to help, to fix it, to make sure his brother pulled through.

Fay nudged the water glass in Ivy's hand. "Take a sip."

Ivy did so but her throat was so tight, she could barely swallow.

"You should call him," Fay said gently.

Ivy didn't pretend not to know who Fay was referring to. She pulled her phone out, needing to hear Clinton's voice, but put it on the counter when she realized he wouldn't want to hear from her. His brother had been severely injured and he hadn't even told her. Hadn't reached out to her.

"He won't want to hear from me," Ivy said quietly.

Fay brushed Ivy's hair back. Squeezed her shoulder. "I'm sure he will."

"Fay's right," Gracie said from the table where she was cutting the crust off Mitch's sandwich. "The cowboy needs you. You should definitely call."

Ivy shook her head. The thought of someone needing her was terrifying. And thrilling. "I hurt him."

Gracie swiped peanut butter from the knife with her forefinger. "We figured as much. But that's not the reason you won't call him."

"It's not?" Ivy asked.

Sucking the peanut butter from her finger, the teen shook her head. "No. You're not worried he's still mad or even that he won't forgive you. You're scared. You've been afraid of him since the night you met."

"What are you talking about?" Fay asked, which was good, since Ivy was unable to form any words.

"There was something between them from the moment they met," Gracie said, twisting the lid back onto the peanut-butter jar. "That kind of connection, especially when it's instantaneous, can be frightening. So it's easier to pretend it doesn't exist. Safer, too. It's scary to want something so much. Especially if there's a chance you won't get it. Or worse, that you will and then lose it again."

Ivy wanted to laugh, wanted to tell Gracie that she was crazy, that her theories were ridiculous.

But she knew, deep in her heart, the teenager was right.

She'd let fear run her life. But no more.

Grabbing her phone, she got to her feet. "I'm really sorry to leave you in a bind," she told Fay, "but I'm taking a few days off."

Knowing how stubborn Clinton was, those few days would probably be more like a week. But she'd take as long as she needed to convince him to give her, to give them, another chance.

Fay waved that away. "Don't worry about us. We'll manage just fine."

Ivy gave her a grateful hug then turned and embraced Gracie warmly. "Thank you," she whispered into the teen's curly hair.

Gracie leaned back and grinned. "What's the point of having friends if they can't tell you when you're being an idiot?"

Ivy laughed for the first time in what seemed like weeks, so happy to have these two women in her life. "Wish me luck."

"Luck," Fay and Gracie said at the same time as Ivy raced off to face her greatest fear.

A man with the power to break her heart.

C.J. PACED THE space between his desk and the sofa in his home office. He had work to do but he couldn't keep his focus. Not when he was so worried about Zach. He hated waiting, but that's about all he'd done since he'd gotten word about Zach's injuries. Wait on call after call, from doctors to tell him how Zach's surgery had gone. From nurses to let him know if his brother had survived the night, if he was in pain, what they were doing for him next.

Once Zach's condition had been stable enough for him to travel, he'd been transported to a hospital in Germany but C.J. had no idea how long it would be before his brother would be stateside again.

He wiped a hand down his face. He hated waiting, and he hated feeling so useless. At least he'd been able to get Zach's mother and younger half sister on a flight to Germany. He knew Zach would rather have them there than any member of his father's family.

But now there was absolutely nothing C.J. could do to help his brother.

The intercom buzzed and he answered it.

"Mr. Bartasavich," Paul from the front desk said, "there's a woman to see you but her name isn't on the list."

Ever since word had gotten out about Zach's injuries, the local media had been bugging his family for the full story. But C.J. wasn't about to turn his brother's sacrifice into a juicy snippet for the society page.

"Tell her I have no comment," C.J. said. He turned away only to have the intercom buzz again.

"I beg your pardon, Mr. Bartasavich," Paul said

quickly, "but the young lady has asked me to tell you that she's not here for a quote. She has something of yours."

C.J.'s scalp prickled. No. It couldn't be. But a part of him, the traitorous part he tried to ignore, hoped it was Ivy. He pressed the button. "Send her up, Paul."

"Yes, sir."

He went into the foyer, ducked into the bathroom and checked his hair. Realized what he was doing and forced himself back out into the hall. It probably wasn't even her. There was no reason for her to come all this way, not after the way they'd ended things.

But when someone knocked on the door five minutes later, he yanked it open, his heart in his throat.

And there she was. Ivy.

He blinked but she didn't disappear. Not a hallucination. It wouldn't be the first time he'd imagined her since he'd left Shady Grove. He'd catch a glimpse of blond hair, and his heart would stop. He'd hear a husky voice, and he'd think she was near. But it was always just his overactive imagination, conjuring her up, torturing him with the memory or her.

He wished he could forget about her, but she carried his baby. They would be tied together for the rest of their lives.

The Ivy before him was bigger and rounder

than the one who'd worn his shirt as he'd begged her to love him.

She was real and she was here.

Shit.

"What the hell are you doing here?" he asked lowly, roughly.

"I came as soon as I heard," she said. "How's Zach?"

Clinton wanted to break down, wanted to lose himself in the fact that she was here. She might not love him, but she was here. For him. But he couldn't. He had to be strong. "He might not pull through," he told her blandly. He didn't want her sympathy, though it filled her eyes. "He's lost his right arm above the elbow and his right leg above the knee. He has massive internal injuries and a head injury. He's…" C.J. had to stop to collect himself. "It's touch and go each and every god-damn hour."

His brother might die, and there was nothing C.J. could do to stop it. To help him. To save him.

"I'm sorry," she whispered, her hand over her mouth. "Clinton, I'm so, so sorry."

She reached for him, and for a moment, he wanted to let her take him into her arms, wanted to rest his head on her shoulder and just hold her. But he couldn't. He didn't trust her. He'd given her his heart, and she'd tossed it back at him.

He stepped back. Told himself he shouldn't feel bad at how crushed she looked as she slowly lowered her arms. "You shouldn't have come," he told her.

"I couldn't stay away. You need me."

Her words blew through him. "I needed you three weeks ago," he reminded her. "I got over it."

"Don't say that." She glanced down the empty hall. "Could I...could I come in?"

"You're asking to come in? Given up breaking and entering?"

She held his gaze. "I am asking. I'm asking you to let me in, Clinton. Please."

He couldn't refuse her even when he wished he could. When he knew it would be better for him, less painful, to turn her away. With a sigh, he stepped aside. She brushed past him. She smelled the same, the familiar scent hitting him like a left jab. Her hair was down, falling in soft waves around her shoulders. She wore a deep burgundy top that molded to her stomach, high-heeled boots and jeans so tight, he had no idea how she'd even got them on her very pregnant frame.

Women and their endlessly fascinating mysteries.

He'd no sooner shut the door behind her when she shoved something at him. "Here," she said, pressing an envelope into his hand. "This is for you."

He frowned. Something told him not to open it but he couldn't contain his curiosity.

"It's a check," she blurted.

"I can see that." It was, indeed, a check. One drawn on her personal checking account made out to him for the amount of fifty thousand dollars. He put it back in the envelope, held it out to her. "I don't want it."

"I figured as much but I need you to take it."

"Why? So you won't owe me anything? So you won't feel indebted to me?"

"So we can start over."

He froze. He couldn't believe what he was hearing. Didn't trust what she was saying.

"I...I made a mistake," she continued. "I was so scared when you asked me to move here with you, when you said you were falling in love with me, so terrified when you brought up marriage and the future. I pushed you away because I was scared."

He narrowed his eyes, not daring to hope. "What are you saying?"

She inhaled deeply, rested her hands on her belly. "I miss you. I miss you so much I can barely breathe. I think about you all the time, and knowing I lost you because of my fear kills me. Please give me a second chance."

He wanted to. It was pathetic how desperately he wanted to take her into his arms and tell her not to worry about it, that he was willing to take whatever scraps she would give him. But he had his pride, and his pride had always been his downfall. "I can't, Ivy. I don't want to be with you on weekends or several times a month. I want more than that. I deserve more than that and so do you and our child."

"You're right. It just took me some time to realize that. And I realize you might not forgive me, but I'm here to ask you to give me a second chance. I'm...I'm asking you to give me your heart, Clinton," she said quietly, her voice unsteady. "I promise if you do, this time I'll cherish it. And I'll do my best to never hurt you again."

He stared at her, wanting desperately to believe her but afraid to take that chance. He couldn't speak, couldn't form the words to tell her to go. To beg her to stay.

"Please," she whispered, tears filling her eyes. "Please forgive me, Clinton. I'm so sorry I hurt you. I'm so sorry I lied to you after I told you I wouldn't."

"You lied?"

She sniffed. Nodded. "I told you I didn't know if I could fall in love with you, but I already do love you. I love you. So much. I've never said that to anyone before, never thought I could feel for someone the way I feel about you. Please don't walk away from me again."

He was shaken to his core. He could see the truth of her words in her eyes. She loved him. She. Loved. Him. He'd gotten his second chance.

Thank God.

He took her in his arms and held on tight. He

never wanted to let go. "I love you, too, Ivy. Please stay with me. Be mine."

She nodded and hugged him hard. "I'm yours. Always."

The baby kicked, and they both laughed. Then he kissed her and knew he'd found his perfect partner, his best friend and the woman he was going to love until the end of his days.

* * * * *

LARGER-PRINT BOOKS!

HARLEQUIN *Presents*®

PASSION GUARANTEED SEDUCTION

GET 2 FREE LARGER-PRINT NOVELS PLUS 2 FREE GIFTS!